I0680687

CULTURE'S SKELETON

ADAM P. KNAVE

Culture's Skeleton
Adam P. Knave

ISBN: 978-1926946-085

Trade edition.
This book is also available in ebook formats.
©2018 Adam P. Knave, all rights reserved.

Published in Canada by Creative Guy Publishing
Victoria, BC, Canada

Cover art ©2018 Valentine Baker
Logo design Frank Cvetkovic

CULTURE'S SKELETON

ADAM P. KNAVE

CREATIVE GUY PUBLISHING
VICTORIA BC

Thanks to:

Lauren for editing and Pete for believing in this strange idea,

to Richard Kadrey whose Metrophage *was the first city novel I ever deeply loved,*

to KC and the Sunshine Band for Boogie Shoes,

and to every city I've ever lived in for the secret reasons.

Calphagas the Weaver of Doom's Engine sat upon the windowsill and considered her next move carefully. The glass caught a ray of light from a split in the clouds and startled her, driving subtle and wondrous plans out of her head. In anger and surprise, Calphagas reared her head back and pecked at the glass. The glare didn't go away under this swift attack, so Calphagas felt no recourse other than a renewed attack, her beak tap-tap-tapping against the window.

One loud *FLUMP* from a pillow hitting the other, interior, side of the window and Calphagas took an astonished step backwards, right off the windowsill. Four feet into free-fall and she'd recovered; stretching her wings, she flew away into her own story and out of this one.

"Fuckin' pigeons," Jake Meyer muttered, waving a hand toward the window, trying to will his pillow to return to him. The pillow, quite stubbornly, refused to obey and sat on the floor sullenly. Grumbling the whole time, Jake got out of bed and walked the few feet over to the window. He grabbed the pillow and walked it back, but as he started to climb into bed, his bladder woke up.

Jake set the pillow down, looked at Casey, who'd slept through the pigeon's needless alarm impression, and stumbled into the bathroom. He peed. He kept peeing. He...this gets awkward after a while, all right? For now, let's go and skitter along the floor, avoiding the dropped guitar picks, padlocks, socks, and other debris of life.

The windowsill – white paint streaked from years of grit and grime until the black streaks merged with the paint, becoming an integral structural element – is of no concern. We slid through it before you even noticed, the way Calphagas only wishes she could. From this vantage point, looking down on Jackson Street from the fourth floor, you wouldn't see many people yet. A small side street, you'd need to shift over to the corner, to Avenue H, to really begin to see life moving at speed.

Enough of people watching, though. If you're going to be a floating, invisible specter you should take full advantage of it. We can head up, right into the sky, past the clouds and brightening sun, into the blackness that should be normal space. This is where it gets weird.

Normal space, it's known, smells like hot metal, a welding-fume type of stench. But here, this space, is different. If you could inhale here, if there were enough particles to draw into your lungs, it would smell faintly of cinnamon and wet wool. No stars.

Nothing to distract. Only void. Which is fine as far as it takes us—which, admittedly, isn't far just yet.

Just work with me here. Let's look back the way we came. See the city now, as a whole? Mur. The Eternal City. Hanging alone in the sky in impossible ways. So let's go back into it. Let's go back down until we can make out the circular, labyrinthian layout of the city. In the center of the city stands the Spire. When first constructed, tens of thousands of years ago and many stories shorter, the Spire was built to be Mur's main temple. Now it serves as City Hall, as well as a more general administration hub. Around it buildings sprawl, done up in every type of architecture imaginable, with no real pattern discernable. Sloppy city planning, sure, but interesting to look at, at least.

People dot the sidewalks on the main roads, stores starting to open as the day shift begins to arrive. The night shift has already moved offstage, mostly, slumping wearily back to beds and food. Not necessarily in that order. Mur sits below us, roughly twenty-five square miles of city, coiled and ready to spring. That sounds cool – it can even sound dangerous, and sure, Mur can be both, but then the same could be said about every major city in the history of the world.

It's time we turn away from the center of Mur, moving further out toward the wall that rings the town, back down toward Jackson street, between Seventh Avenue and Avenue H. That same five-story walk-up, fourth floor, left corner, first window from the edge. The window now stands open. Jake gave up on going back to bed and decided to make coffee. Casey woke up but stayed in bed, sitting cross-legged, tapping a pen against her teeth, a worn and cracked notebook resting on one knee.

Coffee brewing, Jake walked to the window, resting his palms on the only parts of the windowsill not coated in the grime of the city. He looked down at the sill and wished they'd moved in before the damage had been done to the paint.

Either of them could scrape away the old paint, infused with grit, and repaint the sill. He knew that. But he was just as sure their landlord should've done the work instead. Locked in that sort of unspoken stalemate, a contest of wills that neither side is really confident they're having because no one brings it up, the windowsill lost.

A fresh breeze came down along the street until it found its way into the window and brushed against Jake's face. He smiled, inhaling deeply, and pushed off against the sill to stand straight once more. He turned away from the window, back toward the coffee maker, and stopped when he saw the pot hadn't finished brewing. Jake glanced around for something else to distract him for a few minutes.

He worked hard to not bother Casey. With her notebook out – or head down, curled bodily around a guitar and thinking – Jake knew to leave her to thinking and to work. He didn't say a word, avoiding even her line of sight if possible.

Casey Harrison didn't wake up and feel the need to grab the notebook before managing even a hello to Jake very often. She'd learned to not ignore the need when it did come up, though. Thankfully, she'd also finally gotten used to Jake understanding – and, better yet, being all right with – her need. Regardless, a tiny pang of guilt floated through her head, just at the edges. The right corner of her mouth curled slightly upward and she used the feeling, pen scritching over paper in a short bursts.

The notebook was full of a collection of both musical notation and strange glyphs that only made sense to Casey. Combined, and played, they were music. Older notebooks sat stacked neatly in a small, metal safe by the bed. Casey didn't worry so much about her music being stolen, but the older notebooks, also containing notes and strange symbols, weren't *just* music. Those notebooks she hoped to never need to touch again.

The coffee maker gurgled a final time, brewing finished and a job done. Jake stood up from where he had laid down on the floor for no good conscious reason and stretched, biting back a yawn. He made two cups up, black for himself and sugar for Casey, bringing hers over to the bed and setting it down on the floor in her reach, still without saying a word.

Taking his own cup over to the table, placed between the kitchen and the bed in some old, failed, plan to try and split their small loft into different-feeling spaces, Jake scooped up a combination padlock from a box of various locks. He spun the dial quickly back and forth for a few seconds, sipping at his coffee. Lightly placing two fingers on the back of the lock, Jake twitched the dial slowly with his thumb and stared into space.

Sliding her foot over, Casey nudged her coffee mug slightly. Reaching down to grab it, she took a quick sip before returning it to the floor to do double duty as a side-of-foot warmer. She jotted down the next phrase into her notebook and tapped her teeth with the pen again.

In the time it took for her to do that simple set of motions, Jake had the padlock open. He snapped it locked again and resisted the urge to lob it back into the box, setting it down gently instead.

Looking at the loft, it really isn't much. For Casey and Jake, though, it was home. A small, cramped home, but even so. Casey and Jake had lived together for seven months. Before moving in together they'd dated for three months, a time they both looked back on as chaotic in the best of ways.

The night Casey suggested they move in together, they'd left a gallery opening tipsily, walking home through the winding streets of Mur. The air felt heavy with an impending rain, and Jake had tossed the hood of his jacket up over his head. Sound being slightly muffled, he asked her to repeat her idea. Casey started to feel she'd made a mistake, his request coming across like an attempt at dismissal. She took a deep breath and asked again, reaching up to tug his hood out on one side.

Laughing at her gesture, he'd agreed, and they'd started the process of finding a new place to live. Neither of them seriously considered keeping their contemporary apartments, both of them too small for two people – smaller by half than the tiny loft they lived in now. After a search too annoying to detail, they'd found a loft just big enough for them both and broke their individual leases, settling in as smooth as anyone does at first – which is to say not really well at all.

The only lingering issue was Jake's desire to name the space. He favored names including: Hovel Manor, Bonkers Palace, Lofty Loft-loft, The Cave of Forgotten Dishes, and Flappity-Doo. The last being a name he'd been trying to assign to something since childhood, but had never found quite the right object to deploy the name upon. Casey didn't think the loft needed a name; didn't deserve one, being, as she put it, only their starter loft. She described a future loft, with pneumatic tubes going to the theoretical coffee shop that would be downstairs, designed to deliver them coffee and baked goods at speed.

Mostly she just liked the idea of pneumatic tubes. The *whoosh* and *thwump* of them made her smile. Finding small presents delivered as if by magic also had an appeal, she admitted to herself— none of which really had anything to do with where they lived.

For now, though, absent any *thwump* or *whoosh*, Casey set down her notebook, pen clipped to a worn indentation along the cover, and snatched her coffee cup off the floor before standing. Draining the cup, she crossed the forty-odd steps from the bed to the sink before backtracking to the table and sitting next to Jake.

"We should really find some kinda food," he said after a quick kiss good morning.

"Or," Casey countered, "we could go back to bed first."

"How are you still tired, even?" Jake asked, sipping at his own, quickly cooling coffee.

A roll of the eyes answered him, followed by a quick, silent laugh faked for effect before Casey asked, "Who said I was tired?"

"So," he said, "I'm just being dense then?"

"You're just being dense," Casey confirmed as she stood, holding his hand lightly, and led him back to the bed. And with that we'll leave them be for a while, again, letting them have their privacy for a few.

We were, earlier, talking about Mur. Mur, the original city. Mur, the mighty and timeless. The city itself spun around space and time like a child's toy kicked by the family dog on a bender. A word not often used to describe Mur: simple. Words often used to describe Mur: annoying, desperate, and "Where the fuck am I and where are my shoes?"

That last isn't, strictly, a word, but allow for a bit of license.

If you're going to understand Mur, you need to know that this is true. Pure truth, uncut by niceness and concern for the established structures of how most people think the world works. Back when humanity split into three kinds of people – hunters, gatherers, and assholes – there came a time when the existing, easily movable structures weren't enough.

Wait, let's back up. There used to be three primary roles in any sizable grouping of humans:

Hunters – These were the folks who crafted weapons, went out into the fields, and alternatively killed and were killed so that the others might eat something besides berries, roots, and fungi. Humanity wasn't good at those three, constantly tripping over yet another poisonous variation. So there came a diversification in the form of an omnivore shift.

Gatherers – At first these jerks kept killing off large numbers of people by grabbing the wrong berries, roots, and fungi. Later, after *Homo sapiens* started to add meat to its diet, they were in charge of looms and fabrics, as well as general upkeep back at the so-called ranch. Function following form, really.

Assholes – More important than originally thought, the first assholes were the ones who refused to do either of the other jobs, claiming they had to either create or administrate. People didn't look highly at these skills in the beginning, for good reason. Art is fantastic when you have shelter and food. Until then, it's a bit of a hindrance when a key part of your tribe flat-out refuses to help skin lunch because their muse is on them.

Once small, mobile tribes started to wane – due to population increase, which was due to the hunters and the gatherers getting much better at what they did, from speed of the kill to knowing which fucking berries not to shove down their throats – the assholes found their calling. They would organize stable, long-lasting structures to live in. Places multiple tribes could move into and become supratribes, combining forces and creating a leisure class, which sounded much better than "assholes."

Eventually they founded the first city: Mur. Some historians, looking back through broken lenses that could only see bits and bobs of reality anyway, declared, feeling quite informed, it had been named Ur. Others claimed it had been named Mu, and belonged with the lost continent of Atlantis. Either way, evidence of Ur or Mu couldn't really be found, but the existence of such a city made too much sense to let go of. Historians held on to the concept partly because it was actually true, and partly so they could spread the idea of a smarter leisure class being the root of all cities, while removing the idea that they were really just assholes. Historians – back during the founding of Mur – of course, were assholes.

Mur stood as a shining example of what humanity could achieve, if it bothered to care to, for centuries. And then, one day, it vanished. Poof. Gone. No trace remained, except a few stories. What actually happened remains fairly simple, if looked at the right way. The city simply fell out of time and space in a rational sense, going about and spinning directionless across all spaces and times simultaneously.

At fault was an antelope, which became later, among other things, a cat. We'll get there, I promise. Sort of. But for now, you need to know that Mur stood alone and yet accessible.

The city, laid out in a circle for aesthetic reasons by the assholes known as city planners, was built with a wall around it.

Into the wall were cut seven gates. Each gate was fitted with a heavy door, and the ability to secure it against invaders as needed. But like any mass with an irregular spin and orbit through space and time that allows it to touch all points simul-multi-taniously (you'd be surprised how many small objects exist in that state, really), Mur touched, and interacted with, the rest of the world at different points.

Unwary people could walk through certain doors and find themselves in Mur. Unfortunately, if they were dumb enough to walk back out, confused, they would find themselves in a totally different place and time on Earth. Turning back and trying again wouldn't work, as that door to Mur had already spun away. So they were stuck. This happened to many of the people who found Mur. Signs were put up trying to warn folks about the problem at all seven gates to the city, but since language evolves they were pretty damn useless more often than not. But, hey, the city coordinators reasoned, we tried, and past that what can you do, stand there and shout? Not going to happen.

A few lucky ones, for reasons that no one has ever explained, were capable of not only entering and leaving at the same spot, but of finding their way back to Mur as often as they wished. Those people made the rest fairly uncomfortable, possessing an ability others wanted, not to mention the new revenue stream that being able to take people with them brought.

Mur spun on, growing with internal time and population, expanding upward and using as much of its land as it could. How it kept seasons, night and day, and access to crops and fresh water, much less a sun that shone, remained more of those unexplained facets of life that kept many scientists in Mur in money. The closest they'd come was to insist that since Mur was everywhere, it had access to those things the rest of the Earth normally enjoyed. That didn't make more sense than shrugging, honestly. Time passed and people learned to not ask, because answers cost money and made no sense, regardless.

Along the way, Mur gave birth to other cities of myth, such as, but not limited to: Brigadoon, Asgard, Oz, Stars Hollow, and Tartarus. Some claimed Camelot was a Mur analog as well, but that's silly, as Camelot existed exactly where you think it did – north of what would become Vancouver, Canada. But that's a different story and we're talking about Mur, here.

Life inside Mur stood fairly normal, despite all of the previous. Let's face it: humanity is very good at just going about a day without letting the impossible bother them. Plus, the longer the impossible hangs there, the more it seems perfectly possible. Days rolled past and new days dawned and life continued. So why waste too much time fretting about how?

Spurred on by technology, ethical standards, and information from what you might consider both the past and the future, Mur accessed and developed a hybrid of internal ethics and technology that worked better than anywhere else on Earth. They had, if you'll allow, something of a cheat sheet, being able to see where they'd come from and where they would've been going if they'd remained on the chess board. This let them cherry pick which structures to hold tight to.

People born in Mur learned to not venture forth and enjoyed a fruitful life in the city of cities – still dangerous enough to stab you in a dark alley, but also still fabulous enough to elevate consciousness to where even the objectively worst performance art could be appreciated by someone. Once you lived in Mur, you, generally speaking, never wanted to live anywhere else. Some claimed this was mostly because you couldn't pick where and when you would live, if you just left, but they were fooling themselves. It was the best-worst place ever to exist on Earth, and they knew it.

What people didn't know about Mur, but which you're allowed to know about because chances are you won't tell anyone of import, is one of the big reasons for the continued survival of Mur. One of the city's great hidden strengths remained... we'll come back to that, actually. Don't worry, this contains no lies, including that promise. Just remember that every inch of this is true and you'll be fine. But Casey and Jake are laying in bed and busy debating what to do about food, and really, isn't that more important?

"Technically," Casey said, stretching her arms above her head until her hands hit the wall, "we missed breakfast."

"Meal times are a state of mind," Jake said, rolling onto his side to face her. "I thought we agreed that ages back."

"It's true," she agreed, "but the picky places we can *get* the food from don't go along with our decrees in this."

"So it's, what, a search for brunch?"

Casey sat up, feet kicking at the covers to get them off her. "We could go to Ron's," she suggested, knowing it would be rejected.

"Ron's has the worst brunch of anywhere to ever brunch," Jake said. "Why not The Old Chicken?"

"Do they still insist on making everything spicy?" she asked.

"Not *everything*," Jake said.

"All right, their water is decidedly plain. Fine, look, we can just go to the—"

"Square?" Jake said, finishing the thought for her.

"Yup," she agreed, standing and heading for a shower.

Jake lay in bed, waiting for her to finish, for his turn at some hot water, and laughed to himself. Nine times out of ten they ended up at the Square, their preferred diner of choice. They still both insisted on offering up other options in some strange attempt to stave off the restaurant becoming so default that they never even darkened the door of another place. The discussion was ritual – now complete, they could finally start their day for real.

Jake busied himself washing the coffee maker and their mugs, content. Soon enough, Casey traded places with him, letting him grab a shower while she finished getting ready and straightened up the apartment some. Jake got dressed, post-shower, and realized as he grabbed a jacket that they hadn't said a word to each other, moving around in a combination of routine and something close to ceremony.

They locked the door behind them, walked downstairs, crossed the lobby, and Jake pushed open the door, letting Casey sweep past him onto the street. The full light of the day hit them both square in the face, slapping them fully into what remained of the morning.

Turning left, they started the winding path to the Square diner. Walking anywhere in Mur started off as a lesson in frustration. Along with the wall surrounding the city, the paranoid City planners, afraid that they would be discovered for being assholes, had laid the streets out in a labyrinthian pattern. You couldn't go more than three blocks in any direction without needing to turn. You'd find yourself going half a block out of your way, and then back again, just to walk a theoretically straight line from A to B.

Jake didn't even notice it, at this point in his life, having been born there. Casey, on the other hand, having only arrived in Mur a few years ago, couldn't let it go, grumbling to herself at least once a day. Store owners had taken advantage of it over the thousands of years of the town's history; knowing all the ways straight through were blocked by solid buildings, and through-paths being illegal, they'd built stores along many of the switchbacks and deviations knowing people would be forced to traverse them, Mur being a big town for walking.

Two blocks over, half a block Spireward, half a block wallward, another block over, and a block Spireward. Casey kept her morning grumble to herself, letting her love of the city override it. They passed a small deli, nodding at Sharlene, the owner. Sharlene waved back, looking up from her work sketching new specials on the front window in grease pencil.

Sharlene had moved to Mur by accident twenty years earlier. She'd come from a time post-discovery-of-fire but pre-wheel. People walked in to Mur from all sorts of times, including the time before Mur even existed. It works out in the end—trust in that. But Sharlene, nee Klunt, walked through what she'd thought was a very elaborate cave entrance and found herself in Mur. Shocked, scared, and ready to kill anything that moved, she'd been taken in by Emily Frain. Emily ran a small flower shop and hated to be alone. Both her sisters had died recently, leaving her to manage the family store by herself, so the addition of Klunt was seen as a boon. Well, all right, it was seen as a boon once she got Klunt to stop punching and biting strangers.

Slowly, Klunt settled into a feeling of safety. Emily renamed her Sharlene, after the dead sister who she'd actually liked, as opposed to the other one who we won't even begin to get into. They worked well together, Emily teaching Sharlene to read and write, while Sharlene taught Emily how to fight and protect her property. If anyone had thought to offer an award for the least successfully robbed flower store, Emily and Sharlene could've, by year two, won it.

Emily died around the seventh year of Sharlene's import to Mur. Bad luck, really – just the sort of accident that happens in a big city. Construction is rampant, of course, and sometimes chunks of stone or brick, sometimes half the size of a human head, fall off a large structure and plummet to the ground. People get fired over it, of course, but when the path of the falling rock intersects someone, there's not only job loss but monetary repayment. Of course, a bunch of money could not even begin to make up for the loss of Emily Frain, a woman who was willing to take in an almost feral human and discover the happy woman inside, who loved to waltz.

Without Emily, Sharlene found she didn't like flowers and turned the store into a deli instead, using her influx of horribly earned cash. She had no partner, no employees yet, but was planning for it. She was waiting for the right fit, the correct twist of life, to reveal to her the perfect partner.

Until that time came, she worked her deli and worked on her art, enjoying drawing specials on the windows and smiling at regulars as they walked past.

∞

The bell above the door of the Square diner rang as Casey nudged it open with a foot. Jake's hand caught the edge of the door as it swung back toward him in Casey's wake and they took a table near the front window.

The Square didn't actually serve brunch so much as it served everything all the time. That played into Jake and Casey's platonic ideal of brunch: ordering random mixes of breakfast and lunch items like children demanding cereal and spaghetti for dinner.

"What's the plan?" Casey asked as she unslung the thin crossbody bag she wore, putting it between her knees. The top of the bag remained unzipped, and the head of a small, electric travel guitar peeked out.

Casey hated to leave home without an instrument on her, specifically the travel guitar, if possible. Realistically a metal stick with six strings, frets, and some tuners along one side, she'd plugged a wireless transmitter into the jack, paired to a small travel amp hooked to her belt. Jake used to ask, he used to insist she wouldn't need it and that she almost never actually touched it when they went out, but he stopped after a few protests, figuring the guitar worked as her security blanket. As they got closer, he discovered the real reason behind the habit and still categorized it as mostly security blanket – just a very strange and theoretically deadly one.

"The plan?" Jake asked, shifting all of his cutlery slightly until the arrangement pleased him. "The plan is to eat brunch."

"I mean after that," Casey said, adjusting the amp on her belt so it didn't knock into the side of her chair.

"Pay the bill?" Jake asked, smirking.

"All right, jerkbutt," Casey said, sprinkling it with laughter, "you know exactly what I mean. I have a show later, you have a thing—"

"Work," Jake corrected.

"Yeah, a thing, like I said," Casey agreed, smiling, "but that leaves a lot of day. I was just thinking, we could go see a new couch maybe."

"Do we need a new couch?"

"Don't we?"

"We could replace the couch with something better than a couch, is all I mean," Jake said, looking over at the waiter who'd appeared seemingly out of nowhere (but really just out of the back the way waiters normally did).

They ordered without looking at menus, and thanked their waiter, before returning to the matter at couch-like hands. Not that couches have hands. Well, sure, all right, some do, and Jake thought that if he found a couch that had arms that looked like arms, with hands at the end, he might be into that particular couch, but otherwise a couch was just a cushiony butt-bench and a place to feel bad about accidentally napping and he could take them or leave them.

"What would be better than a new couch to replace the horrible thing we have now?" Casey asked.

"A daybed, maybe," Jake said. He sipped at his water and reached down to twitch the placement of his fork again.

"A daybed is just a couch without a back," Casey pointed out.

"Right, but that would open the room up."

"And be annoying for sitting on – no way to lean back. How about we just get a really nice couch?"

Jake shrugged. "We can do that, too. I just think there are other options."

"Such as couches that are missing part of their couchness," Casey said, nodding.

"Or a few armchairs, instead of one big couch," Jake offered.

Their food showed up: eggs, sunny-side up, a cup of tomato soup, and a salad for Jake; pancakes and chicken wings for Casey. They started to eat, Jake crumbling crackers into his soup. They ate in silence for a while and then started to snicker and laugh as they snarked at people walking by outside.

"Oh, see," Casey said, using a wing bone stripped of all meat to point at a man walking by outside before dropping it onto a side plate, "that guy isn't a native. He's been here maybe two years?"

"Hey now," Jake said, laughing, "careful casting stones, newbie."

"I've been here five years," Casey protested, "I'm a native, now, retroactively."

"Are you, though?" Jake asked. "I mean a native is someone born here. You weren't. So…"

"So even when I'm eighty, I won't be a native?"

"Technically, no," Jake said, swallowing some salad. "That's just not how it works."

"I don't see why not," Casey said, "I mean, I know the city, I live here – I love it here, in fact."

"But you weren't born here," Jake pointed out.

"Better, I choose to stay here," Casey said, raising an eyebrow. "Or is that not better?"

"I think it's terrific," Jake said, "but it still doesn't make you a native."

"See, it's that sort of attitude that makes people feel like people born here are just smug."

"We're not *just* smug, and you know it. We're *also* occasionally rude and pretentious."

Casey sighed. "I'm serious, though. I can feel the city in my bones as well as you can, at this point."

"Sure, and if we had a term for native-in-all-ways-except-born-here, you'd be dead on. But we don't."

"So let's use native," she said, chewing on another wing.

"It just feels wrong," Jake said, poking at his eggs. He didn't want to fight, and even though this wasn't yet a fight, he knew it could become one fairly quickly. He had a problem – the same one as Casey, actually – avoiding a fight just because it wasn't wanted. Stepping back, even when they thought they were right, was a problem they both shared.

Somehow, though if asked neither of them could explain how, that hadn't sunk their relationship yet. They'd each go at it along rigid lines, neither of them actually wanting the fight, both of them wishing they could let themselves back away. Along the way to complete implosion, though, one of them would just fizzle out. Both of them would swear the dissolve remained unintentional, but the move was as reliable as their ability to forgive each other seamlessly for the fight itself.

Today, though – well, today Jake decided to actively try something different. He chewed, swallowed, and nodded at Casey. "Then again," he said slowly, "what do I know, right? I can't be the arbiter of nativeness. Nativosity. Nativity...no, that's totally wrong. But, you know, I mean it's not up to me, right?"

"I..." Casey thought for a second, feeling the shift out carefully. "Well, let me ask one question."

"Shoot."

"Do you all have meetings where you dole out flash cards of people in town and decide who is and who isn't a native yet?"

"We're not supposed to talk about it," Jake said, smiling.

"Then I guess," Casey said, throwing the same sort of argument life-line Jake had thrown her, "you might be the nativeness arbiter but couldn't admit it, so no, you're not. And I only say that to preserve your cover, sir."

"Why, thank you," Jake said, nodding slightly. "So furniture hunting, then?"

"Sure…no, wait, we can't. I mean we can later, but I should go by The Alibi and check the new sound system for tonight."

"And I guess I should have a quick meeting about tonight myself," Jake agreed.

"Calling one, or forgot about one you had planned?" Casey asked, knowing full well what the odds were.

"Forgot," Jake admitted.

Casey nodded and set her napkin on her plate. "Then we should probably get moving."

"I'll grab the bill—meet you outside?"

"Sure," she said, standing, guitar bag in hand. She fished in her pocket and left a tip as Jake went to go pay the bill.

Jake hadn't wanted to tell Casey that there was a bad side to being a native of Mur. He ran his fingers over some money in his pocket, waiting in line to pay the bill, and thought about the cost of it all, as he saw it. Well, he thought wryly, all your childhood friends *and* enemies still lived in the same city, and if any of them moved you never heard from them again, period-full-stop.

There was no place for your best friend leaving but keeping in touch and running into each other later. Stories like that fascinated Jake. People would come to Mur with them and share them over a drink, always told in hazy ways that kept their past at a distance, and Jake would just be swallowed by the very idea of it. But that hazy distance was the other thing. People didn't talk about their history outside of Mur much. It made sense but also left Jake, and all the other natives, with this annoying blank space.

His history, on the other hand, was routinely dragged from him by strangers once they knew he had been born here. They were somehow more fascinated by him then he was by them. And it grated after a while. A silly, stupid sort of annoyance that was easily shrugged off, but it was there.

The woman ahead of Jake was taking forever to sort out a tip while she paid, and Jake caught himself idly watching the till. Tracking how the guy behind it moved, how often he glanced down at the open money drawer, or moved enough of his body away from it that you could pass by, bump into him, and probably slip some money out of the till and into a pocket.

That sort of lift wasn't what Jake did, but as a kid he'd found his innate talents aligned well with removing bits of money from people in ways they didn't see coming. Picking locks and pockets, small con games, even plotting a decent robbery – these were the life skills Jake discovered and explored.

His parents both worked honest jobs and wanted Jake to do the same. He liked music, they knew – even if he showed zero aptitude for learning to play it, he could run a music shop, or work in a concert venue. Plenty smart, they felt he could even own such a place after a few years if he really applied himself.

Instead of any of that, Jake and his first boyfriend, Sylvan, had decided to teach themselves how to steal things. They held each other to what they thought were exacting standards, inventing from whole cloth how to pick pockets and do card tricks. They actually weren't bad, considering they had no idea what they were doing. They practiced on each other for a good long while and then decided to try their newfound skills on random people in a park near where they lived.

They got arrested inside half an hour.

The scare of it made Sylvan back away and declare that he really did want to be a cobbler like his dad. For Jake, though, the sheer failure of it forced him to double down and try harder. Without a friend by his side, Jake ended up talking with shadier and shadier people, trying to find an in. Mur, like anywhere else ever to exist on Earth that contained over three hundred people, had organized crime. Really, the only difference in settlements was that the larger your urban area, the more organized your crime tended to be. For Mur that ended up very organized indeed.

Jake worked for them for a while, but never warmed to the idea that crime would be a job like any other – you worked for a boss, did what you were told, and stayed in your lane. So he tried to leave. The problem with organized crime and leaving is it makes said organizers feel bad. No one wants to put in years of training, and by that time it *had* been a few years, only to have their worker up and go freelance.

Jake was barred from doing anything big, and he was all right with that rule until he found out that it really meant not doing anything at all crimelike if he got noticed in the least. He ended up working for the same crime bosses he hated a second time, out of frustration.

The second time, his leaving took. He made it clear that he didn't want to step on their toes and that, honestly, it would be way worse to have someone in their organization who worked actively against them. When it was pointed out to him that he could simply be disposed of – either killed or bodily tossed out of Mur – Jake shrugged, laughed, and asked a simple question: "But what if you didn't do that?"

Havelock, the big boss at the time, laughed in return and nodded at the little snot standing in front of him. "Then you'd get what you want."

"I mean..." Jake said thoughtfully, "that sounds like a good idea to me."

"I bet it does, Meyer," came the reply, "but it doesn't answer why I should. You go solo, you could expose our inner workings—"

"Which would get me killed."

"Or work against us, hit targets we're working on. Meyer, this isn't something we do. You work for us or you don't work."

"There was a guy," Jake said, jerking a thumb over his shoulder at an imaginary person, "playing some Find the Queen in the park the other day. He work for you?"

"No, of course not," Havelock said.

"Some rich guy Spireward. Last week he got robbed. You care?"

"Of course not."

"Then there you go. I don't want," Jake told his boss honestly, "to be some giant fish laughing as I mess with you. I'm just good at this stuff. And I don't want to do it for you. No offense, right? I just wanna be my own guy. That's—"

"That why you got into this line of work in the first place?" Havelock finished for him.

"Exactly," Jake smiled.

"You're fearless, Meyer, I'll give you that. Most of my guys, they wouldn't dare just stand here and pitch this to me. You could stay here and go places."

"Thanks, but..." Jake trailed off and finished his sentence with a shrug.

Havelock nodded. He understood and – despite the general rules he worked with, rules that kept things in check for him – he agreed, and let Jake leave. Even after Havelock retired, in that way almost all crime bosses retire, in the middle of the night with a gunshot, Jake worked alone or with a small group of friends on slightly larger jobs. Just nothing too big, ever. The current organized crime working in Mur didn't like the fact that he remained one of the few exceptions but also hadn't been able to scare him into working for them, so Jake followed his own path, watching his step exactly as much as he thought he absolutely had to.

He smiled, the woman ahead of him finally having worked out a tip, and paid the bill, overtipping out of habit. He felt you should reward good service.

Casey learned against the building, near the door to the Square. She made sure she kept out of the way and that she leaned without taking either leg off the ground. None of that one-foot-propped-against-the-wall business for her. Instead, she managed to look relaxed, slouching along the wall like it'd paid her to promote something. She knew she was doing it, unnaturally seeming relaxed even as she kept an extra-close eye on her surroundings; situational relaxation, her Commanding Officer had called it. All right, fine, the CO'd called it SitLax, because military people love to shorten things. Casey refused to call anything SitLax on principle, given how it sounded to her.

Either way, she scanned the street quickly, making it look slow. Big, obvious head movements coupled with quick eye scans; drumming her fingers on the wall behind her to keep count of things, setting a rhythm up to make the counting automatic. The guitar bag barely even touched the wall, no pressure on the instrument itself, but if you glanced at her – hell, if you looked right at her and stared a full minute – you would walk away swearing she was slumped against that wall.

So yeah, Casey knew she was doing it; she also hated that she did it. But reflex bests us all at times. Worse, to her mind, she knew she did it, caught herself doing it, and still didn't stop. She wanted to stop—she told herself to at least twice, but couldn't. Casey sighed even as she thought the word 'couldn't,' knowing that abdicated responsibility yet again.

Her annoyance with herself reached a definitive middle as Jake came out, the bell above the Square's door ringing as it opened. Snapping back at the waist lightly, Casey bumped her ass against the wall, pushing off and taking a quick step to match Jake's gait. She reached out and took his hand; he squeezed it tightly, once, while he searched her face. He could feel, just that sense of a partner, that something was off. A thrum in the machinery that didn't belong there. Casey looked away from him, shaking her head just enough for him to notice. He took the hint and smiled at her.

"So off to The Alibi?" he asked, letting her set the agenda for the conversation.

"Yeah, you got your meeting?" she replied, feeling her tension ease with the regaining of the familiar.

"At home, yeah. Probably take about two or three hours, that work for you?"

"Yup," she agreed, "have to run through the new sound system, can get some practice in while no one's there—three hours, then a couch maybe."

"Then a couch," he agreed, "maybe."

She squeezed his hand once, hard, and let go. They walked together for a few blocks until the next block twist, Jake going back to the apartment and Casey turning the other way to head to The Alibi.

The Alibi inhabited a two-story building, wedged between a shoe store (Bob's Sole) and a pawnshop (Eight Pawns). The Alibi's façade contained three things besides brick: a door, the bar's name painted in big, dark-blue letters against black above the door, and a single, wide window painted black with house paint, the thick brush strokes still visible in the final, dried effort.

The owners of The Alibi, currently the third set of owners, actually, didn't want the place to seem uninviting, but they also didn't want to actually invite people. They needed to, to keep the doors open and lights on – they'd admit that quickly enough. When Billy and Rhona had bought the bar from the previous owners they'd wanted a place they could hang out with their friends.

Their friends could bring other friends, all right, that would be fine—but strangers? You never knew what you would get with strangers. Rhona felt that whole scheme smacked of too much risk. Billy pointed out to her wife that specific risk came with owning a bar, so they kept the place open to the public and just friendly enough to get people in.

Then they started bringing back live music. This was, in both their estimations, where the whole thing had gone sideways for them. Suddenly The Alibi was not only getting strangers, it was becoming popular; the bar threatened to become a place talked about far further out than their immediate neighborhood.

Billy had just grown sick of the jukebox and wanted some live music to listen to, and the idea snowballed from there. So they painted over the window and darkened the bar a bit more and hoped the balance would be restored. Which it may have been, except both women were fans of good music so they kept booking artists people enjoyed. One of their, and the crowd's, favorites was Casey.

Casey, had a standing invite and filled in any quiet nights The Alibi had so long as her schedule allowed for it. Casey didn't want to be a famous rocker, she had no big dreams of stardom, but she adored playing for an audience.

Brightly lit, while the place stood closed but setting up, The Alibi revealed its scars and bruises to Casey. She took in the small, red, round tables that dotted the floor, each meant for two to stand at and each routinely hosting four. She smiled at the booths, done up in blue vinyl, remembering as she did most nights how she and Jake had talked until closing the first night they met, sitting in one of them, the cracked and worn vinyl creaking and sputtering like a trapped mouse. As she looked at the low stage, its lone stool shoved into a corner next to the empty mic stand, she felt she could see the bar, in her mind, from the angle she normally saw it, standing there, cheap, ugly rug under her boots. Simply put: Casey loved The Alibi.

"Case," Oscar said from behind the bar, "you know you don't go on for...eight hours, right?" Turning away, he reached up to put a bottle on a high shelf along the bar back. "I get it, I get it," he continued, over his shoulder, "you like to be early, but girl..."

Crossing the floor to lean both hands on the bar, Casey smiled at the six-foot-three bartender. "What'd I tell you about calling me 'girl'?"

"You'd break my hands with my own tie," he said, facing her again and slowly straitening the yellow tie sitting around his neck. It rested along a blue shirt and tucked into the silver vest he wore, buttoned tight. "But you don't know," he said, "I might like it."

"You have issues, Oscar," Casey said, unslinging her bag.

"I'm black," he said, drawing a glass of water for her, "you're Hispanic. This bar? It's white as *hell*. We both got issues, being here this often. "

"Seriously?" Casey asked. "You're gonna...Oscar. Come on. Also, I'm German. My parents were German. We've been over this."

"No one with your looks and your skin color is German," Oscar insisted. "Unless, wait, *when* are you from?"

"Oddly racist, Oscar – there are all sorts of people in Germany, just like there always were, so nope, nice try," Casey said with a laugh. "I'm here to check the new sound system. Rhona around?"

"She'll be back up in a few. Go wander, maybe. Come back in a bit."

"You're kicking me out?" Casey asked, surprised.

"You know Billy's been on a tear recently, even for you. Just give it a good fifteen and I'll make sure she thinks it was her idea you come by super-eight-hours-early, all right?"

"Well, you're dressed like a carnival barker, so I guess wrangling is part of..."

"You're going to stand there and mock my outfit?" Oscar asked, smoothing his tie unnecessarily.

"You're going to bring this all down to race, again, *and* call me girl? What's really off the table today, huh?" She sipped the water, slinging her guitar bag back over her shoulder.

"You and me hooking up, that's what. After this, no way. Sorry...*Chica.*"

"You're gay, you *unbelievable* ass," she laughed, shaking her head.

"It isn't unbelievable, just the product of a lot of hard work and..."

"Not *your* ass, that you *are* an...oh fuck off, Oscar. I'll be back in fifteen." She nudged the water glass an inch and stepped back from the bar.

"Thank you, Case. I love you, Case," Oscar said, laughing.

"You're welcome, Oscar. I love you, Oscar," Casey said, finishing their personal ritual.

Outside, Casey kicked lightly at the street, took a deep breath, and started to stroll around the block. She reran her conversation with Oscar, laughing at his attempt to get a time location out of her. One of the early things she'd learned in Mur was to not discuss when you came from often. Where was fine...mostly. Even then it could be awkward. People wanted to know what happened when they came from New Amsterdam and heard that you came from New Sprawl, but mentioned the same geographic markers.

If you said you were from somewhere in their future they wanted details; they expected everyone *else* to have a degree in history. Residents didn't expect to go home again, so they treated any detail as important and could grill you for hours about the smallest ones. What happened to this deli, when did busses start to have eight wheels, why did Canada come into existence, and who defeated the black plague?

Of course, if they found out you were from their past, they grilled you on the same sort of details, wanting to ferret out information about ancestors and so on. There was no winning the game, only refusing to play it. Your personal history vanished, for the most part, once you were in Mur. The remaining important part of your own personal story became only that you were currently in Mur. Friends, good friends, would dig into their lives, of course; humans are human after all, and sharing overly personal details is a species-inherited fetish.

Casey hesitated even saying she was German, even though it was only kind of true. Mostly she did it to annoy Oscar.

The facts were as follows: Her father was born in Germany, sure, and he met her mother when she fled from Belize, but that was the 2400s C.E. in a nutshell. People moved around frequently, avoiding catastrophe and wars. Borders were supposed to be tighter but, as they often did during such times, ended up being far looser. Casey herself was born in Boston, her parents having fled Germany not long before the German-Italian War broke out.

But, in some cases, though we don't often like to admit it, facts are just that: facts. In this case they tell the tale of the tape, but not the reality of a family. Casey Harrison was, in her own head, from Boston. Before Mur, Boston was the only home she knew. She'd lived in many places, traveled the globe far and wide, to be sure, but home sat off Hanover Street. Her parents didn't define themselves as being from somewhere else, either. They were just Bostonians, the pride of the area creeping into their behavior quickly and cementing itself there for the rest of their lives.

Casey turned a corner and wished she still smoked. Waiting and passing time seemed to faster when all it took was some fire and patience. Without the fire, the patience took a critical hit, for her.

She passed an alley, wedged between a run-down used toy store and a nail salon. Then, blinking and playing the situation back, she turned on her heel. Considering the replay, Casey reached over her shoulder and drew out her guitar, nudging the portable amp on her hip to life with an elbow. She didn't want a fight; she resented the idea at a bone-deep level. Then again...

Casey walked back to the opening of the alley. What she saw confirmed what she thought she'd seen. Three guys, apparently sent from Central Casting, harassing an old woman who seemed to be trying to shrink against a wall. The three wore wallet chains unironically, which says everything, regardless of time or place. They were mooks—you know, the type of people who get labeled 'Street Toughs' by the elderly and 'Problem Children' by the courts that eventually seize their throats in a grip that does nothing to help or change them.

"Snap to!" Casey said sharply. She held her guitar in front of her, left hand resting lightly on the strings, right braced to strum. She stood, back straight, looking like a piece of forged metal dropped from the sky to impose order. In reality her body was totally relaxed, poised to move quickly and efficiently, the way she'd been trained.

"Fuck off," one of the mooks said. Casey decided he would be the leader, given the way the other two just nodded at him. So she designated him Mook One, with the bright red crew cut. Mook Two, to his left, tugged at the bottom edge of his drab green jacket and grinned the grin of those who try to hard to look 'crazed' to outsiders, to present themselves as a danger. Casey figured Mook Two would fold fastest. Mook Three stood to his leader's right, the small gang's tough, muscles straining again the ripped long sleeves of his shirt. He'd be a problem, she figured, unless his joints worked like every other human's.

"I said snap to!" Casey repeated. The mooks all laughed this time. She nodded. "Ma'am," she asked the old woman, "are you all right?"

"I'm fi—" the woman started to answer.

"Don't talk to her, talk to us," Mook One said, stepping away from the old woman and turning his attention fully on Casey.

He took her in, giving her a huff of contempt: around five-eleven, her mother's dark skin, hazel eyes, and brown hair, but her father's German cheekbones and bone structure, upon which she'd developed enough muscle to be clear even under a jacket. He, blessing it with its own snort of distain, noticed her guitar as well: a metal stick that had looked like a weapon before it had been carved flat on one side to add strings.

"You gonna play us a song?" he asked, curling his lip in what he felt was a grin of pure evil.

Casey flexed the fingers of her left hand slowly, drawing a small laugh from Mook Three. "If you don't back away in about three seconds, I sure as shit am," she said, her voice flat and cold.

"Oh, honey," the old woman said, "no, I'll be—"

"Shut *up*, woman!" Mook Two said, raising his hand to slap her.

Casey's eyes tightened at the motion. "Three," she muttered, out of formality. She played a quick set of arpeggios, all G in the third position, then shifted up the neck, body of the guitar braced by her right arm, and played a succession of notes, all a half-step out of harmonic relation to each other.

As she played she focused her will, her raw spiritual intent, down through her body, along her arms and into her fingers. It was with that that she plucked and held strings. The strings vibrated, the pick-ups resonated, and the electric impulses were converted to sound by the amp on her hip. All perfectly normal, if dissonant after a few notes.

The results weren't quite as normal.

Mook Two felt a force wrap around his body and lift him into the air. He started to scream but couldn't get it out before he met the wall face first. Mook Three watched in growing horror, but Mook One realized the source of the problem.

"You fucking—"

"Shhh," Casey said with a mean smile as she played more notes, hands moving faster across the strings. Mook One felt his body vibrate as if pinned down by an earthquake, and he dropped to the ground.

Casey walked the few steps over to him and looked down at him as she continued to play. He looked back at her, pain clear in his expression. He could feel his joints starting to separate from the vibrations – all of them at once. She looked down at him, understanding full well what he was going through, and nodded.

Then she kicked him in the face.

Mook Three ran. Later in the day he would describe the way five large men attacked them in an alley and try to rally his friends to do something about it. They wouldn't, mostly because they didn't believe him, but partly because Mooks One and Two would stumble back before anyone could decide what to do and, after seeing them, no one wanted to go anywhere for at least a day.

Casey grabbed her guitar, flipping it over her shoulder and slotting it back into the bag with an ease of habit. "You all right, Ma'am?" she asked the old woman, stepping over Mook One as she did.

"Oh, honey, I'm fine," the woman said, standing up straight. Casey could see her clearly now: Her face was a web of wrinkles, but her eyes were as alert as anyone on Casey's old team. She wore an ensemble that could only be described as "hasty." Her hair was looped up in a messy bun that tilted to the right and wobbled as she spoke. "You didn't need to do that, any of that."

"They were going to beat the fuck..." Casey stopped and clicked her tongue, "oh, uhh sorry about the langu—they were going to rough you up, Ma'am."

"They were going to try, but I knew I'd be fine," the old woman said. "The city provides."

"Well this time I guess it provided me, so it's a good thing I did step in, huh?" Casey offered the woman a hand.

"When you put it like that," the woman agreed, taking Casey's hand as she stepped around the mooks on the ground. Casey walked them both out of the alley. "Even so, not many would have come back, once they caught sight of these boys."

Casey laughed. "They weren't exactly a threat, not to me."

"Even so. You didn't *want* to get involved. Did you?" The old woman smiled sweetly at Casey.

Casey felt a trap closing in on her, and she took a sharp breath, holding it for three seconds to stop the rise of foreboding as best she could. "I thought I could help, so I did," she insisted, suddenly sure her best option would be to leave the woman there and get back inside the safe enclosure of The Alibi.

"Oh, sure," the woman agreed. "But," she patted their clasped hands with her free one, dry, papery skin pressing against Casey's hand, "you didn't want to—I mean you wanted to help, but I could see it in your face, you didn't want to fight."

"You should never *want* to fight, not really," Casey said softly, "but you were in trouble."

"This town – well any, I suppose—that isn't as common as you might think. Honey, what's your name?"

"Huh? Oh, Casey. My name is Casey."

"Well, Casey, thank you," the woman said, patting their hands again.

"You're very welcome, Ma'am."

"Stop with that Ma'am stuff, honey, we're friends now." She smiled warmly when she said it, but Casey felt a small chill along her spine.

"Sure we are, Ma'am – so, then," Casey asked, "what's your name?"

"Ahh, well, yes. Most people just call me Grandma, I suppose."

"That's not really a good name, though, is it?" Casey gave the woman a smile of her own, knowing it would come off as guarded and fine with that.

"I like it, sure enough, but some people call me Key, if they really want to."

"Key? I like it," Casey said.

"I thought you might," Key agreed. "So, would you like a job?"

"Excuse me?" Casey let go of Key's hand and took a step away from the woman.

"I need a young person for some odd jobs," Key said, clasping both her hands behind her back as they continued to walk, "and you seem to be nice, and caring."

Casey realized she'd been heading back to The Alibi but didn't feel like leading this strange – and growing stranger by the minute – woman there. She turned at the next corner, Key still walking beside her.

"That's nice of you to offer, a bit sudden, but... you know, I'm good, thanks."

Key nodded, watching the sidewalk as they walked. "I'm not asking for a bodyguard. I just need someone to help me out with a few simple tasks."

"Then you should have no problem finding someone," Casey told her.

"I already have," Key insisted. "Please trust me, you'll love this. It won't take up much time, you won't have to fight anyone, and you'll help me to help people. Just, once. For me."

"Once?"

"One time. Just meet me," Key looked around and pointed to the corner, "at that corner, tomorrow. You'll help me once, I'll pay you, and if you think it's still not a good fit I'll never darken your door again. Deal?"

"Against my better judgment: deal. You're a strange woman, Key," Casey said, looking at the corner to work out where they had wandered to. She felt her jaw tighten when she recognized it as just down the block from the loft.

"No stranger than you, I think, honey," Key said. She waved a little grandmotherly wave and stopped walking with Casey, crossing the street instead.

Casey lifted an arm to wave back but stopped herself, not sure why she kept playing this old woman's game. She stood there like that, one arm in a static wave, for a full minute, watching Key walk away, making sure the woman kept going and didn't look back.

While Casey gathers her wits and unfreezes from confusion, let's talk about her some more. Casey Harrison was a Combat Musician – retired. She celebrated her twenty-fifth birthday by signing up for the military to help the U.S. fight the tail end of the German-Italian War, which had spread to Australia, by then a land contested by both countries.

During basic training she took a few aptitude tests and was yanked away from an infantry position and handed a guitar. Casey had never played an instrument in her life. The next years were all training and practice. She learned to fight, discovered her ability to lead a small troop, and played a lot of guitar.

Along with playing came the concepts of Combat Music. To put them as simply as possible: vibrations can be deadly, harmonics can fuck your day up, and your force of will can be electronically transmitted and used to do some truly strange shit if you know how.

Her troop came in like the cavalry, playing music both to lift spirits and melt tanks. The military didn't have many Combat Musicians, and those it did have strained under the pressure. Lifting a person wasn't too bad; the things Casey did in the alley were all standard technique. But for real combat you needed bigger effects. Sometimes that meant multiple instruments layering harmonics and intent over each other, but it also meant, more often than not, hurtful levels of focus. Pushing your will into another container, and using it to harm objects, cost. It cost your health, and it cost a bit of your soul. Casey grew sick of it.

So she deserted. Shamed by her choice, she also couldn't find a better option. The army wouldn't let her go. She couldn't keep on as she had without losing herself so fully that she wouldn't be recognizable to herself anyway. There was only one door left in her mind at the time. She ran. She spent a year hiding, living on the streets in different countries, sneaking across borders and oceans, until one day in 2495 she saw an army outpost, panicked, and took a door she hadn't noticed before in the back of an alley.

Mur took her in, and she'd made a new home of it.

Three people reached for weapons when the sound of a lock's tumblers snapping open rang out into the room. The fourth person held up his hands as he started to stand.

"Whoa there!" Jake said. "Let's not shoot anyone in my place, all right? Maybe we could see who it is first. If we were getting busted, would they unlock the door? Seriously?" he talked fast as he hurried to the door, grabbing it open like a magician's reveal. "See, it's just Case." Turning to Casey, he gave her a confused glance. "Hi, Case, everything good?"

She shrugged and kissed him on the cheek lightly. "I need to go back to The Alibi but...shit," she said as she looked at the people in the loft, "I forgot you were having a...I'll go."

"Yeah, good idea, *Casey*," one of the people at the table said, voice dripping ice. She crossed her arms, her right hand still holding a gun.

"Hey, Lane," Jake said, turning back to the table but keeping a hand on Casey's arm. "You might want to shut the fuck up."

"I'm sorry, are our women allowed to interrupt our meetings now? I'll get my wife right over," Lane said, shaking her head angrily. "Fuck your feelings, Meyer, this is business."

Jake squeezed Casey's arm before letting go and stalking back to the table. "*My* business, that *I'm* running, that *you*," he leaned on the table with both hands, "benefit from. So if you want to keep the arrangement, you'll shut the fuck up about now."

"Ach," one of the other table occupants, Benok, said, "Jake Meyer, you are not a fighter. Do not threaten us as such, eh?" He laughed as he said it, leaning back in his chair comfortably.

"I'll take bets on it," Quyto, the final person sitting at the table, said, nudging Benok with an elbow. "A Meyer/Lane fight? At the least it'd be funny and worth a few bucks, right?"

"Shut up, Quyto," Jake said, "no one is fighting anyone. Just give me a minute and fucking relax, all right?" —this last with a glare turned toward Lane.

Jake left the table, taking a deep breath, and walked the few steps back to Casey. She seemed calmer now, herself. Jake ran a hand along her arm. "What can I do?" he asked.

"I should really just go," she told him, looking around the loft.

"No, ignore those idiots," he insisted, lowering his voice, "they're just nervous we're still operating around Ferdinand's declarations."

"Well, I just had the strangest thing happen," Casey said, in quiet tones, her voice going a mile a minute as she ran down a simplified version of her encounter with Key. About halfway through, Jake's eyes widened. By the end he kissed her cheek and muttered, "Yeah, just hold on a sec," before turning back to the table. "We're done for the day."

"This is bullshit," Lane said, standing fast enough to knock over her chair.

"Yup," Jake agreed, "sure is. But we'll talk tomorrow. Same time, back here, and finish this."

"Meyer," Quyto said as he stood, "your shop, your rules, but we can't just put off business."

"Oh sure we can," Jake told him, "it's just some light crime. Come on, it isn't like we're on an actual schedule, outside of our wallets. It's all good, trust me. I'll explain the plan tomorrow, you'll agree because you always do, and we'll make some cash."

"You better be right," Quyto told him as he walked past him to the door.

"You only work with me because I am," Jake reminded him. "Hey Benok, tell your kid hi for me, will you?"

"Of course, Meyer," Benok agreed, sorting through a large bag he then slung on his back. He smiled at Lane and walked with her to the door, making sure to be between her and Jake.

"And Lane," Jake said as she and Benok reached the door, "come at me again like that and I'll break your nose."

"You could *try*," she huffed, slamming the door behind them.

Jake shook his head at the door, trying to will the annoyance he felt to push through the door and hit Lane square in the face.

Casey crossed her arms. "I was freaked out. Still am a bit, I guess, but you didn't need to toss everyone out."

"But come on," Jake said, growing excited and letting it show now that they were alone, "you met The Grandmother of Keys!"

"I did what now? No, I met some old woman who said her name was Key," Casey told him, "that's all."

"Grandmother of Keys," Jake insisted. "I mean meeting one of the Three Forces is a big deal. I wasn't even sure they existed. All right, fine, I mean I knew they had to, right? Because look at this place." He swept his arm in a gesture taking in the loft. "Not *this* place, but the city, the whole of it. They have to be real. And you met one."

"You've lost me," Casey said, crossing to sit at the table, falling into a chair heavily.

"You don't know about—"

"I think we're past that. I don't. You want to maybe—"

"Yeah, yeah, sorry," Jake said, sitting next to her. "They're these stories we hear as kids, growing up in Mur, you know? Like urban legends."

"But you think they're real?" She shook her head and wished, for the second time that day, that she still smoked.

"Well...yeah, I think I do," he admitted. "So there are these three forces, and they're called—"

"Hold on, don't tell me. They're called the Three Forces?" Casey shook her head with a bit of a laugh and just waved a hand toward the collection of bottles along the kitchen counter. "Please?"

"Sure," Jake got up and poured them each two fingers of scotch. "And yeah, the Three Forces. The stories name them The Grandmother of Keys, who I think you met, The Cat With No Face, and The Heart...well The Something Heart, but I always hear it different, from people. I grew up with it being called The Beating Heart, but I've heard Silent Heart, Waiting Heart, you get it."

Casey took a glass from Jake as he sat back down. "All right. I'm still with you."

"So The Cat—"

"With No Face. How does it eat?" Casey sipped at the scotch, pulled a whiskey face, and set the glass down.

"That's the thing. The Cat eats souls, I always heard. Wait, let me back up." Jake sipped his scotch, twirling the glass in his hand instead of returning it to the table. "So The Grandmother walks Mur to protect it, the way your grandmother looked after you as a kid, all right?"

"We had very different grandparents, I think. My grandmother worked on an assembly line into her eighties and hated everyone."

Jake laughed hard, setting his glass down almost too hard. "Fine, fine, but Case, just work with me here. She protects us. Quietly, you know? Not like she fights crime or anything, but she watches over Mur. All of it in service to The Heart. The Heart is, well—"

"Let me guess, The Heart is the heart of the city?"

"Literally, the embodiment of the soul of the city. Grandmother works for The Heart."

"All right, sure, why not." She drained her glass in one slightly ill-advised gulp, held it in her mouth while she reconsidered the move, and then swallowed. "So, tell me," she said softly, then shook her head and continued, "what is this Faceless Cat about?"

"The Cat With No Face eats souls. It's a cat. Just kind of a boogeyman figure in the whole thing. Watch out or The Cat could get you."

"But you think this is all real?" Casey asked, looking at Jake differently that she had before.

"I think something bigger than just happenstance runs this city." He waved his hands around again. "Mur is its own thing, so why wouldn't it be run by forces beyond what we can really figure? There has to be some reason the city works."

"So instead of turning to science, like you do with everything else," Casey pointed out, "you go right for magical cats and living cities."

"This might be one of those things you have to grow up here for," Jake said.

"Nope," Casey stood and took her glass to the sink, rising it out, "nice try though. We all have superstition. I just didn't expect to find you had a giant one. So hey," she leaned on the counter and looked at him, "why did this Grandmother need my help, if she's this powerful force?"

"Obviously she wants you for something, and this was her way to lure you in," Jake said with a hint of smile. Casey couldn't tell if he was joking or not. She decided he wasn't, if only because he really seemed to believe the rest of what he'd said, and she'd have to come to terms with that.

Casey held science tight, as did most people from the 2400s C.E. It never crossed her mind that Jake might be up for holding spiritual and scientific beliefs next to each other without worry. She had no experience with it, and clustered people into simple boxes of 'science' or 'non-science' even if those boxes were, for many, unfair and reductive.

So she shook her head at Jake with a ghost of a smile, for effect. "I think she's, at most, an old lady who might think she's this Grandmother of yours. Which, I don't even know. I'll go with her this one time and humor her."

"You also realize," Jake said, smirking, "that this is just further proof you're not a native, right? Not knowing these stories."

"Don't start that again. I know them now. So there," Casey replied, smiling some herself.

"Here's what I want to know," Jake said, rising and crossing the room to take her hand in his, "if this is all just one old woman who is slightly off, why did it freak you out so bad?"

"I, uhh, I didn't..." she pulled her hand from his. "I used the guitar."

"To deal with those guys?"

"Yeah, I mean I *used* it," she said softly.

"No, I get that," he told her, looking at the floor, "but why? You didn't need it, there were only three of them, right?"

"I don't know!" Casey insisted. "Instinct? I don't know. I just don't want it to be desire. And I can't tell if it was—does that make sense?"

"Of course it does. Why don't you take the night off, I can stop by The Alibi and cancel for you, and—"

Casey reached for his hand and gave it a hard squeeze, "No, I need that tonight, playing for real and not to destroy. You'll be there?"

"I can be there tonight, of course," he said squeezing her hand back.

She smiled at him. "It won't derail crime?"

"Nothing derails crime," Jake insisted. "But before you go back, why don't I grill you a cheese?"

"That would be lovely," she agreed, letting go of his hand to walk to the bed and fall into it, trusting the mattress to catch her, as it always had.

We brushed up against the hidden strengths of Mur earlier, and you were promised a return to that. Once more: no lies here. Accordingly, here we are, and it turns out that Jake is both right and wrong about them. Not surprising – after all, most of us hit and miss with our belief systems. It's close to impossible to be fully right, or wrong, in what we believe. You might believe in a God, and maybe you're even right – but if you are, you'll be wrong about the details. You can't know God the way you know a pet dog, or your cousin. The motivations just wouldn't make sense, by necessity.

Along the same line, you might be superstitious and be right that some actions can wobble luck more than others. Luck being just a quantum field projection, it can be tossed about to limited affect. That part is certainly right on the nose. Where people go wrong is in how they assign the oscillation in the field. Breaking a mirror was long considered bad luck because a reflection contained your soul; thus, disrupting it with breakage would disrupt your very soul, leading to bad luck.

That's just wrong on a few levels. Breaking a mirror will ripple the fields and change the odds for your life, a bit. Certainly not for seven years, closer to three months if you did the math, and the reason unquestionably has nothing to do with reflections and your soul. No, mirror luck is all down to common multiverse theory. Your reflection shows you a very close slice of a different universe; it's an entanglement problem. Shattering that creates multiple, close-event-horizon universes all at once and disrupts fields that determine luck all over the place.

See? Simple. And yet we all tend to grab an explanation, share it, and take it as gospel.

How does this relate to Mur, you might be wondering. It comes down to the simplicity of reality versus the layered belief systems that gather crust and grime over the centuries. The Three Forces are all real, and all important. Going into detail on each of them right now would be a huge mistake, so that won't happen, but let's peek at one, at least.

The Grandmother of Keys is the current Walker. It's a job she's held for the majority of her roughly thousand years of life. But she isn't the first Walker, only the current one – Mur being far, far older than a thousand years. The job of The Walker is to wander Mur endlessly and take care of the city; Jake's long-held belief in her is based on that much truth. However, the thing where he believes her to be a giant powerhouse who never needs help is just silly.

We all need help, and none more than a city itself. Taking care of a city isn't about stopping problems; it is, instead, all about helping other people take care of it, enabling them to be good citizens. The reasons for that might, again, seem obvious – and they might be, but they can also be wrapped in something else.

Also, just because The Grandmother of Keys has a job to do, a seemingly endless one at that, doesn't mean it's the root cause for everything she does. No one does their job all the time. Sometimes they fuck off at work, right under the boss' nose.

Also, do keep in mind: just because The Grandmother of Keys exists doesn't mean Casey met her. Then again, maybe she did.

Jake and Casey ate a small snack, each ending up having half a grilled cheese, and she went back to The Alibi to check the sound system. Jake went with her, framing it as his need to walk in the same direction to go calm down Lane, but they both knew that reason landed squarely at half-truth.

He did go see Baozhai Lane after leaving Casey at The Alibi, but the route to see her lay in the opposite direction from their apartment. He had a tense conversation with her at her shop, a small boutique scarf store – which should have been a big sign that it was really just a front, because who needs scarves that often or in an amount that would support a whole store?

Jake had never warmed to Lane, but he needed her in enough of his ventures to put up with her, and she felt exactly the same about him. Working freelance crime in a town like Mur posed problems, and having a few people you could trust, if not like too much, became essential.

So they talked, came to the same uneasy accord they normally came to, and set a meeting for the next day, Lane promising to tell Quyto and Benok. That settled, Jake went back home and worked on plans a while longer. Since he did work freelance crime, and didn't really ever want to hurt people, Jake focused on small theft. They would never rob a bank, for example. Light, low-level scams were Jake's preferred motivation for getting out of bed in the morning.

Working quickly, he roughed out a nice grift involving a man who sold illegal electronics and a way to get the guy to pay Jake (and his compatriots) to relive him of his merchandise. It'd be tricky but doable, and would net them a decent sum of money. Enough to keep Jake afloat with his half of the bills for at least four months. Ideally they'd need a five-person team, but four could work, and would have to since Jake couldn't think of anyone else who he could trust, or who had the needed skills for this particular scam.

The hardest part, for Jake, was that most con artists and petty thieves skipped town when things got hot or went wrong. Jake didn't have the luxury, so he needed to, when planning something this big, make sure that he would not only get it right – he had to get it locked down in such a way that, six months from now, when he ran into the guy he'd scammed on the corner, nothing would be awkward, angry, or deadly.

The rise in difficulty there made many thieves in Mur choose to not work freelance but gather under a bigger, protective banner. Well, that and the fact that the bigger, protective banner in this case liked to harass people who didn't find shelter under his particular umbrella. Jake held tight to the idea that he'd gotten into a life of crime to not answer to someone else every day, to not have a big boss – and so, really, joining up would have been akin to becoming an accountant to him. So he worked hard to stay under everyone's radar, and he really did mean everyone.

Finishing work for the day, Jake measured the space for a possible new couch, making notes on a scrap of paper he shoved into a pocket. He always remained mindful that he was a freelancer, so it would be easy to just never stop working, and in response set times for himself to Not Work.

Casey came back, but they put off couch shopping for another day, choosing instead to sit and be quiet around the apartment together. Jake read, while Casey listened softly to the radio.

Mur, being a giant mash of cultures yet fairly isolated, had an entertainment problem. People came to the city with the stories they carried with them. People also, obviously, remembered things from their past. Some of them arrived with books, or memory sticks full of music, TV, movies, and other visually recorded art. But there was no access to it, unless you not only found someone with that particular media, but also a way to play it back.

Engineers were in short supply and high demand, as were laptops and other playback devices. A market rose up early on for duplication and recreation, but they didn't have TV stations, or an internet. They relied on radio, theatres, and live performance.

Cell phones didn't work, having no satellite access or orbital access to speak of, but landlines were run early on to enable communication. To be fair, stronger solutions could have been developed, but the people who came to the city without cell communications and constant internet didn't miss it, and the people who arrived and found themselves disconnected – assuming they stayed in Mur – tended toward being relived all of that had vanished, so they weren't in a hurry to recreate it.

Day gave way to night and Casey packed up a guitar, got dressed for the show, and grabbed her travel guitar as a precaution, hating herself a little bit as she slung it across her body.

Jake tossed on a light jacket and they left, walking in silence to The Alibi together. At the door to The Alibi, Jake felt a hand grab his shoulder, stopping him. He turned, tensing as he did, and spotted Casey turning with him.

A large, fit, Korean man stared hard at Jake, flanked by two bodyguards. Well, they seemed to Jake like bodyguards, unless the guy'd taken his pet rockslides for a walk.

"Ferdinand," Jake said, giving as much of a greeting as he intended.

"That's Mister Vink, Meyer. Mister. Vink. We're not friends," Ferdinand said, letting a sneer grow to accompany his stare.

"Call me Jake, Ferd," Jake replied, forcing his body to look relaxed. Jake stood all of five foot eight to Ferdinand's six foot three. Jake's blindingly white skin, the product of generations of shut-ins and sun avoidance, grew pinker around his forehead, right up to the line of his shaggy haircut and down to the perfectly straight diagonal of his beard.

"You still operating without me, Meyer?" Ferdinand Vink asked.

Jake sighed. "Ferdinand. I'm not scared of you, or your stacks of muscle here. Could you break every bone I have, vanish the body, and get away it? I mean, sure. We both know that." Jake gave him a shrug. "But there's zero reason for it, and if you start doing stuff like that for giggles, we both know how long you'll last at the top. I don't step on your toes, man. So leave it be."

"They are all," Ferdinand said slowly, "my toes, in this town."

"That didn't come out the way you meant, I'd bet," Jake told him, stifling a laugh. "Hey, Case, did you know Ferd owned your toes?"

"Pretty sure he doesn—"

"Enough. Both of you. You want to continue in this town a free agent? There's a price for that."

"Oh for—no, there isn't," Jake said, "otherwise it wouldn't be free agenting. You want to have another sit down, *another* one, and go over this? We can. Next week. Have your avalanches call my people. Set up a time. But right now I have a job to do."

"You intend to rob The Alibi?" Ferdinand asked, honestly surprised.

"No," Jake smiled, "I intend to drink like it's a profession, though. Unless you also own fingers, as they apply to rum."

"Make your jokes, Meyer. You expand, you make alliances, it makes me look bad. And I can't have that."

"We'll talk soon," Jake said, turning his back on Vink and walking into The Alibi, Casey next to him.

Inside, the door closing behind them, Casey leaned over and whispered in Jake's ear. "You do know he might try and kill you, right? You also know you can't fight him. These are things you one-hundred percent know, yes?"

"Of course," he told her, walking her up to the side of the stage and helping her unpack her gear and set up for the night. "But he isn't sure. Which seems ridiculous, but he isn't. So I get to keep him off balance and he never becomes sure enough to just deal with me. It works."

"Right up until it doesn't," Casey said.

"Then I'll shift plans. Don't worry—seriously, don't. Have a good show, I'll be over with Oscar."

Casey stood on the edge of the stage, bathed in darkness, while Jake wandered over to the bar. Giving Oscar a wave, he sat and turned to watch the stage. A single spotlight came on and Casey walked into it, sitting on the paint-chipped stool. She plugged in her guitar and looked out into the crowd. Not that she could see it at all, given the light in her face, but she still looked out to make a connection, to get a sense of the quality of the silence that the seated bar-goers let fall over them as she settled in.

Oscar pushed a rum and soda to Jake as Casey began her set. Jake took it, sipped, and nodded to Oscar. The crowd gave Casey some polite applause as she introduced herself, and Jake settled in to watch.

A few blocks away from The Alibi, Ferdinand Vink walked with his bodyguards, heading to check on a warehouse he owned that had recently started to slip on timely payments. Ferdinand felt something hit his leg and looked down as a cat, its fur seeming to shine almost blue, ran past him. Following it with a gaze, he caught a flash of blueish light at the intersection up ahead.

Seconds later, Ferdinand Vink watched as Ferdinand Vink ran past him, followed by Jake Meyer. They both looked far worse for the wear, clothes torn, hair astray in every which direction, and dirt caking their bodies. Vink noticed that the other him wore different clothes, and Jake's clothes were different from what he'd been wearing when Ferdinand had seen him only minutes before outside The Alibi.

"Boys," Ferdinand said, "after them...I mean, me. And Meyer. Those guys," he finished, pointing. He took off, not waiting for his men to acknowledge him.

The other Vink and Meyer were locked in a struggle. Jake fought hard, moving in ways Ferdinand was sure the Jake he'd left behind couldn't do now. His head hurt. What was he seeing? Himself. Losing a fight, he guessed.

That didn't help.

His men caught up to him. "Boss, should we go help him...you?"

"I don't even know if that's actually me – I mean, I'm right here. This has to be some sort of trick of Meyer's, right, boys?"

"I dunno, Boss," one of his men said softly, "it sure looks like you, and him."

They watched as the fight continued, growing more desperate by the second. Jake had Ferdinand pinned, then Vink took a shard of something out of his shirt and tried to stab Meyer with it. Meyer grabbed his wrist and twisted, then picked up the shard and stabbed Vink in the heart, saying something none of them could hear.

"Boys, get him!" Vink roared as his double fell, sprawling along the sidewalk, blood pouring freely from his chest.

The other Jake looked up at the shout and dropped the shard, sprinting away. Vink's men ran after him and Ferdinand went to his own side, kneeling, feeling his pants grow wet with blood.

"Kill...him..." escaped the lips of the Vink on the ground.

Ferdinand nodded at himself. "How is this possible?" he asked his double. No response came, and he asked again before realizing that the body

57

he knelt by could now be sorted definitively into the 'corpse' category.

A few minutes later – Ferdinand lost in thought, watching his own dead body – his bodyguards returned, without Jake. "We, uhhh, we lost him Boss."

"Never mind that right now," he said, feeling anger grow in his chest. "Get me—this other me—get me up and let's get back to the house before anyone sees."

They nodded and draped the body in their jackets so people couldn't see who it was. Lifting him, they walked slowly, struggling to maneuver in the street with a dead body.

"Today!" barked Vink.

They sped up as best they could, and hurried home.

∞

At the same time, Jake and Oscar sat in The Alibi, listening to Casey play.

"She doing anything new tonight?" Oscar asked.

"Not that I know of," Jake said after a long sip of his drink.

"She just doesn't normally play with that other guitar in a bag hanging off her knee, I thought maybe—"

"It's all fine, Oscar. Just a precaution. In case she...breaks a string. You know how musicians are – paranoid. Right?"

"Not generally, no," Oscar said. "You guys all right?"

"Yeah, it's—like I said, it's all fine."

"If you say so."

"I say so," Jake said, turning away to watch the stage again. Casey moved from the end of one song to the start of another with no flourish or rush. She just shifted and started back up, as if there was no reason to rest left in her.

Jake looked over at the booths that lined the wall. Their blue vinyl, cracked and worn, made him smile, and he thought of the first time he'd seen Casey play, the night they'd met.

She'd been in town a year or two by then, and started performing at The Alibi tentatively at first, just trying to start using her skills with a guitar to make people happy instead of injured. Her early shows, she didn't have songs – no lyrics or real plan. She just got on the stage and played guitar for as long as they would let her, crafting melodies from nothing and then building on each one to tell a winding tale of notes that captured the audience's attention.

After her set finished, she'd hung out at the bar with Oscar. They laughed and drank and Jake sat nearby, trying to not watch. Oscar would come over and refresh Jake's drink, and every time he would slip in a wink, or slight head tilt, to make it very clear he knew exactly who Jake wished he was talking to.

Jake wondered now, listening to Casey play a song he loved about some birds that learned to swim and traded air for sea, if Oscar ever knew that his prompting almost kept Jake from saying hi to Casey then.

He hadn't wanted the pressure, he remembered, of not only being turned down – that was fine and normal – but of that happening in front of a bartender he'd just started to get to know, which would taint the whole bar for him. He knew even then that Oscar would bring it up for ages, and he liked The Alibi enough he didn't want to abandon it so soon.

Eventually, as the night drifted later, Jake got up and walked over to Casey, introduced himself, and asked if he could buy her a drink and maybe, if she agreed, chat a while. She did agree, after getting a reassuring nod from Oscar, who tried his level best to keep people he knew were creeps away from both his regulars and the performers.

She suggested they move to a booth, laughingly insisting that they get away from Oscar's ever-present super-hearing. They talked until Oscar kicked them out, but Jake couldn't remember what they discussed no matter how hard he tried. His memory of those hours existed in a simple, free-floating space filled by happiness and the too-quick passage of time. They left The Alibi together, standing both too close and too far apart for their liking, and then went their separate ways after an awkward good-bye hug.

They'd met there again the next night, Casey not playing, and started to date and eventually ended up right here, Jake thought to himself with a smile. Not a bad life, he told himself, and drained his drink quickly. Oscar appeared equally quickly to refill it, and as he put a new, full glass on the bar top, Jake looked the bartender up and down.

"It's been years, right?" he asked.

"It has, man," Oscar agreed. "Why?"

"Your closet. I mean, look, I respect the hell out of you, man. We've *cooked* for you, but did a clown car explode in your closet one day and you just had to live with it?"

Oscar smoothed his yellow tie, then tugged down his silver vest. "I have two questions for you in return."

"Oh I need to hear them, Oscar. I need to," Jake said, grinning. "Please?"

"First, how long have you waited to ask that – like specifically how long did you work on it and then hold it in?"

"Oh," Jake said, stopping to sip his drink, "you don't even know. Year or more?"

"I figured," Oscar nodded. "Second – why unleash your hurtful barbs now, man? What set off the proximity alarm?"

Jake shrugged and raised his glass, tipping it toward Oscar, who grabbed the metal water bottle he kept behind the bar and clinked it against Jake's glass. "Sometimes the moment is just right, I don't know. Let's blame the song for putting the idea in my head."

"You do know this song is about a woman who steals a car and uses it to run over her ex, right?"

"Shhhh, just let me have this," Jake said, ducking his head to sip from his drink so the laughter wouldn't be audible.

"You're a strange guy, Jake, but I like you," Oscar said. "But you being this...cheerful, it might just start to worry me."

"Oh trust me, Ferdinand was grumbling at me just outside – I ain't happy, overall. But I can't listen to her without...you know."

Oscar shook his head, smiling. "I know."

Once her set ended, Casey joined Oscar and Jake at the bar, having a few drinks with them. Before closing, Jake and Casey left, hitting the street and wandering off in search of food. The air outside was cool and crisp – mingling with the normal stench of a large city, a breeze cut through, making them feel like a clear, pleasant air ruled around them.

Two people, one of them in a large, furry cheetah costume, stumbled into Casey before throwing up violently in the street. It served to remind them where they actually were. Casey stepped over the vomit and looked at Jake. "Is it bad I love this town?"

"Because of or in spite of the random street vomiting?"

"Little of column A, little of B, you know how it is."

Jake laughed, "I really d—"

He stopped short as a couple slammed into him, showing up seemingly out of nowhere. The man wore a black suit that seemed to mostly fit him, the woman wore a burnt orange three-piece suit of her own, complete a blood-red ascot. "Could you not?" she asked Jake, sounding tired.

"Lady, you hit me," Jake said, giving her a shrug.

"Sorry," the guy in the black suit said in a low voice, "we're on business here."

"Oh, well, then in that case," Casey said, waving her arm to let them pass, "don't let us keep you from your important ascot-related business."

The woman smoothed her suit, rolled her eyes, and started walking fast, the man following without another word.

"Thank you," Jake said, "that ascot was bugging me, too."

"I'm not sure which is worse," Casey said, "her ascot, or the fact we both instantly had the name for it right on hand like that. Why do either of us know what an ascot is without thinking?"

"We were both raised by wolves?" Jake suggested.

"Do wolves wear ascots?" Casey countered.

"I think I read that book when I was a kid. Oh hey," Jake said, forgetting all about ascots, "is Samir's still open?"

"Did neckwear blossom into a need for tandoori?"

"If I say yes," Jake asked, "can we go *get* some tandoori?"

Casey gave Jake's hand a squeeze. "Sounds like a plan. So tomorrow, I have to go meet that old lady—"

"Grandmother," Jake corrected.

"If you say so," she conceded. "I just wondered, you really think this is a good idea? I worry she just wants muscle. That's not what I want to—"

"Make it clear, remind her, and if it goes that way just back away and leave her."

"Wait, you could do that? Seriously, you could leave some old lady twisting in the wind like that?" Casey let go of Jake's hand and stopped walking.

"If she used me, lied to me, and set me up to take the damage for her? Yeah, I could." Jake reached for her hand and sighed as she moved it just slightly out of his reach. "I mean, I guess, if she's The Grandmother of Keys maybe not? But then I wouldn't think she'd need me for that anyway, so it would be a different thing."

"No, but who cares who she is – you don't just leave someone like that," Casey insisted. "That's not right."

"If they set you up for it?"

"Then you deal with that, separately, after," she said.

"That's just not a great way to make sure there is an after in which to deal with it. If someone creates their own problems—"

"And needs help, even if they're jerks about it—"

"I call people who actively put me in harm's way a bit more than jerks."

"You know what I mean, Jake."

"I do know what you mean," he agreed, "but I also know that self-sacrifice for people who wronged me isn't something I'm down for."

Casey took a deep breath, held it, and thought. "Everyone deserves help," she said at last, eyes closed, not wanting to see Jake's expression when she said it.

"I agree," Jake said, "right up until they try to do me harm."

"I mean, sure – if they're trying to hit me, or kill me, even, I wouldn't help them do it," Casey agreed.

"Then—"

"But if, in the middle of a fight, let's say the building we're in catches fire..." Casey trailed off, remembering. "You help them—even then, you help them," she finished after another beat.

"Do you, though?" Jake asked, unconvinced.

"If not, I wouldn't be here," she said, meeting his gaze firmly.

Jake sighed and reached out for her hand again. "I'm sorry," he said, "I didn't—"

"Doesn't matter," she insisted, "the point stands. You don't stop being a human being just because you're in a fight. You can't, or you risk sliding all the way down the ladder straight to being some sort of monster."

"I just think there's more middle ground than you do," Jake said, taking her hand when she offered it and squeezing it.

"Can we agree it's far more situational then anyone, including us, should be comfortable with?"

"That I would drink to," Jake agreed. "Except I probably shouldn't have anything else to drink."

"Just one when we get home, maybe," Casey said, moving close enough to half-lean on Jake while they walked.

He let go of her hand and wrapped an arm around her shoulder instead, and they walked the rest of the way home like that, in what appeared to be a comfortable silence. In reality, they both chewed over their tiff like an otter with a squeaky toy. Neither of them got to anywhere new, so they kept quiet, but couldn't find it in themselves to stop replaying things for their own viewing displeasure.

They litigated, relitigated, declared mistrials, and otherwise continued the small fight for themselves, each in their own head, thinking the other was satisfied with how they'd left things. They stewed, and it was only a few blocks of walking. Regardless, the human mind is boundless in its ability to rehash uncomfortable moments, and by the time they got home they were well and truly annoyed with each other, but determined to continue to hide it since, they both thought, the other was fine with things. Neither of them wanted to restart a fight when they were sure the other wouldn't understand where things had even flared up from again.

Instead of a last drink when they got home, they both begged off and got undressed, exchanging basic pleasantries, trying to hide their individual frustration. They got into bed, still partly drunk, and clung to each other, each trying to will understanding without communication into the other.

The night didn't go nearly as quiet for Ferdinand Vink, though his evening also contained much frustration. After finally getting back to his base with his own dead body, he set about proving the body wasn't actually him at all. People moved around him, past the body on a gurney, and fretted as Vink yelled and ranted at them. Most of his explosions contained the basic sentiment to hurry up or be tossed out a window.

Vink's place was a set of apartments that he called his house, considering he owned the building. He used the full third floor for himself, knocking out walls between apartments to create a giant, circular operational home and base.

He kept a medical assistant on retainer, just in case one of his people got hurt, and it was that same, small man who looked over the body on a gurney now. "It does look like this is you, Mister Vink," the medic, Ralph, said. He hated his job with Vink, but he loved drinking and being a doctor, so after a few years, working for Vink remained his only option. Worse yet, he spent his nights feeling like a cliché and plotting ways to be more than that.

He spent those same nights drinking himself to death, however, and so he wasn't exactly making great progress.

What he needed was help and understanding – a lifeline to hang on to and drag himself out of his own hell back into the light. What he had, instead, was a job working for Ferdinand Vink. So he poked and prodded at the corpse in front of him. He tested the blood and the eye color, took fingerprints and compared them under a microscope, trying to think of other ways he could prove that the body dead in front of him was not also the body yelling at him.

"If it's me, then tell me: how am I standing here?" Vink demanded.

"I don't know, sir," Ralph answered, handing over his charts, "but every test I've run shows the same thing. Do you...do you have a twin?"

"A secret twin?" Vink slapped the gurney hard, making a strange *bonging* noise that Ralph might've laughed at in a different situation. "Is that something you think actually happens? Even in this town? Hell, especially in this town—where would a twin hide out, huh? You tell me!"

"I don't know, Mister Vink, maybe he lived on the street and—"

"I didn't actually want a crackpot hidden twin theory, you idiot," Vink said, shaking his head and trying to work out whether any of this was real. "I want you to tell me what is actually going on here."

"Unless someone duplicated you, Mister Vink, then I don't know. The body seems about the same age as you—maybe it's from the future? I mean, it could be the past, but if it was the past then you'd be dead, too, since this is you, and—"

"The future?" Vink asked. "That's the best you have?"

"Right now, yes, sir."

Vink walked toward the door, opening it a crack. "Do better," he said darkly, before leaving, closing the door quietly behind him.

Ferdinand worked to push the mystery down deep. He needed to solve it – of course he did – but he also needed to get work done. Running a citywide criminal empire didn't allow for early evenings very often.

Vink also had a plan to set in motion. One he'd been building to for years. He wanted to help Mur, as a whole. Honestly he always had. That's why he'd gotten into crime in the first place. Growing up in Mur, he'd witnessed out-of-control crime and lawlessness keep people down. Crime would happen, regardless – he never even considered becoming an arm of the law; he thought that would be a futile waste of his life.

Instead, he wanted to run it all himself. That way he could try to rein crime in and direct it. Mur had a mayor, The Honorable Peri J. Haimes. But Haimes could only try to put a stop to crime, and took credit for the constantly trending downward slope of criminal activity he saw on reports. The reports were true – the more of a stranglehold on crime Vink amassed, the lower the crime rate went.

He backed people good at their job, and their crimes often went unnoticed or under-reported. What reported crimes there were tended to be controlled. Yes, people got hurt on occasion, and scared often, but keeping a firm grip on things let Vink limit the fallout.

So he went to his study and analyzed his own recent internal reports. They, obviously, contained much more detail than anything Mayor Haimes, or his police chief Commissioner Dawes, had access to. Home break-ins were up, as requested, mostly scattered around middle-class areas.

Vink's requested thieves were after people who used a specific brand of home security devices, trying to wedge that company out of the market. Vink had recently purchased that companies' competition and wanted to make people feel safer if they used the brand he made profit from.

He saw himself as the true mayor of Mur. He wanted to help people. He never wavered from his belief in that, or in himself. And so he kept working. Muggings were up, something he'd asked not to happen. He made a note on a small notebook next to him to 'talk' to a few people, intending to stop the behavior, or the people involved from walking, for a while. Either would do.

As he kept reading, he thought over his One Big Plan, as he liked to call it. Then he reflected on the body double he'd just walked away from and what Ralph had said. Him from the future. It fit, given what he would be attempting and what he knew of how the city really worked.

The idea that the city, that Mur itself, would also try to send him a warning like his own dead body from the future felt more reasonable the more he deliberated the facts and data. But what was Jake Meyer involved for? He had no tie to the city that Vink knew about, at least none that ran that deep.

A tie like that might not matter, he thought, as much as the facts at hand. Jake Meyer had killed him and run into the night. If that was his future dead body, then he could assume the Meyer who killed him was also a future Meyer.

All of which added up to Ferdinand still having time to derail events. He stood up and walked around half the length of his floor of apartments until he reached his communications hub. The two people in there, dictating to messengers and sitting near a small bank of phones, looked up at Vink's entrance. The boss could be hands on, but messages normally came second- or third-hand.

As Vink entered, the individual messengers all sidled out of the room, hoping to not be noticed. Just in case the message wasn't for them, if Vink was sending it himself, they didn't want to overhear it.

"I need you to let everyone know, we're putting a price out on someone's head," he said, not bothering to greet anyone.

"Of course, Mister Vink," came the quick reply from both of the seated workers.

"Who is it?" one of them asked, grabbing a pencil.

"Jake Meyer," Vink told them, "triple the normal rate, when they show up with proof."

"You want a head specifically, or—"

"No," Vink said, cringing a bit, "the last guy who thought to bring me a head as proof, it dripped all over the place. Some of these guys, they ain't thoughtful. Cost me a lot of rugs and paint, you know? No, just bring a body, or tell me where it is and we'll go to it, I don't care. Proof of death is required for payment."

"You got it, Boss," the other message-taker said, "we'll get that out to the heavies now."

"Get it out to everyone. I want everyone we got on this. I don't care if they just pick a few locks, they should consider how to kill Meyer for me."

"That'll cause some problems with the rank and file, Boss," the message-taker said. "Plus, if they go for it, this Meyer guy will know you're after him and—"

"Did I come here for advice, or to have a message sent?"

The first message-taker slapped the second along the back of his head and nodded at Ferdinand. "Of course, sir, apologies. We'll get this out to everyone. Right away, sir."

"Better," Vink said, leaving the room.

The first message-taker closed the door after Vink had left before turning to look at his partner. "You're a special kind of annoying, you know that?"

"Hey," the second said, "I just wanted to make sure—"

"That we get fired and tossed out a window? Just...shut up and send the message. I'll get the runners back in here. You idiot."

The next morning, Jake woke up and lay there as long as his bladder would allow, just watching Casey sleep. The remnants of the previous night's fight lingered, swirling around his consciousness just low enough to render him grumpy, but not enough to instantly remember why.

He went to the bathroom and then started the coffee, recalling more in greater detail as he went. Meh-ing at himself over it all, he let the coffee brew and hopped in the shower. By the time he got out the coffee was ready, a mug prepared for him at the table, with Casey sitting there, her own mug cradled in both hands.

She took a long sip from her mug as Jake sat and then set her coffee down, watching him. Jake knew the look; that expression of Casey's meant she was waiting to see if they were still fighting or not. That was, of course, up to her as much as him, she knew. Regardless, Casey liked to gauge the weather before going outside, so to speak. Jake reached a hand out for hers and she took it, giving it a squeeze before muttering a small good morning and going to grab herself a shower, leaving the rest of her coffee to cool.

Jake sat and waited, drinking his coffee. He needed to get down and talk to Lane et al., but first things first. There was time for coffee, for getting dressed and fully waking up, he knew. There was also time for dealing with whatever still stood between him and Casey.

Jake felt bad enough for letting things sit overnight – he didn't want it to bleed into the next day. As he sat, he saw clearly they'd both squirrelled away their anger and kept it away from one another. On the one hand, that felt polite and sweet of them. On the other, Jake knew, it was a problem waiting to be attended to. They couldn't just sit and fume individually, or everything would blow up far worse than it might if they directly confronted their issues.

Let's not paint this as all Jake wanting to deal with things and Casey not. In the shower, Casey worked around ways to bring it up to Jake that wouldn't set off a fight again but would, instead, allow for discussion, with room to differ and yet also agree the other was right, if not right for both of them. She hadn't gotten far, but she kept trying, knowing she didn't want her coffee to get cold, either, while she showered for too long.

Wrapping her robe around herself, Casey came back to the table and sat slowly, reaching for her mug. Halfway there, her hand was grabbed by Jake, and squeezed. "So, last night?" he asked, letting go of her hand so she could take her coffee cup.

"Last night," she agreed.

"We're jerks, huh?" he asked, swirling the last coffee in his mug and watching it spin.

"We kind of are," she said. "I just think we need to be able to really get it from the other angle, you know? Even if we stay where we are for ourselves."

"I mean, yeah," Jake agreed, "but we also can't just sit on resentment. I may never be some big self-sacrificing hero, like you."

"I'm not—"

"You are," Jake insisted, "and we both know it. And I'm a street rat."

Casey laughed. "No you aren't."

"Yeah, Case, I am," Jake said, draining the dregs from his mug, "and that's not a bad thing, either. But we both came up so different—we do what we need to, to sleep at night and survive."

"Sure, no, I agree," Casey said, finishing her own coffee, "but I need there to be more than just the next day, I think. That was so much of my life. It feels..."

"Empty?" Jake asked.

"Sometimes, yeah. Mostly, even."

"I get that, but for me, so much of my life has been just finding that next day. Maybe I can find my way out of that trap."

"Do you want to, though?" Casey asked seriously.

"I do," Jake said, closing his eyes. "I think? I can't know until I do or don't." He opened his eyes slowly, looking at her.

She shook her head. "You need the intent to make the change if it's going to be made. Otherwise it's just an empty target in the field for you to miss and long for."

"Please tell me you didn't hear that said that way for the first time on a combat range," Jake said, with a bit of a laugh trailing after it.

"That doesn't make it untrue," Casey insisted, letting herself laugh.

"Might make it a bit creepy, though."

"Hey, it might," she agreed, "but it's still true."

"Well, I do mean to try, and see if it fits my head," Jake said.

Casey nodded and stood up, grabbing both empty mugs. She walked them to the sink and rinsed them before setting them back down. "That's all I could ask, really."

"Yeah." Jake tipped his chair back and craned his neck to watch her. "So hey, I have to go to some meetings today, after yesterday's—"

"I was there," Casey reminded him, then laughed again. "Shit, I was the reason for you needing meetings today."

Jake shrugged. "They'll live. You get to hang out with Grandma today though, right?"

"I get to see if this old woman wants me to be her muscle, yeah."

74

They each got ready and left, Jake wandering off first, and both agreeing to come back for dinner, at the worst, if not sooner.

Jake wandered toward his meeting slowly, taking more time than he strictly needed. He just didn't want to deal with crime today. Sometimes you need a day off your job, even if it's your passion. People who like to claim that doing the thing you love means you never work a day in your life obviously don't do the thing they love for as living.

The dirty secret is you work harder, that way.

The even dirtier secret is that if your job, and passion, is illegal, then you work even harder than that. It's akin to building a tower out of blocks. Most people think that sounds like fun, and it could be.

When your job involves building the tower, you realize the blocks you stack have to also be able to stay standing when bumped into by the cat from next door, without being secured by anything.

When your job and passion are crime, you could use the same metaphor, except first you greased the blocks. Then you gave acid to the cat.

Jake kept walking, sneering at the occasional garbage can and thinking about kicking random street poles. Really he just felt like breaking out his cards and a box and playing a little 'find the lady' for a few hours.

Connecting with people, even if you're pulling a light card scam on them, made Jake smile. He found a joy in it. He also didn't work with a ringer, instead letting people win a bit here and there to really keep things interesting and his hands sharp.

Instead he gave in and turned a corner, taking a half-block switchback the long way around thanks to the layout of the city, and entered the Fitz and Family Jewelry Store. The guy behind the counter, seemingly all long hair and piercings, waved at him and lifted the Employees Only counter, letting Jake through.

There had never been, to Jake's knowledge, any Fitz. Lucius Benok just used the name in the least clever dodge ever. Jake pushed his way into the back room, then took the stairs down to the lower storeroom, and there he went through one more door, unmarked and half hidden by a bookcase, into the meeting room.

"Meyer," Benok said from inside the darkened room. A flick of a switch and a small light came on. This wasn't how Benok normally did things. He didn't hide in the dark, despite the location of his meeting room. That was simply practical. The room itself, as Jake knew it during other times, was well-lit and warm.

"Benok," Jake replied, growing warier by the second, "what's going on here? Where are the others?"

"No one is coming. You should leave, yourself. I only let you back here because you have made us some money in the past. Always been fair, Meyer, you've always been that."

Jake sighed and sat down at the table across from Benok. If this was going to go south badly, Jake intended to look relaxed about it. "What happened, Benok? Tell me that at least."

The door behind Jake started to move, causing Benok to leap to his feet, gun in hand. Jake turned in his seat, the door to his left, and waited. While he assumed that whatever had caused this cancellation would now come through that door for him, he also knew Benok was a good shot. If he was reacting, he had a better chance at stopping things than if Jake got in the way.

Baozhai Lane stepped through the door, speaking quickly: "Don't shoot, Benok, you idiot."

"What the hell are you doing here, Lane? We agreed—"

Lane sat, Benok sitting as she did. "I decided Meyer deserved this much respect from me, but after this all bets are off."

"Thanks, I think," Jake told her, still wondering what the hell was even going on here.

"Quyto wouldn't come," Lane told Benok, "he's firmly against all of this and went to ground."

"Mikael Quyto is a fool and a coward," Benok declared.

"You're *both* sitting here," Jake said, "still not telling me why you're cancelling our job. So from where I sit maybe you're all—"

"Vink has a kill order on you, Meyer," Lane cut in. "Knows we're working with you, thought we could do it for him at our next meeting." She rested both her hands flat on the table. "As you can see, we're not doing that, so maybe cut the strident shit."

"Wait, what?"

"You heard Lane," Benok said. "This is a courtesy, and one we're taking at a fair amount of risk, I might add. So yes, dial it down a bit, my friend."

"Oh, I'm your friend? Then why are you bailing on this? Fuck Ferdinand. He's in a mood. I'll talk to him."

"I would not do that," Lane told him. "This is not a *mood*, this is a serious, full-kill order on you. Triple rate, Meyer – this isn't some hurt feelings. What did you *do* to him?"

Jake slapped the table. "Nothing! I did nothing to him. He got in my face outside The Alibi, but it was all the normal song and dance. I can straighten this out."

"You can't," Benok said, shaking his head and grabbing a bottle from the floor near his seat. He set glasses down as well and started to pour dark brown liquid into each.

"Bit early for a drink, even with this conversation," Jake said.

"It's tea, you idiot," Lane said, grabbing a glass and sipping. "Shitty tea, but tea."

"You always insult my tea," Benok complained, "and yet you drink it like water."

"Well if you made better tea, I could respect it and drink it slower, you—"

"The tea doesn't matter," Jake said loudly. "Hi. Hello. There's a price on my head?"

"Which is why you must leave and not contact us," Lane told him.

"So that's it?"

"Meyer," Benok said, putting the bottle of tea back on the floor, "we are risking ourselves giving you a warning at all. Leave while you can, and run far. Perhaps you should leave Mur for a while, and—"

"Leave? And get back how?"

"You could hire a Knocker," Benok suggested. "Give it a few months and come back."

"Hire a Knocker," Jake repeated. "I'd have the money for that, maybe, if we pulled this job first."

"Then go to ground and pray," Lane suggested, "but either way, you need to leave here now and forget we talked. Lose our contacts, Meyer. Please."

Jake stood, slowly and carefully setting the chair he left back where he'd found it. "Yeah, all right." He opened the door and moved through it, starting to close it behind him. "Thanks, I guess."

Jake left the jewelry store and walked down the street, now paranoidly glancing behind him every few steps. He cursed, forced himself to stop, and considered his next move. All options came back zero, and, cursing again, he started over.

Casey, while Jake's meeting went any way but how he expected, found herself having a much different time of it. She'd gone out early to grab more coffee at a nearby bodega, then circled the block so she could meet Key on the corner she'd wanted to and yet also not be seen just walking right from the apartment to it. Casey knew there was an above-averagely creepy chance the old woman knew where she lived, and that this was some sort of long con, but she refused to play along even in the small moments, knowing, from living with Jake, how even that much twist to a plan can throw people overboard when they aren't looking for it.

Casey kept an eye on every person walking toward her corner from any direction. She stood, seemingly relaxed, at the corner and casually glanced around her at irregular intervals designed and spaced to look random. The way she moved her head had been thought of – each time she scratched her chin, or neck, to keep count – all habits and training from her time in the army. She knew it, hated it, but accepted the help anyway. She touched the strap of the guitar bag slung across her body, her small guitar held snugly, top of the bag undone just in case.

"Waiting for me, honey?" a voice behind her said, causing Casey to startle. She spun on her heel and looked at Key, the smiling old woman just standing there as if she'd been waiting with Casey the whole time.

"Where did you come from?" Casey asked. "I didn't see—"

"Looking is good, but feeling is better," Key said. "Now, we need to—"

"No," Casey said, leaning against a light pole at the corner, "there needs to be a ground rule or two to this first."

"We discussed those," Key said, waving her hand dismissively.

"We're going to add a new rule before we go. No riddle-talking, sage-old-woman stuff. Talk plainly and let's avoid confusion."

"You don't like being snuck up on," Key said, then shook her head. "No, I suppose no one does. I'm sorry, honey. You were just looking the other way, is all. I was in that store there," Key pointed back the way she came, at a small flower shop, "talking to a friend. That's all."

"Sure," Casey said, not quite buying it, "so what did you mean by 'feeling is better than looking,' then?"

"In this town? Mur? Oh, honey, it's easy to not notice people, is all. You can get distracted by watching a man from the early days of France clashing with someone from your local idea of the far future. It's hard. The patterns of people aren't the same."

"Uh-huh," Casey muttered. "Sure, sure. So, then, where are we going?" she asked, giving up on working out where Key had actually come from for the moment. For the record, though, Key hadn't lied. She'd been in that flower shop. Casey hadn't gotten soft, either, but she hadn't noticed that the people walking between her and the flower store when Key arrived had been perfectly timed to allow Key to walk right up on her, almost as if Key'd paid them to coordinate the timing. Which she hadn't – just sometimes you get lucky and take advantage of the windows life gives you.

Now, Key could've explained that to Casey, but that would have decreased the mysterious air Casey let drift around Key, and though she didn't actually need it, Key enjoyed it just enough to let it stand, taking the chance to keep it going for a while longer. She led Casey down a block, around a switchback, and further wallward in silence. Casey followed, waiting to see if Key would make her ask again where they were actually going.

"You didn't have to bring the guitar," Key said after a while.

"I don't like to go anywhere without it," Casey shrugged.

"You might have to, if you keep working with me – is that going to be all right?"

"Let's find out when we get there," Casey said, not intending to make this a repeat attraction anyway.

Casey waited the majority of the twenty-minute walk before asking where they were going again. Key slapped a hand against her leg and apologized. "Oh honey, right, we're going to see a man about a dog."

"Not a horse?" Casey asked, waiting for a punchline.

"No, he couldn't keep a horse. But he does have the dog of a friend of mine. We're going to get it back."

"So you *do* expect me to be your muscle," Casey sighed, feeling defeated suddenly.

"What?" Key asked, looking at Casey while they kept walking. "No, I said that wasn't why I needed you along and I meant it. I wouldn't lie to you, honey. I wouldn't."

"So why do you need me along, then?" Casey asked as they walked up to a five-story apartment building. The brick itself looked tired somehow, and the front security door's glass was cracked and grime coated. Casey tried pushing on it and it swung freely, the hinges in oddly perfect shape.

"I just like company, honey," Key said with a smile. She started up the stairs, going slowly, and Casey offered her an arm to lean on. Key ignored the arm but used the railing. Casey noticed how lightly Key touched the railing, not actually using it, but making a small show of holding onto it.

They only went up to the second floor, Key wandering down the dried-paste–colored hallway to a door marked 2H. She knocked twice and waited, turning to flash Casey a warm smile that Casey didn't return.

A guy opened the door about halfway, and Casey could see he was a bit taller than her, hair buzzed tight, and with muscles straining against the short sleeves of his shirt. "What?" he asked, not sounding angry or impatient, only busy. Behind him a dog could be heard barking. "Shush!" he called over his shoulder, but the barking continued.

"I live downstairs, Key said, "and just wondered if I could borrow your kettle."

The man blinked twice, looked behind himself and then back at Key and Casey. "I'm sorry? My kettle? I don't have a—"

"Thank you, dear," Key said, happily pushing against the door with one light hand. The man backed away and let her in, baffled. Casey followed, figuring that even if she wasn't actually being brought along to protect or fight for Key, the extra body would be required to make sure this guy didn't do anything stupid. "Oh, Casey? Could you grab Scraps for me, while we're here?" Key asked as she kept walking down the long hallway of the railroad apartment to the kitchen.

Casey nodded, realizing Key couldn't see her, then looked at the guy standing next to her. "So, yeah, I guess I'm here for uhm, Scraps?"

"You want my dog?" the guy asked, incredulous.

"Oh, dear, he's not your dog, is he?" Key called from the kitchen, where she could be heard rattling around in cabinets.

"Look, Mister—"

"Trent."

"Trent," Casey repeated, "just hand over Scraps and—"

"Why should I give you my dog?!"

Casey held up a finger, stopping Trent cold. She walked quickly down the hallway and found Key sorting through things in a cabinet. "I need some reason here, Key."

"It's his girlfriend's dog. Martine," Key said softly. "Trent here took the dog when they broke up – Martine wants Scraps back, that's all. Can you take care of it, honey? I need to find something."

Casey walked back to Trent, grumbling to herself. "Look, Trent, I get it."

"Get what? What do you think you understand, huh?" He was growing impatient with strangers in his house. "And what's she doing back there?" he asked, trying to move past Casey.

Except Casey didn't budge. Trent stopped, trying to stare her down, intimidate her into moving. Casey felt her left hand itch, as if fighting to move by itself to grab her guitar, but she wasn't going to. There was no call. Instead, she just blocked Trent and smiled.

"Looking for your kettle to borrow, I guess," Casey said. "So about Scraps?"

"That dog is mine," Trent said, turning to yell, "I said shut it!" at the endlessly barking dog again.

"All right, but listen, between you and me?"

"Who *are* you even?" Trent asked, splitting his annoyance between the barking of the dog and Casey.

"Case, I'm sorry, we weren't really introduced." She held out a hand for Trent to shake and he stared at it for an extra beat before reluctantly letting manners take over. He shook her hand quickly and then dropped it, scowling.

"And why am I giving you my dog, and who the hell are you to come *take* my dog, anyway?"

"Since Scraps hasn't stopped barking since we got here, I'm going to guess he does that a lot?" Casey asked, swerving around the questions.

"He won't shut up," Trent admitted.

"So let me take him off your hands. I can return him to Martine, no more annoying constant barking, and you'll be remembered as a good guy, right? Who doesn't want that? It solves your problem."

"Wait, what?" Trent was trying to keep an eye on Casey, look down the hall to see what Key was up to, and think of away to shut Scraps up all at once.

"No Scraps, no barking, right? Let me help you, Trent."

"You know what, fine, this stupid dog, just—" Trent cut himself off, opening a door right near Casey and grabbing Scraps from inside it. He held the dog cradled, not seeming angry at him, though he was, and shoved the dog into Casey's arms hurriedly. "Just go, and take the old woman with you."

"Key," Casey called, "I have Scraps – let's go, then?"

"Just a moment," Key called from the kitchen, where she could still be heard shuffling things around.

"Get her," Trent told Casey, "out of my...lady, what are you *doing* in there?" he shouted down the hall, trying to walk past Casey again, who, now armed with a fully functional and operational barking dog, barred the way still. "Look, you have the dog, right? Now get out of my apartment before I call the police or something."

"Hey, we don't want trouble," Casey reassured him. "She'll just be..." she turned to look down the hallway. "Key, we should be going."

Key appeared from the kitchen, waving. "You don't have a kettle," she told Trent, helpfully.

"I *know* that. I told *you* that," he said, looking at Casey with frustration clear in his eyes. "Can you get her out of here, please?"

"Of course, Trent, sorry about this," Casey told him, waving Key out the door and blocking the old woman's body with her own as she passed Trent in the hall. Scraps kept barking, and Casey hugged the dog closer to her.

They left the building quickly, Casey clutching Scraps to her and wishing the dog would hush. Once outside she looked at Key, annoyed.

"What were you doing in his kitchen for so long?" she asked, shifting the dog in her arms as he squirmed.

"I needed to get something, but Trent, well," Key smiled at Case, "he wouldn't want me to have it."

"Does he have a leash or something? I don't want to put him down just to have him run off," Casey asked, unsure of what to do with the dog. "And what thing? Did we just steal a dog as cover?"

"We," Key said, holding her hands out for the dog, "helped my friend Martine get her dog back."

Casey started to hand Scraps over then stopped, thought better of it, and hugged the dog to her again. "But you were there for something else."

"Well, that too, yes, honey." Denied the dog to hold, Key reached over and petted Scraps' head softly. "But really I wanted to help Martine."

"Sure," Casey agreed distantly. "So what did you steal?"

"I didn't steal anything," Key insisted.

"You took something that wasn't yours from a guy who didn't give it to you." Casey shrugged and turned a bit as they walked so Key couldn't easily reach Scraps anymore. "That's pretty much textbook stealing. And no more dog pets until you tell me what."

Key laughed, taking a large coin from her pocket. "I just took this off of him. It wasn't his to have, anyway. It would've gotten him in trouble, eventually. We did him two favors, really."

The coin was half the size of the old woman's palm, and thick. It didn't glint in the sunlight at all, the metal of it flat and uninspiring. An inner ring of tarnished silver circled the imprint of three circles, each overlapping their outlines into the circle next to them. Three rings, interlocked, stamped into the face of the coin.

"Is that..." Casey shook her head, shushed Scraps, and looked at the coin again, "...is that an Exchangers coin?"

"Sure," Key said, slipping the coin back into her pocket. "Like I said, he would've gotten in trouble for it anyway."

"We can't have it either," Casey insisted. "We have to...how do you even give one of those back? I've never met an Exchanger. This is bad. I could ask Jake. He'd know some. He has to."

"Don't ask your Jake."

"My Jake? Wait, how do you know who—"

"The way you said his name, honey. But it's fine, trust me. Let's just get Scraps back to Martine."

While the two of them continued to walk, and argue about what do with the coin, we should stop and discuss Exchangers and, really, Knockers, even though Jake can't afford one. Mur, remember, is cut off from the world outside. Given its size, there are some hydroponic centers underground – and a few above, as well – but space is at a premium, and there isn't exactly a large stretch of farmland to support the life inside the area.

When Mur first separated from the world – and more on that later, really and truly – the city suffered, containing barely enough farmland to make do a single season. They needed to trade with the world outside their walls. That world, however, had since become everywhere and everywhen. At first they couldn't even open the gates.

Except for Delondra, the first Knocker. She found that she could leave Mur, and then, impossibly, re-enter it. With practice, Delondra discovered she could also return to places and times she'd seen already. She tried to teach others, but no one could manage it. She could, however, go get them when they failed, if she'd gone with them to see where and when they'd left to.

Quickly, she monetized her ability, and, over time, did find a few others with the same ability she had. They set up a system of codes – knocks on the gates they would use to call up a certain area of space/time on the other side. The knocks were in no way needed, but they made the people with them feel better. Obviously, they started to think, this was a high-level magic trick.

Taking the name Knockers, after their little scam, they gave their newfound guild a prestige that also allowed Mur to begin to set up trade with the outside world again. Food and goods could come and go from Mur back to the people who might pay for it.

Which also managed to exacerbate an entirely different problem, one that grew as fast as the city did. People came to Mur accidently, for the most part. When they did, they possessed only what they happened to be carrying with them at the moment. For many people, that included currency, of some form.

But an 1873 United States dollar bill and a 2692 German Galleon weren't exactly compatible. People thought about a trade-only economy, but what was a really nice clay pot worth versus a titanium quartz watch? So the Exchangers were set up. All foreign currency, foreign being designated as anything not issued by the Exchangers offices, was turned into them and converted.

The Exchangers set the rate, including working out any new currency they came across, and issued bills, which came to be known as bucks in general speech, that were then used by people in Mur for all their currency needs.

All of which ignores a thriving black market for alternate currency and so on. Look, any decent settlement of humans will contain not only a made-up money scheme that makes internal sense and seems generally ridiculous outside of it, but it will also include an underground trading market to act as a secondary money scheme. Mostly the undermarket actually helps enable the uppermarket, so they leave each other alone and never speak of it.

Exchangers and Knockers worked together, of course – out of necessity if nothing else. Both parties also worked with the Mayor, who might as well have been President, or Chancellor, since the office didn't work under anyone else. There was no larger state or national government for Mur to liaise with, after all.

So while the Mayor's office oversaw the day-to-day operations as well as longer-term planning for Mur, the Knockers enabled and helped run trade, and the Exchangers took care of the money.

Exchangers also carried coins as a badge of office, instead of – well, instead of an actual badge. Knockers carried their own coins, figuring they would be overlooked as trinkets instead of a badge they might have to explain while outside of Mur. The Exchangers just thought they looked cool. Sometimes that's all it takes.

Jake thought about Benok's advice, hiring a Knocker to get out of the city for a while. Tying up a Knocker to either stay with you for a few weeks or to make sure they'd come back and get you – either way cost an arm and a leg, money Jake couldn't think of a way to raise.

So, instead, Jake walked. He wandered Mur aimlessly, keeping to the shadows of buildings, and considered where he could go to ground. The apartment felt like a no-go for him, they'd be sure to look there. But that meant he couldn't warn Casey.

Good relationship tip: if someone is sending people to try and kill you, it is considered both polite and appropriate to warn your significant other before they get home so they might be aware they could be walking into a kill box.

Jake decided to avoid the apartment for the time being and, instead, make sure he was seen on the other end of town. He headed Spireward, grabbing a bus to gain ground quickly, sorting out a bill from his pocket to pay the fare and climbing on the electric vehicle (all motorized engines in Mur being electrical to avoid needing to source gasoline from the outside).

Approaching the Spire, Jake got off the bus and continued walking, this time making sure he kept to the center of the sidewalk, making himself as visible as possible. He searched his pockets and came up empty for what he had in mind, so he stopped into a bodega along the way and bought a pack of cards. He'd been twitching for exactly this earlier and felt his sprits rise as he unwrapped the deck.

Breaking them in and shuffling them as he walked, Jake looked around until he found a cardboard box, discarded in the trash, and a bench to sit on. He set the box up in front of him and laid out three cards. Then he waited, fiddling with the cards idly as he did. He also considered what to do about Casey. Best guess he had a few hours, worst only a few minutes – but since nothing could be done in a few minutes, he thought he'd split the time and get noticed. That should draw them away from the apartment while he worked out a plan. He kept nudging the cards around, faster and faster.

After a few minutes – it never did take long – a guy walked by, watching Jake closely. Jake gave him the old patter and roped him in, starting to move the cards faster. He grabbed a bill from his pocket and put it down on the box, and the man across from him put a matching bill on top of the first.

The cards, under Jake's guidance, moved, spun, and danced faster still. Then suddenly they stopped. The man pointed, Jake flipped the card, shrugged, apologized, and swept both bills into his pocket before the guy could protest. The guy tossed down another bill, Jake matched it, and they went around again. And again, the guy lost, Jake sweeping the bills aside. Then he smiled, shrugged, and put a bill down, the guy taking the bait. By this time there were two other people watching.

Like pigeons after bread crumbs they watched Jake's movements, waiting for him to toss scraps their way. And this time he did; the guy pointed, Jake showed him his winning card, and the guy swept the money up himself, clumsily, almost knocking over the box. Having won, the man felt proud of himself, but Jake smoothly talked him out of playing again, letting him leave a winner.

Having the guy leave helped convince the others he wasn't a plant. Which was, if they had thought about it, ridiculous. He well could have been a friend meeting Jake later, but Jake showed them what they needed to believe right then, which for once was the truth, and roped more of them in. He kept his rousing game going, keeping half an eye out for any of Vink's guys.

Victor Botha left Jake that afternoon feeling lucky. Walking into his job at the grocers, he slipped on his apron and waved cheerily at his coworkers. No two came from the same place, his boss, the store's owner, having a habit of hiring newly minted Mur occupants if possible. It wasn't that he didn't like second-, third-, or other-generational inhabitants, but he wanted to give the new folks a chance to settle in, get some money and a feel for how the city worked. Victor himself had shown up in Mur while out walking his dog, Mrs. Dancer, one night outside of Johannesburg in May 1963.

He had a lot to unlearn, and his boss took him in under the condition that Victor get the fuck over his racism as fast as possible. He tried, never having understood the need for apartheid but having ingested it as normal and correct. Which was, of course, horrible and wrong, as Victor quickly learned. He struggled here and there, still, but two years of living in Mur – surrounded by people from, well, everywhere – helped burn a lot of it off. Though, to be honest, Victor still carried a bunch of it with him, just in silence. He would never treat another person as less than himself, but he would often catch himself thinking of them that way.

When he caught himself doing so, however, he would try to reason with himself and correct it. Victor faced an uphill struggle, and one that was both admirable, in that he wanted to climb that mountain, and damning, in that he still needed to.

Jake let himself play for another hour or so, until he was certain he'd been seen by someone who knew someone who considered someone a friend who worked for Vink. Then, letting the last player win a round for karma, though he in no way believed in it, he swept the cards up in a single motion, ending with the deck vanishing into a pocket.

Picking up and taking his empty box to a garbage can, Jake set it down and stalled, looking around. He saw Mur, as he expected to. Obviously, he saw Mur, but what he expected, and got, was: People moving down streets in various directions, a decent split between bored strollers, head-down purpose walkers, and people looking around them trying to figure out where the architecture for *that* building came from, or *that* one. Busses, cars, and other small vehicles fought for space on roadways. He smiled at his city and felt it was, indeed, his. He could close his eyes and feel it, like a living creature whose heart beat along with his.

Jake stayed there, breathing slow and steady, for a good minute before opening his eyes again. When he did, he looked around, seeing if anyone appeared to be coming straight for him in a 'not just walking and paying no attention' sort of way. Seeing no one, he started to walk, himself, heading slowly wallward in a roundabout way. He took switchbacks, winding a trail of nonsense across the city.

Keeping an eye out for anyone following him, Jake noticed two guys trying to be subtle. He wanted to laugh, they were so bad at this. But he didn't, knowing they intended to kill him. Luckily, he knew they wouldn't call for help since they wanted the fee for themselves.

Jake stopped walking and leaned against the apartment building he'd happened to stop in front of. They caught up with him quickly, swerving off at first to try and make it look like they weren't following him. They gave that idea up after Jake waved at them.

"So first," he said as they came closer, "I want to say congratulations. There are a lot of people who got the word today and are here to kill me, but you two are the first responders. Hold that close, you get me?"

"Man," said one of the guys, tugging his ugly blue canvas jacket down, "we're gonna kill you."

"That's...did you listen to me?" Jake asked, then turned his attention to the second guy, who was busy slowly opening a folding knife. "You need to get faster at that. I gotta ask you both, *how* did you manage to get here first?"

"We saw you," Folding Knife said, "and followed you."

"No, I get that," Jake said, "I mean you're obviously not good at...wait a minute, neither of you has killed anyone before, have you?"

"We don't need a test run," Ugly Jacket reassured Jake.

"No need to get defensive," Jake said, taking a half-step back. He didn't have a plan past talking to them, and it occurred to him they might not be the best listeners. "I'm on your side, really. Against all odds, here you are. That's what I'm hoping for, too."

"You're hoping we kill you?" Ugly Jacket said, sliding on some knuckle dusters.

"No I'm hoping that you don't, against all odds." Jake ran a quick mental check of the contents of his pockets and came back with some money, a deck of cards, a few lockpicks, and two or three mints. Not great fighting odds there. Unless, he thought... "Hey, are either of you guys allergic to mint?"

"Is anyone allergic to mint?" Folding Knife asked.

"Someone has to be, right?" Jake said, suddenly unsure. "Anyway, thought I'd check."

"What, you're gonna stop us with mint?" Folding Knife asked, stopping in his tracks, confused.

"Well, if you happened to be allergic to it I would've at least considered the idea. But you shot that down. See, you're doing pretty good at this so far, boys." Jake looked around, wondering if there was anything nearby he could use, but saw nothing.

"Shut up," Folding Knife told Jake, waving the knife around, "and stand still."

"Not sure either of those'll be happening," Jake admitted. Then, sighing, he shook his head. "No, you know what, come stab me, buddy."

Jake stood there and flung both arms out to his side, letting his wrists go limp, hands dangling. Folding Knife froze, totally unsure what was going on. He'd never really expected Jake to go just go along with a light to medium stabbing.

"Stab him!" Ugly Coat yelled.

Folding Knife went in for the kill, thrusting the knife out in front of him. He didn't want to kill anyone – him and Ugly Coat were just low-level bag men for Vink. They didn't even ever have to rough anyone up, though they told themselves they could, of course, if they needed to.

The knife darted toward Jake's chest, clutched tight in a hand whose knuckles had gone white with tension. Jake did the only thing he could think of, the one way he'd learned to deal with a knife fight when he was younger. He turned quickly, bringing his arms in, and took the knife in his left arm.

Clamping his jaw shut, Jake wrenched his arm away, yanking the knife out of Folding Knife's hand. He wanted the knife out of him, but knew that the arm would stay numb for a while due to shock and wouldn't bleed freely with the knife in. So he left it there and forced a grin to unfurl.

"Well," he said, doing everything he could to make his voice sound calm and level, "now I have your knife. *Now* what?"

Folding Knife charged, only a step or two away from Jake. Jake held his left arm out a bit so it wouldn't get tangled and leaned toward the guy, taking the body hit and twisting so they both fell.

Jake flailed, really, managing to land on top. Knees raised and lowered, his right arm punching Folding Knife anywhere he could reach, Jake just went wild, attacking him until he thought the guy would stay down.

His left arm hurt now, distracting him. Jake struggled to get up, making sure to step on, and kick, Folding Knife a few more times while he did. He also banged his left arm against the ground once while he did, sending a shot of pain right along his nerves that almost dropped him.

"You...!" Ugly Coat yelled, coming at Jake while Jake was still trying to stand. The pain from his arm was fuzzing out details and he blinked quickly to clear his vision.

Jake caught a flash of fake gold glinting and turned his body again, raising his right shoulder as he ducked his head in against his chest to take the blow from Ugly Coat's knuckledusters. It hurt like hell but didn't break his jaw, and Jake took that for the biggest win he could hope for.

He fell against Ugly Coat, thinking that not only had it worked on Folding Knife, but it would put him inside the range of those brass knuckles. But Ugly Coat saw it coming and threw a rain of knees and elbows, hitting Jake all over. None of them very hard, with no momentum behind them or real strength, but Jake still instinctively curled in on himself, losing ground.

He screamed as Ugly Coat smacked the knife still stuck in Jake's left arm. The world shrunk to pinhole size for Jake, and it spun. He tried to crawl away, only to feel his ankle tugged hard. Kicking back with his free leg, Jake got lucky and caught Ugly Coat right in the face.

No one offered to help, people hurrying past the fight, not wanting to get involved, until one person started yelling for someone to call the cops. Ugly Jacket knew he had to kill Meyer quickly and escape. Folding Knife still laid on the street, moaning, but if he stayed there and got pinched then the whole reward would be Ugly Jacket's, who discovered quickly he was all right with that.

Still, he had to end this fast, he thought as he wiped blood from his face. Jake's kick had spread his nose across his face and he huffed, breathing hard through his mouth as he looked at Meyer, on the ground, bleeding from his stabbed arm, unable to stand. Ugly Jacket smiled, though it hurt to do it, and stood up, looming over Jake.

All he had to do, he knew, was stomp Jake's head into the ground. He'd need proof, but decided the police report would serve for that. He walked, haltingly, along Jake's body, lining up his shot.

Jake rolled over onto his back and kicked out again, catching Ugly Jacket between the legs and dropping him. Jake, still not feeling up to standing, rolled over again so he was next to Ugly Jacket, who was curled up, making his testicles the center of his body, trying to catch his breath, sucking air in through his mouth, his nose a bloody, gagging mess.

Meyer slammed Ugly Jacket about the temples a few times with his right elbow. He didn't want to kill anyone, just leave them unable to follow. Jake knew he, too, had to get out of there before anyone did show up to help. The chances were about even that one of them would be involved with Vink enough to want a bunch of money.

Another few blows to the face, ears, sternum, and kidneys convinced Jake that Ugly Jacket was going nowhere. Gathering himself as best he could, Jake stood. He looked back over at Folding Knife. Stumbling over to him, Jake kicked him once more, this time in the face, and started to walk off. He couldn't get on a bus in his condition, but even if it was walking into a trap, he needed to go home, get the knife out of his arm, and patch himself up. Also possibly have a drink, some sleep, and about seventeen more drinks, he decided, as he tripped generally forward, keeping upright with the help of building facades and force of will.

Tiffany Stern poured herself a cup of tea and leaned back in her chair. She considered putting her feet up on her desk but knew that Alyson, her boss, would give her 'that look' again. So she kept her feet firmly on the floor and stared at the ceiling while her tea cooled toward a drinkable temperature.

Her office had computers, but – Tiffany rolled her eyes – they used keyboards for input. No one in Mur seemed either able or willing to make a subvocalization input, much less a decent AI speech-to-text program, of the kind she'd grown up with in the late twenty-first century.

Tiffany was one of the few who'd found Mur via hunting it down. She'd started to hear stories about it, on and off – a hidden, secret city that could be gotten to from anywhere if you were lucky enough to find the right door – from a few different sources.

Which was, for everyone else, the problem. Tiffany's sources were considered crackpots. She was writing for a weekly paper best described as a trash rag. They covered vampire babies, alien abductions, and the like, treating them all with the focused intensity of someone half asleep. Tiffany had wanted be a journalist when she grew up, and had managed to do exactly that. But pissing off an editor led to losing a job and bad references, and the need to keep paying rent took her straight to such journalistic heights as 'My Daughter's Baby Is Prince of the Moon.'

She did some legwork on a few different hidden city stories and noticed that – unintentionally, she was sure – a lot of the details repeated themselves. That sort of thing was fairly common with alien abduction stories; since they got so much coverage, people just took on details from other stories and became convinced they'd experienced them. But these were under-reported and Stern couldn't see the link.

So she played a game she had fallen back on before: to get at a story and try to treat it with some version of journalistic integrity. She'd start assuming it was all true, just running with the theoretical facts to see where they took her.

It was while searching for one of these doors that every account claimed were real – from people who said they came from the city and left, not realizing they couldn't go back, to people who swore they had a friend or loved one who had vanished into the city – that Tiffany overheard someone talking about meeting a Knocker later that day.

She followed them, figuring it would make good color for an eventual story, and when they went through a door into what should have been a storeroom, Tiffany dove through with them and found herself in Mur.

Most people in her place would've backed out again and started telling the same stories she'd heard, or assumed something wildly strange and different. But Tiffany ran from the shouting Knocker and his passenger into Mur. Believing the stories that she couldn't go back, she spent a day or so living on the street and confirming stories before she decided to stay and make a new life, with no baggage, as a journalist in town.

She didn't miss her old life, but she still missed a lot of the tech. She sighed, sat up straight, sipped her tea – now the perfect temperature – and got back to work before Alyson came by to check on her.

∞

Casey tried to stop smiling as Martine and Scraps played with each other. Seeing the woman reunited with her dog was wonderful. She brushed aside the thanks, assuring Martine she hadn't really done anything, while Key swore the opposite. Casey shook Martine's hand one last time, dodging a hug, and they left, walking down the stairs of the apartment building and back onto the open streets.

"I'm still pretty annoyed," Casey told the old woman as they stood at a corner waiting for the traffic to stop, a sea of bicycles whizzing past.

"Because you think I intended you to beat Trent up to get Scraps back?"

"That," Casey said, "and that you used me as a distraction. If I hadn't thought to just talk him out of keeping the dog—"

"But that was why it was good to have you along," Key insisted. "Someone else might've just decided to be violent, and that wouldn't have solved anything."

"Still would've gotten Scraps back," Casey muttered, starting to cross the street.

"Not for long. Trent would've been even madder, and then what? He goes to Martine and the whole thing starts up again, except now he thinks she will use violence against him, so why not use it against her, and then the whole situation ends far worse then when it began. That's not a solution, honey, it's an inciting incident."

"And you're going to claim you knew all this beforehand?" Casey asked.

Key sighed and stopped walking again, on the other side of the street. She turned to face Casey and pin her with a stare. "I am," she said softly, "and

I'm glad I was right. But before you go for the day, there is one other stop I need to make, if that's all right?"

"Sure," Casey said, shrugging broadly for effect, "why not?" She adjusted the strap of her guitar bag and waved a hand across the widening street they faced. "Any particular direction? And will it take long? I should get home in not too long, I need to put in some practice." At this last she tugged the strap of her guitar bag lightly.

Casey didn't actually want to go with Key; she felt used and still twitched a bit internally at the game the old woman seemed to be playing. It was all well and good to take credit for knowing things and being sure about how people would react, but Casey didn't really believe it. More to the point, she felt lucky she had diffused the situation, agreeing with Key about where things might've gone had she simply knocked out Trent and made off with Scraps. Which is why she hadn't in the first place, she knew, but the whole thing just ended up in a knot in her brain.

She agreed to go on this last side trip, she told herself, because it would provide her some insight into Key, maybe; seeing someone at work a second time told you more and gave you a hint of a baseline to go with. But she knew she wouldn't work with the old woman again.

They walked, Key leading, for a while – long enough for Casey to suggest a bus or cab, but Key liked to walk. It kept her, she said, young. Shrugging unseen behind her, Casey kept walking.

After a long, silent walk, which Casey spent chewing over the same set of thoughts, they arrived. Wilhelm's Flower Shop was painted across the glass, and the small store burst with color. Plants and flowers of all sorts grew, bundled into arrangements and wreaths or just erupting from pots and seeming to scream 'Hey! We're flowers!' to Casey. Her idea of a good houseplant was something simple, and preferably not in her house.

Key pushed the door open, a tiny bell tinkling a welcome as the door swept past it. "Alfred? Are you here?" she called out, not seeing anyone.

"In the back," came the reply in a rich baritone. Alfred himself appeared soon after, wiping his long, thin hands across his apron. As he saw Key a smile spread along his face. "Granny," he said, "you didn't have to come by."

"Oh, Alfred, you knew I would. This," Key said, nodding toward Casey, "is a good friend of mine, Casey—"

"Just Casey is fine," Casey said, nodding at Alfred.

"Any good friend of—"

"Of course," Casey cut him off with a well-faked smile.

"So is it true?" Key asked Alfred as he waved them over to the counter.

He slid behind it and busied himself with small tasks as he answered. "He's a good kid, Key," came the eventual reply. Casey blinked.

"If he was a good kid," Key said, "would he have—"

"Of course not," Alfred said. "But he didn't know that when he bragged about having access to the shop...Key, he wanted to show off to some friends.

104

Let them in at night, like a bragging party to make him cool."

"I'm sorry," Casey cut in, "letting people into a flower store at night makes you cool these days? Because..." she trailed off and shrugged.

"No, I'm sorry," Alfred said. "Tomaso, he's a kid who helps out in the shop. Always reliable and good and never stole anything, at least that I noticed – and really, if he did, it was a buck or two for a drink, you know?"

"Sure, sure," Casey agreed, waiting for understanding to creep into the conversation.

"His friends, they thought he was just a boring kid—"

"How old is he?" Casey asked.

"Sixteen, he's a friend of my neighbor—but anyway, he let them into the store, to prove he could break rules. That was it. But one of those other kids must've seen the code on the alarm and sold it for some cash, and they got in and robbed the place."

"Do you know *who* did it?" Key asked, resting a hand lightly on Casey's elbow. Casey took it as a sign to hang back and let the old woman ask the questions. Fine by her – she wasn't sure what they were even doing here. Just being sympathetic? That would be Casey's first guess, if she had to make one. Surely, she thought with an internal groan, Key didn't expect them to fix this. Maybe she was rich, and seeing if she could afford to fund it? Casey set her shoulders and braced herself for the worst.

"Tomaso does, yeah. And it isn't even the money," he said, making Casey sigh internally, knowing this meant Key would insist on something that Casey wouldn't like. "When they emptied the register they took my husband's locket. It's all I have left of him."

"Oh, honey," Key said, reaching across the counter to pat Alfred's hand warmly. "Well, give me the name and I'll see what I can do."

"Granny, no!" Alfred insisted. "These aren't nice guys, I don't want you putting yourself in danger. It'll be fine, I'm sure. The police will—"

"Possibly get the money back, but the locket will get lost in the shuffle – we both know it, Alfred," Key insisted.

Alfred sighed, something Casey wanted to let herself do but didn't. "Don't do anything silly, Granny, seriously. I'm pretty sure it was this guy Torok Ox."

Key nodded. "I can't promise anything, and I *won't* do anything silly – not that I ever do," she maintained, "but I'll let you know if I can help, all right? And let poor Tomaso know he *is* a good kid, I said so. But he has to stop caring what the others think of him. It'll just get him in more trouble."

"I will, thank you, Granny," Alfred said

He described the locket to them and Key turned and started toward the door with a soft "Let's go honey," to Casey. Casey waved to Alfred and left, the door chime going off again and sending them into the slowly darkening afternoon.

Outside, Casey sighed loudly, causing Key to stop and stare at her. "What is it, honey?"

"Torok Ox," she replied.

"You know him?"

Casey waved a hand around, stirring the air. "I know *of* him. Never met him, myself. I'm pretty sure I know where he works out of, at least. But Key," she told the old woman, trying to impart extra seriousness in her voice, "you don't want to...he's not..."

"Reasonable?" Key asked. "I didn't think he would be. But I don't think we need to go fight them – it isn't the money, we just want—"

"Wait, 'we just want'? I didn't know this was a done deal," Casey said, letting the anger she felt building start to show on her face.

"Well, you know where he is," Key pointed out. "You said so yourself. I assumed that meant—"

"It meant that we should stay away."

"Alfred's locket is worthless to anyone but Alfred," Key said softly, "there's no reason this Torok would want to keep it. I don't see why he wouldn't listen to reason."

Casey rubbed her right temple slowly. "Oh for... because he isn't a reasonable sort of guy. He's the sort of guy who would want to keep it just *because* it means something to someone he views as not worth his time. He's mean and petty and—"

"I thought you didn't know him."

"I don't. But I do know of him, like I said. Can you trust me on this?" Casey started walking away, sure this was it, and she was done.

Key kept up with her, though. "I don't know, I mean you don't know him, not really, and I think it's worth a shot."

"Worth getting shot, you mean."

"It won't come to violence," Key insisted. "If he says no, at all, I won't challenge him – I'll back away and we can leave."

"I'm not sure he'd let us leave. Don't you get it?"

"I just don't think it's as simple as you do," Key said. "Just give me the address and I'll go. You can go home if you want."

Casey considered it for a quarter of a second, frowned internally at herself, and shook her head. "If it does go south, I can't let you twist in the wind like that. I just...I can't, all right?"

"All right with me," Key said, smiling. "See, I knew you were right for the job. So," she asked, looking around, "where are we going?"

Casey started walking, stopped, and waited for a bus wallward. They got on and rode in silence, Casey still wishing she could've let Key go alone but knowing she wouldn't have been able to do it. They got off at the last stop, so close to the wall itself that a few of the buildings – older, early ones – actually leaned against it, badly needing repairs but having no scrape of money to fund them.

"Down here," Casey said, remembering the time Jake had brought her. She hadn't gone in with him, at his insistence. He wasn't protecting her so much as he hadn't wanted to be there, either, and if he just ducked in, dropped something off, and left, it would raise no questions. Unlike bringing in a new person. New people, Jake warned, meant questions, and questions meant answers and so on, none of it good.

So she remembered the location, at least. Which assumed Torok hadn't changed his base of operations, but from what Casey'd heard, she doubted he would. The name felt like a giveaway, too. Torok Ox felt to Casey like either someone from an early enough time to think that was a sweet, sweet name, or someone who thought they would sound cooler if they were thought to be from some earlier time. Either way, it left him as someone who clung to that image.

Two guards lounged outside a doorway. They wanted to look like they were just hanging out, two people from the neighborhood, but Casey could see the tension in their bodies change as they noticed her and Key.

"I have an idea," Key said, and she moved herself in front of Casey.

Casey felt her shoulders tense and forced them to relax. Key getting turned away right at the door would be the best Casey could hope for, and she pulled for that outcome. Key walked right up to the guards – both wide, annoyed-looking guys – with a smile on her face.

"Excuse me," she said, prompting baffled looks from both guards. "I'm here to see Torok Ox. I just need to pick something up."

"And who," the guard on the left said, moving his hand toward his back at waist level, slowly, "the fuck are you?"

Casey knew the guard was reaching for a knife, she could feel it. The other guard, she saw, kept his hands in his pockets, which didn't bode wonderfully for them, either. Key reached a hand into her pocket, very slowly, and took something out – Casey couldn't see what. Her best plan was to stand where she was, a few steps behind Key and to her right, but it meant she couldn't see what the old woman held in her left hand clearly. Whatever sat in Key's hand did the trick, though.

"Just need to pick something up, all right, boys?" Key said again, the smile never dropping from her face.

The second guard looked at the first, with his hand still hovering near his back, and nodded at his colleague before vanishing into the blackness of the dark doorway they stood around.

Jake, while Casey and Key waited to see what the returning guard would bring with him, tried to keep to the shadows. He'd pulled the knife out of his arm, managing to not scream mostly thanks to biting down on his wallet, and used the knife to cut his pants leg short. That fabric made a decent enough tourniquet, though Jake's leg was now cold. Worse for his personal comfort, he realized he had to cut his other pants leg the same to at least pass for something ignorable. So Jake – limping, nerves lit up from all sorts of directions, and half delusional – tried to make his way home wearing the ugliest pair of cut-offs in Mur.

Stumbling in the direction he thought he needed to go, Jake took a switchback slowly, winding along the streets of the city and staying to the buildings as much as possible, a hand trailing along the facades he passed. Jake tried his best to not outright lean on a building, worried he wouldn't be able to start back up if he stopped moving for long, but dragged his palm along brick, glass, wood, and stone to reassure himself he was still upright.

Convinced he could feel the heat of a target on his back, Jake kept moving. Home might not be the smartest place to head, but a hospital, he knew, would only be worse. He passed a bodega and looked in. Harsh light filled the space, and his eyes zeroed in, only slightly blurrily, to a row of juices. He nodded to nothing and went in.

Using what money he had on him, Jake bought some bandages, rubbing alcohol, and a bunch of orange juice. The juice was, as always, at a premium. Since it needed to be imported, like most of the food Mur ate at this point, good-quality orange juice remained hard to come by. Most bodegas carried some anyway, knowing people would happily pay for the good stuff, just as Jake had.

Outside, Jake started walking again, still afraid of stopping forward momentum for too long. While he walked, he undid his pants tourniquet, poured the alcohol over his wound, nearly passed out from the pain of that, then wrapped it tightly in the fresh bandages.

Somehow, he managed to keep taking a few steps while he did everything. Dropping the bloody, cut-up pants leg, Jake opened one of his small containers of juice and drank deeply. A deep breath, another extended gulping of juice, and Jake put one foot in front of the other and kept moving.

The second guard came back and leaned in close to whisper something to the first guard, who waved Casey and Key inside. Key looked behind her to make sure Casey still hovered there, caught the look in Casey's eyes, and winked. Casey felt her anger rise again. This wasn't, she knew, no matter how much Key wanted it to be, a game.

They walked down the unlit entrance to the building together. Just enough light from the stairwell ahead seeped in to let them feel they could tell where they were going. Casey, moving closer to Key, asked her softly, "What did you show that guy, anyway?"

Key reached back without answering, found Cassey's hand, and pressed something into it. Casey felt it, running her fingers over every surface. Pressing the coin back into Key's hand, she asked angrily, "Are you serious? You pretended to be an Exchanger?"

"I didn't pretend anything," Key said, "I just showed him that I had the coin. Anything he did after that is on him."

"Key, no," Casey said pleadingly, "this doesn't end well."

"I'm just going to ask, like I promised," the old woman said as they started to climb stairs. A flight up, a guard met them and pointed down the hall. Down the hall, another guard – Casey keeping count and trying to plan an escape route that would leave as much of the building intact as possible – ushered them into an apartment.

Walls draped with dark, blood-red rugs, light coming from raw exposed bulbs, Casey felt like she'd entered a warlord's cave. Which was, she knew in her gut, the exact feeling Torok aimed at. She liked him even less for it, her elbow hovering near the switch for the amp at her hip. She really didn't want this to turn into something. She begged, pleading to no one in particular, that they would be able to just walk out once Torok told Key off. She didn't believe it, but she hoped.

They were led through the claustrophobic apartment quickly, right to Torok himself. Casey nodded to herself when she saw the shape of his head. Large, sloped forehead, wide jaw, and thick facial hair all placed him as having arrived in Mur from somewhere far, far back in history. That he'd managed to make a place for himself as a small king in a big pond didn't surprise her. Tin-plated despot, her C.O. would've called him. The sort of man who kept power through cruelty and would be in power exactly as long as he kept everyone afraid of him. The second he slipped up, one of his men would try and take over, and a knife in the back, out of darkness, had felled plenty of people who thought they were in perfect, complete control.

"You're the new Exchanger?" Torok asked Key.

Key shrugged and showed him the coin. Casey wanted to scream. Instead she stood there, looking as calm and confident as she could project.

"No need for Exchangers right now. What do you want?"

"You robbed a flower store recently," Key started, "and—"

"You get no cut of that," Torok said, growing angry, "you should know that."

Casey braced for impact and strained to hear the whispers of the guards around her. "This have to do with Vink's offer, you think?" one of them muttered.

"Couldn't, could it? Why would an Exchanger give a fuck about Meyer? Vink wants him dead, Exchangers don't do that."

The name drop caused Casey to flinch visibly. "What is wrong with your guard?" Torok asked Key. "She afraid of us? Shit guard. Leave her with us, I'll dispose of her, you can leave."

"I really hope the boss don't kill off an Exchanger today," one of the guards whispered. Casey was both offended by their sloppy attitude and grateful for their unprofessionalism.

Casey took Torok in with a slow, steady look. She made sure to lock eyes with him, long enough to show him that she didn't intend to back down. Carefully, she broke eye contact and put the back of her hand to her mouth, as if stifling a yawn. She didn't want to rile him, but given his threat, she couldn't let him think she was easy meat, either.

"I don't expect part of your score," Key told Torok, ignoring Casey on purpose, "but there was a locket mixed in with it, and I need it back, if possible."

Torok looked back at Key, slight confusion playing across his wide, pale face. "This locket, it's worth enough to drag an Exchanger out here to take it back?"

"Sentimental value," Key said lightly.

"You think I care?" Torok said, letting his question trail off into a loud burst of laughter. His guards all joined in late, in that special way only lackeys have to try and make their leaders feel special.

"I think you—" Key started.

Casey cut her off fast, realizing that, in no way shape or form, did the old woman intend to back down and just leave, despite her promises. "Hey, Boss," she said to Key, "pretty sure it's right in that bag there." Casey pointed and then thought fast. She could pull this off, she decided. She had to, because the alternative spilled a lot of blood. Hopefully not their own, but that wouldn't diminish the loss for her.

"Oh, thank you," Key replied casually. "Just grab it and we can go, then?"

Casey walked over to the bag, shadowed by Torok's men, who looked confused but were just going with it since they didn't yet have orders to the contrary.

"What the fuck are you doing?!" Torok roared. "Don't let her—" he shouted at his guys, who moved to stop Casey now, happy for the clear direction, if not the tone used.

"I figured we could save you the trouble of digging it out," Key said, following Casey's lead. Casey appreciated it, even as she wanted to throttle the woman.

Casey kept her back to Torok's minions and started to dig through the bag. She grabbed a locket, opened it, and discarded it. Then she grabbed another and did the same. The third locket she opened and nodded. "Yup," she said, clutching it tightly in her hand, letting the chain dangle freely.

One of the goons grabbed her wrist, and Casey forced herself to not smile. She twisted, looking and feeling to him as if she wanted to get free of his grip. Instead, she put the goon's body between herself and Torok, leaving herself next to the bag.

Casey dipped her hand in quickly, grabbing and closing the second locket she'd opened. She made sure to ball the chain up with it and went to move her hand toward her pants pocket, slowly enough to not be noticed and quick enough to not be seen.

Her move would never rank in the halls of the great lifts. Pickpockets and thieves would never sing songs about Casey and The Locket, but the lift worked. Her distraction paid off and the correct locket sat in her pocket, feeling like it could burn a hole through the fabric and scald its imprint into her leg for all time.

All they had to do now was leave. Luckily, Casey's plan included that bit. Sort of.

Torok took the locket from the lackey who had snatched it from Casey and grinned. "Why would I give to you?" He turned to stare at Casey and let the grin fall. "And you, I should skin you for just reaching into my—"

"Forgive her, she's a screw-up," Key said, "I'll kill her myself later, if I have to. But it is mine to do—"

"If I decide it is," Torok said.

"Of course," Key told him, smiling. She caught Casey's eye with a questioning look, and Casey just returned a brief nod. Casey hoped it would be enough. "I am so sorry we bothered you, we'll just go. With deep apologies."

"You think I intend to let you leave?" Torok asked.

Casey took a deep breath, subtly enough that the goon *still* clasping her wrist wouldn't notice. She started to brace herself to fight their way out any way she could. "I think you might," she said. "If only to—"

"I said I'd deal with you later," Key cut her off. "But yes," she replied to Torok, "I do think we'll leave here. And the next run, we'll work for two percent cheaper," she flipped the Exchanger's coin in her hand and then slid it into her pocket. "But if I were to go missing, well...it'd be annoying to have to smooth over and explain, no?"

Torok considered her words at length. Casey twisted her arm again, seriously this time, and jerked it free of the goon's grasp. He made a small noise and started to reach for her again but stopped, catching sight of her expression. After all, he reflected, no one had told him to hold on to her. Didn't seem hardly worth it when the woman shot a look that very clearly involved a promise to remove limbs.

Torok thought some more. Casey looked at Key during the long silence. Key looked at Casey. They kept character, Key glaring and Casey nodding, almost sadly, accepting her fate, just in case a goon was watching.

"Go," he said at last, and with that turned away from them. "One of you, see them out," he said without turning around, "make sure they don't do anything to make me regret my choice." He busied himself, then, ignoring the room.

Key led the way, Casey behind her, and bringing up the rear was the muscle who'd grabbed her wrist earlier. He didn't try it again, and didn't seem inclined to try and force them to go where they seemed happy to go anyway.

Again down the darkened hallways and stairs they went, passing guards that ignored them once they caught sight of their own comrade with them. Back into the fading daylight they moved. Their guard left them there, at the door to the building, and turned, without a word, to head back upstairs.

Casey touched Key's elbow lightly and whispered, "We need to move," before starting off as fast as she felt the old woman could keep up. And Key did exactly that, letting Casey lead her down the street and turn clear of the block.

"Why are we rushing?" Key asked once she'd decided they were clear. They'd turned a corner, and the light somehow felt brighter around them.

"Torok isn't letting us go, he's letting us not be traced back to him. There'll be some idiot, and soon, trailing us to deal with us," Casey said, trying to keep her voice calm and level.

"Oh, honey, I don't know about that," Key said.

"Really? You're going to keep doubting me? This is getting old." Casey turned again, seeming to follow a route in her head that made no sense to Key, who followed, shrugging.

"All right," she conceded, "and good job getting the locket. I mean, I saw you grab it but—"

"Yeah, I'm not a pickpocket," Casey said, "but I had to think of something, he was about to just drag us in the back and make stew."

Key laughed. "Dramatic, no? He isn't a cannibal."

"Yeah, sure, if you say so. Look," Casey said, "when they come for us, just get behind me, all right?"

"But honey, I know you don't want to fight."

"I don't, but I want to be killed even less." She fished in her pocket and handed the locket to Key. "Give this to Arthur. As soon as we're clear, I need to get home. One of Torok's guys said something about Jake – I think he might be in trouble, and he needs to know about it."

"Of course," Key said. "If you need to go now..." she trailed off and shrugged quickly, then realized as she was just off Casey's left and a step behind the woman while they walked, she couldn't see it.

"Would love to," Casey admitted. "Sort of. But we're either going to get hit or not in the next few blocks, so just bear with me."

At the next corner, Casey took a switchback, going a half block around to loop a half block back and continue the way they'd been headed, Spireward. As they neared the corner, ready to turn Spireward again, two men started coming down the block in the opposite direction.

Casey glanced at them and started to dismiss them as just random people on the street, like many others they'd passed, until she saw they both had their eyes pinned right at Casey and Key. She tensed, looked away from them, and decided to just keep going as if she hadn't seen them. The two guys would have to catch up, which meant that if Casey turned now, they would fall in behind her and Key. But if she went straight, then they would meet face to face, which suited her much better.

Pointing at a store window they passed, Casey muttered softly to Key, "Two guys coming right at us, keep walking, just fall another few steps behind me," making sure to look like they were discussing what the store sold. They kept walking, Key doing as Casey asked, and Casey, herself, counted off steps until they met the men head on.

As one of the men reached in his pocket, the other started to speak. "Stop right th—"

Casey spun on one foot, spiraling down as she turned as if she'd drilled into the street, and shrank out of view. As her body came around, halfway through the turn, her other leg shot out, speeding her up even further. On the full turn she hooked the foot of her extended leg and grabbed the ankle of the man trying to speak, sending him to the ground hard.

Casey kept her outstretched leg moving, while the rest of her stayed still, until it was in place to push her back to standing. She looked at the other man, hand still coming out of his pocket. "Just run," she told him, "tell Torok some story about how we had a big gun or something. Save face and don't," she said as she placed a foot on the neck of the groaning man on the sidewalk, "feel bad for your friend. He'll want to lie, too."

The guy took out a knife and held it out in front of him, but hesitated. His partner had hit the ground before he could even get his knife out of a pocket. What were, he thought, the chances of him actually being able to stab this woman? Then again, if he didn't try...

He waved the knife a bit, then yelped as Casey grabbed his wrist and twisted. She leaned into it and he found himself without a knife, upside down, and falling. As his back slammed into the concrete of the sidewalk he finished the math in his head, sluggishly, that would have told him to do as she asked.

"Do I have to break it?" Casey asked, twisting his wrist harder. "Or are we agreed about the story you'll tell?"

"Story," he said softly, blinking back the burning feeling of tears welling up in his eyes.

"Good," she said, and waved Key over. She let go of his wrist and started walking, Key with her again. She walked, first, in the direction the goons had come from, just to make sure they wouldn't be followed further.

Jake panted, out of breath, as the light faded above him, the sky darkening with intent. Leaning on the side of a building, Jake wondered how much further he could go, and how much further he needed to go to get home. Both answers came back from the magic 8-ball of his brain as hazy. He pushed off from the wall and kept moving.

"Meyer!" came the shout behind him.

Jake groaned and turned his head to see who'd called out to him. He recognized, faintly, Cassandra, a small-time delivery woman for Vink. She liked, Jake remembered, violence, but had never managed to move up the ranks to muscle. He couldn't remember why and supposed it didn't really matter. Right then he knew he couldn't outfight or outwit most kittens, much less a grown human.

"Cassandra, right?" he asked, learning against the wall again as he turned to face her. "Didn't I buy you a drink last month at The Alibi?" Jake's voice wavered, and he paused for breath a few times.

"You don't sound good, Meyer. I almost feel bad for how easy this'll be," she told him, making a big show of trying, and failing, to crack her knuckles.

"Come on," Jake said lamely, "I bought you a drink." He took a slow, long breath. "Just last month."

"That's it?" she asked, slowly walking toward him. "The great fast-talking Jake Meyer reduced to begging?"

Jake pushed off the wall, forcing himself to stand up straight. His leg almost gave, but he cursed himself out mentally until it supported him. "That wasn't begging," he said, as firmly as possible, "that was a distraction. I just needed you to," he stopped to cough a few times, "hold on a second while I got ready to kick your ass."

"All right, this is pathetic," Cassandra said. She advanced on Jake, taking her time and considering how she intended to kill him. Getting him down would be too easy, she reflected. A shove would do it, no reason to even punch him. Once he sprawled out on the sidewalk she could easily stomp him until he stopped breathing.

She took another step toward him, and Jake held his ground, trying to hold a grin in place as if he was waiting for her to make a move. She kept thinking. Indiscriminate stomping would be good, but it'd take a bit longer than she might like. No, she'd target his head – no, she revised, his neck.

Then she'd just have to hold him up, put him in a cab and pretend he was drunk and passed out, get him to Vink, and she could cash out. More importantly, she could demand a new job.

Yeah. That worked for her. She took another step.

Pain exploded across her back and she felt herself falling forward. Catching herself with her hands, feeling concrete scrape skin off her palms in a hot burst of pain, she yelled and turned to see what'd happened.

She caught the sight of a boot sole just before it crashed into her face. Her vision swam, and then there was a second impact to match the first and she collapsed to the ground.

Oscar stood over Cassandra, a wooden bat in his hands, and looked at Jake. "You OK?" he asked, stepping over the woman.

"Where'd you come—"

"You're leaning against The Alibi, man."

Jake looked at the wall he'd allowed himself to lean against again. "I thought the brick felt familiar," he said, trying to sound casual.

"No you didn't," Oscar said, sighing. "What happened to you? You look like you tried to sleep with a meat grinder."

Jake let Oscar put an arm around him and help him stand up straight. "Well," Jake said slowly, "I was out alone, and there was, you know how it is, a meat grinder, and—"

"Do you ever stop?" Oscar opened the door to The Alibi and started to help Jake in.

"No," he admitted, even as he resisted. "No, not The Alibi. Take me home."

"Can you hold up the wall a minute while I let them know inside? I'll be quick."

"I'll be here," Jake agreed, leaning against the building again. He waited what felt like a week and a half while Oscar ran inside, yelled that he'd be back in twenty, and helped him upright again.

"Why not come inside?" he asked, looking around. "And shit, where do you guys live again?"

"People," Jake said, "are after me. Don't want them in the bar."

"Nice of you. Where am I going?" Oscar asked again, trying to act like Jake's weight wasn't a problem at all.

"You've been to our place," Jake said, walking as much as he could by himself. "A bunch. Fine, it's this way," he pointed, "now stop slowing me down."

They got to the loft and Oscar took Jake's keys from him, wrangling the door and helping Jake in. He steered him toward the bed but Jake insisted on sitting at the table in a normal chair. He collapsed into it, leaning on the table heavily.

Oscar, at Jake's request, made some tea. Jake convinced him, when the tea was drunk and the world had started to spin again, that he would be fine. Oscar doubted him, but he also had to get back to The Alibi, so he left, swearing he would be back in a short while to check in on Jake. Jake agreed, not wanting to bother him but knowing it would be futile to resist.

$$\infty$$

Casey looked at Key. "I really should get home. Like I said—"

"Your Jake is in trouble, I remember," Key said.

"You can just call him Jake. This 'Your Jake' stuff is a bit—"

"Old?" Key asked, laughing. "Like me. Let me have this, honey. And thank you for your help." She grabbed Casey's hand and patted it. "Tomorrow night, can you come to a party?"

"I told you, we're done. What you did back there was reckless. You almost got us both killed." Casey shook her head. "And you lied to me. We're done here."

"Honey," Key said sadly, "please reconsider. Just come to this party. I'll call you tomorrow morning with the details. Sleep on it, at least."

"I..." Casey trailed off. She needed to go, she knew, if she hoped to catch Jake before he went anywhere. "Fine, fine – call me tomorrow and we'll see. I'll think about it," she promised. "But no guarantee, got it?"

"Of course," Key said, "now go."

Carson Delancey sighed, checked his watch for the fifth time in two minutes, and looked at the door again. Delancey was an Exchanger, one of the fastest, and he hated lateness. Most of his regulars knew it, too. Word spread, easily, that you didn't keep Carson waiting unless you were being stabbed. Even then, it was a good idea to call and reschedule while the stabbing went on.

But here he sat, at his desk, in the middle of the day. Carson decided to get back to some paperwork while he waited so the time wasn't a complete waste. Exchangers, it was thought, had a fairly simple job. You took currency and changed it into money usable in Mur. That was it. There were, everyone knew, tables for different rates of exchange. All you had to do was count, people snidely thought in Delancey's direction – when his back was to them.

Of course they all realized that some currency was worth more than others, but then they stopped considering it at all, because unless you worked with exchanging money a lot, that sort of thing wouldn't hit your radar very often. Parties and places you might try to look smart, a bar maybe, but otherwise? Meh.

What Delancey knew, however, was that money exchange complicated itself greatly. Most people could decide a dollar was worth X and, say, a franc was worth X plus or minus Y. Exchange rates, taadaa and scene – until you brought in the factor of time period.

When someone showed up from 1922 Arkansas and 2003 Arkansas with the same one hundred dollars, those dollars were worth far different amounts. So Exchangers worked off of approximate buying power. One hundred 1920s dollars had about ten times the buying power of the same amount of cash from the early 2000s. You could not avoid factoring that in. So the entire system ended up being built off of tables kept and expanded constantly each time a Knocker came back to Mur with new information.

Carson had memorized most of the hard tables, which was what made him so fast at his job. When you hired him to exchange your money, either into money workable in Mur or into a currency where you wanted to do trade, you could rely on it taking far less time, and being far more trustworthy, than many.

Which is why he hated to be kept waiting. Another five minutes and he would let his greeter know to turn the appointment away. Just on principle, he didn't want to take the meeting anymore. The move might cost him money based on how much he had to exchange and what his cut would be, but he could afford it.

He checked his watch. Sighed. Jabbed at the intercom. Stupid clients.

Casey pushed open the loft's front door with her knee, one solid motion from unlocking it to open. "Jake?" she called out as the door whuffed against the end of its hinges' rotation. She caught it on the bounce back and closed it behind her.

Jake sat at the table, head down. "Mmyeah?" he muttered, not moving.

Casey rushed over to him, sitting down next to him. "I heard...I was out...and one of Torok's goons said that there was—"

Jake's head came off the table and he stared at her, trying to focus. "Torok? What the fuck were you—"

"Later," she said, starting to run her hands down his body softly to assess the damage done. "What happened to you?"

And so they caught each other up, running at different speeds, like band members playing in different time signatures. As they talked, Casey went to the bathroom and came back with a large metal toolbox. She opened it and started digging through it.

"You know we could have a normal first-aid kit, like normal people," Jake told her, not for the first time.

"This one is bullet-proof," she said, as she always did.

"I get that," he said slowly, "but do we need to protect the bandages from gunfire?"

Casey shrugged, then laughed, while she threaded a needle. Dipping it in alcohol and passing it through the flame of a match, she undid Jake's hasty arm bandage, cleaned the wound again, and started to sew him up.

Caught up on each other's days, neither of them believing somehow it had only been a single day, they sat together and tried to each of them breathe slowly.

"I should…" Casey trailed off, standing and moving to grab her acoustic guitar from near the bed. She returned to the table and sat down, pushing her chair back to account for the guitar in her lap.

"Case?" Jake asked, watching her.

She didn't respond but started to strum softly, playing the opening chords to the song Jake knew as "Safe." She never named it, when she played it on stage, so he just took the name from the chorus. A slow build of a tune, "Safe" stood as one of Jake's favorites from Casey's writing. Having no idea why she would be possessed to play the song through right then, Jake found he didn't mind, the chorus swelling and starting to speed as she went into her guitar solo.

The solo confused Jake a bit, and always had. It stuttered and slid in a way that almost none of her songs ever did. That was one part of why the song stood out to him. She didn't play it every set, but it remained one of the songs in heavy rotation at her shows; he'd heard it the first time he met her, in fact. Solo ended, Casey transitioned back to chorus, then verse, then chorus and let the song die out, as it always did, with a final chord ringing softly.

Casey set the guitar down on the table and leaned over to check Jake's new bandages.

"Hey, Casey?" Jake asked, watching her.

"Yeah?"

"Why did you just—"

"Protection spell," she replied quickly, "makes sure no one can find where we live unless we invite them, or tell them the address specifically. Wait," she sat back, looking at him, "you didn't know that?"

"How would I have known that?" he asked.

"I must have told you. That's why I play it as often as I do, keeps the protection fresh – it wears off." She shrugged and, satisfied with Jake's injuries being at least stable, leaned back in her chair.

"No, I would remember that," he said. "So even if they've been here before..."

"If I've reupped the protection since then, it would become unknowable to them again."

Jake sighed. "I mean, thanks, but yeah, I didn't know. Anything else I should know about?"

"Oh so much," she laughed, "but no, that's it, I think. I'm sorry! I really thought you knew. So, that solves that."

"How does it solve anything?" Jake asked, as Casey got up to make more tea for both of them.

"Do you want some pasta?" she asked, already filling a pot with water.

"Sure," he agreed easily. "How does it solve anything?"

"We won't be attacked in our sleep, for one," she said, "since Vink's people can't find you now. And you can just lay low here until this blows over."

"That's not gonna work, "Jake said, sipping at his tea.

"Sure it will," Casey insisted, salting the water and waiting for it to boil. "We have decent drugs, and you'll be...I don't know about fine, but fine *enough* in a few days, but Jake—"

"Until I know why he's decided to come after me, this won't blow over," Jake said. "I won't just hide in the dark for months and hope he gets bored. All that leads to is him picking it back up when I resurface. It's a delay, not a solution."

Casey tossed the pasta into the pot angrily, splashing scalding water around the stove. "If you go back out there and try to, what, to ask him? He'll kill you. That's literally what he wants to do."

"It's a misunderstanding," Jake said, starting to get up to go over to the stove, "it has to be." He slumped back into the chair as soon as he put weight on his leg. "I'm not saying," he said softly, "I'm going to run back out this second, of course."

"Of course," Casey said, wincing as she watched him land in the chair again. "So fine, you're going off to get killed—"

"Your wild, unshakable faith in me is noted and appreciated."

"—and I guess I'll talk to the old lady who wants to get me killed tomorrow," Casey finished.

"Good plan with Torok, though," Jake said, "but I can show you how to do that lift and palm if you want."

"Please," she said, coming back to the table. "And maybe, before you do head back out, I can teach you how to fight a bit?"

"I can fight," Jake said, then laughed. "Obviously not well enough. Just don't injure me worse."

"Not even by accident," Casey said, resting a hand on his shoulder.

"I just mean, I know it'd be easy to, even just to stop me from leaving a while longer."

"I wouldn't. Ever. And I'm really good at this," she said, and went back to stir. Satisfied with the pasta's progress, she started tossing together a light, oil-based sauce. Soon enough they ate, the first round of drugs in Jake's system starting to wear off. The shock of it had left, and more juice and tea helped with the blood loss. While he could, he thought thankfully, speak normally again without feeling like he would pass out, moving remained a problem.

After clearing the dishes, Casey sat down across from Jake and he proceeded to show her the basics of a clean lift and palm. They practiced while the drugs kicked in again for him, and then, as a stomach full of food and narcotics took their toll, she helped him into bed where they lay, talking.

Well, trying to talk, as Jake drifted in and out not only of consciousness but sense. By the time he passed out, Casey had given up asking what he rambled about, just letting him go until he kicked off fully into dreaming.

She got up and grabbed one of her electric guitars, not plugging it in, just playing as softly as possible at the table, thinking. She'd been trained to fight battles on multiple fronts, of course, but it required her to have people under her who were similarly trained. Managing it herself, while not letting Jake get hurt or anyone know what was going on, would be a challenge.

Casey knew, for herself, she had to keep working with the old woman. Torok would still be mad, though he *probably* wouldn't come after either of them again. He'd only tried the once to prove a point, and since he didn't think they'd even gotten what they'd wanted, neither of them would be worth the effort, even for someone as bloodthirsty as he seemed to be.

That was also somewhere Jake came in handy, to be cold about it. Torok knew Jake, and if he did decide to go after Casey he would do some research, come across that, and probably back off then, figuring that with all the details he had, a continued effort wouldn't be worth the knock-on effects from Jake and his friends deciding to not work with Torok anymore.

Regardless, the old woman had seemed to do some good – small-time good, to be sure, but Casey enjoyed it. She'd have enjoyed it even more if she'd been braced for the details and able to manage threats beforehand, but she could continue to work on that. For now, she'd be in, against her better judgment.

She looked over at Jake, sleeping the sleep of the drugged and exhausted. She wanted to think of a way to save him, to remove the threat of Vink, but couldn't. Not one that didn't make things far worse. Added to that, of course, would be Jake's own reaction if she did.

He enjoyed her help, on his own terms – but only then. Jake didn't want to drag her into his world any more than being simply close to him already did. It changed you, he pointed out, in ways you might not see coming.

When she tried to help with crime, as he put it, without checking with him, without seeing the angles through his lens – an experienced one that was running the game in progress – she threatened to topple unforeseen consequences. That would just leave Jake running around trying to juggle new factors in play – a huge risk. She knew he was right. She didn't have him check her levels at shows because he didn't know how to set them. He might guess – he could listen and make a good stab at it – but being wrong cost you something.

So Casey sat and fretted a bit, getting it out of her system. Jake would be fine, she decided, because he knew his job. The only reason he didn't run the town was because he wasn't bloodthirsty enough. No, she corrected, he could probably fake that and find a way to sleep at night and be all right with himself, even, if he had to. He didn't run the town because he didn't want to. He liked being a small-time crook, carving out his little section of reality.

That landed on similar ground for them both, really, she knew. Doing things because they made you happy, even if the goals were smaller than other people felt they should be, defined them and drew them closer together. They both believed, with everything they had, that your goals for life should make you happy. Sounds easy, but cutting away expectations – from friends, family, society – that sort of culling and focus came as a cost. A cost both Casey and Jake had agreed to pay before they'd even met. A cost that they both felt remained cheap at twice the price.

Casey watched Jake sleep while she practiced as quietly as possible for a while longer. Shaking her head, she looked down at the guitar. She tried a few ideas out for a solo, seeing how it felt to play more than how it would sound. An hour flew by before she noticed, and only realized when she started to yawn. Taking herself to bed, Casey determined they would solve things in the morning.

A three-shift town, like most large cities, Mur didn't have a bed time. It had a three a.m. last call, but no real bedtime. Most bodegas, many diners, and some laundromats were open twenty-four hours. What wasn't open all night at least tended to close late enough that an overnight shift worker could still eat, shop, and get errands done without fear or frustration. More than normal, at any rate.

Gustav showed up for work a bit early, at around nine-thirty p.m. Clarissa, his boss, nodded as he walked in and unlocked the door to the backroom. There, he unlocked the gun safe, took out a pistol and holster, and strapped them to his waist. Working the overnight shift at the Pawn To Queen pawnshop came with risks that Gustav didn't like, but he needed the job.

He sat in the backroom and opened his lunchbox. His husband called it his dinnerbox, but that just sounded strange to Gustav. As he ate one of his sandwiches – the roast beef, saving the ham for later – he thought about how he couldn't get exactly the same bread he'd grown up with, here in Mur.

It was, for him, the little things. Gustav wasn't upset that he had left Iceland in 1740, drunkenly going through a door to the town, passing out in an alley, and waking up to a whole new life. But he still missed things, and supposed he always would.

Thankfully, when he'd woken up in the alley a woman had spotted him, saw the look on his face, and recognized it from when she had first landed in town. She stopped him from leaving by the nearby gate and ending up somewhere, and somewhen, different.

The current reigning language in Mur was English, though that changed every few centuries as the language evolved, and inhabitants moved along with it. He'd learned modern idioms fast enough, and had adapted to the concept and feel of the city handily, in most respects.

But Gustav had a problem holding down jobs. Something about Mur messed with his internal rhythms just enough that, until he'd gotten a night-shift job, he couldn't adjust. Once he'd gotten the job at the Pawn to Queen, though, he started showing up on time, feeling better – generally adjusting more and more to the town. Just last year he'd met his husband, himself a transplant to Mur from 1975 Utah, and settled down.

Even so, he missed the little things: the taste of bread, the particular smell of the air at night, the stars above in the patterns he'd learned as a child. These were the pangs that tugged at him when he forgot and then remembered them at random times.

Nothing for it, though, he figured. He could raise enough money to go back home, possibly, with a Knocker hired and all – but would Donald, his husband, want to make the move? Doubtful. And what would his life be? He hadn't had much of a future before he came to Mur. That was why he'd drank so much – searching for answers, or at least silence, in the bottom of a cup.

But since Mur he'd cut way back, feeling hopeful. Not that he thought a night-shift job at a pawnshop would be his path to fortune and prosperity, necessarily. But being married, and having a stable job for the first time; these things mattered to him, and changed him and how he thought.

Plus, he had a suspicion that Clarissa might offer to sell him the store within a few years if life continued along the same path, and he would say yes. All of which assumed he stayed safe and healthy in the interim. He sighed, resting his hand on the butt of the pistol. It seemed, as always, to weigh three times as much once he strapped the holster on. Gustav wasn't a fan of violence, and unlike one of his coworkers – the little snot Stefano, as Gustav considered him – he didn't feel powerful for having the weapon. He felt, if anything, weaker.

He also acknowledged it worked as a deterrent that they had needed in the past. Gustav finished his roast beef, brushed crumbs from his beard, and put away his lunchbox. He went out to the main floor and logged into the records book, taking control of the store, formally, from Clarissa, letting her go home and have her night.

He counted the till, watched the monitors, and listened for the door chime to go off, signaling a customer. Past that he stood, and waited, thinking of the taste of the bread of his youth.

Morning, somehow, seemed to come earlier than usual. Casey woke up to the sound of the phone and rolled out of bed. Really, she fell toward the floor, catching herself and making it look intentional. Stumbling over to the table, she grabbed the phone, glancing back at the bed as she did. Jake slept on despite the noise.

"Honey, are you there?" Key asked over the phone.

"Oh, sorry, yeah, morning," Casey muttered, trying to focus her brain on being awake. She didn't often get up after Jake, and as a consequence found herself far too reliant on his making the coffee and allowing her to wake up on her own time. She smiled, enjoying feeling spoiled.

"Tonight, you will come to the party, yes?" Key asked, pushing the conversation.

"Yeah," Casey agreed. "What type of party is it? Where is it?"

"I'll take you there, it'll be easier," Key told her, "but the dress is formal, wear something nice – a good dress, a suit, something for rich people."

"Rich party, got it," Casey said, wanting to start making coffee.

"And honey," Key added, "you can't bring that guitar with you."

"No way, where I go it goes." Casey frowned. Now, she thought, she really needed that coffee.

"Not this time," Key told her seriously. "Even if you did, they would make you check it, and I figure you'd rather have it at home where you knew it was safe than in some coatroom. Besides, it doesn't fit the dress code."

"Key—" Casey started to protest.

"Honey, you can't – I'm sorry, but that's the way it is. We'll meet where we met yesterday morning at eight tonight, all right?"

Casey sighed, quietly, hoping the phone didn't pick up the sound. "Sure," she agreed after a moment's hesitation.

They exchanged pleasantries by rote and Casey hung up, turning to go make coffee. She started it brewing and leaned against the edge of the kitchen counter, facing the rest of the loft. Jake stirred and started to stretch, then made a tiny yelping noise. Casey hurried over to him and sat on the edge of the bed.

"How're you feeling, tough guy?" she asked, smiling at him.

"Worse than last night, somehow, I think," he told her, getting out of bed with only a little difficulty.

"Naw, you're doing great, just stiff. It'll pass. Go take a hot shower, you'll see."

Jake nodded, kissing her cheek, and made his way to the bathroom. The sound of the shower running followed the toilet flushing closely, and Casey went back to thinking of nothing while the coffee finished.

Jake came out of the shower, looking far closer to his normal skin tone, and sat heavily at the table. Casey brought him over a cup of coffee and he drank greedily from it before talking.

"What's the plan today?" he asked, setting his mug down.

"I got nothing," Casey told him, "until tonight. I agreed to go to a party with Key, I meet her at eight."

"Well," Jake said with a short laugh, "I think most of my plans are cancelled for today. Mostly I guess I'll let these bruises turn fun shades of yellow."

"They'll heal faster than you think," Casey said. "One of those pills you took last night was from my old days, should speed you up quite a bit. But we shouldn't spend today just sitting around."

"You've got better ideas?" Jake asked.

"I'm gonna run to the Square and get us breakfast, bring it back, and then I think I should show you some simple fighting things."

"We can trade," Jake said, nodding.

"You'll show me fighting techniques?" Casey asked, taking their empty mugs to the sink.

"Shush, no, but you'll see," Jake said, inspecting his bruises as well as the stitching on his arm.

"That sounds...promising," she said, smirking at him.

"Hah, no. Not like that," he told her.

"Well fine," Casey said, heading to the bathroom. "Let me grab a quick shower and I can go get us some food."

"I could cook," he told her.

"You could," she agreed, "but this way we can feel decadent and lazy. That's worth something, I'm pretty sure."

"You're part cat, I think, sometimes," Jake said, rising to go get clothes on himself.

"Sometimes," she agreed, "sometimes."

The bathroom door closed and Jake laughed softly, pulling a t-shirt on over his head.

The alleyway smelled of squirrel. A soft blue light lit a stretch of the brick-sided, asphalt-floored pathway, swinging back and forth. A snuffling sound could be heard as well, if you listened closely enough under the general background city disruptions. Tiny feet, four of them, settled against the ground, one after the other, as the hunt continued, each foot making no sound.

The Cat tensed, feeling the eyes of another predator scanning. She felt a hiss starting, low in her chest, as she stood there, fur starting to rise. She reached out, tail twitching, trying to get a feel for the possible danger. Then, without warning, she sprang to the side, pushing back into what shadow she could find, daring the danger to come find her in the edges of the alley.

The other predator, a raccoon that had found its way to Mur with a trader, hiding in a basket and dumped without ceremony onto the streets to fend for itself when it'd been discovered, hissed and chittered. The raccoon excitedly scurried down the alley, sure it smelled something it could use as food – something rancid, something sustaining.

Instead, it saw a flash of blue and screeched, tiny hands flexing in panic. The raccoon ran back out of the alley. Let someone else have the garbage and possible squirrel.

The blue light shone from those shadows, from where The Cat's face should have been. It reduced her ability to be a creature of stealth immensely, but even though she'd been around for thousands of years, she'd never quite coped with the idea that the glow came from her.

Her sleek fur carried a tiny bit of the same blue, somehow always looking almost wet so that it might be blue, but could be black, but no one felt qualified to decide for sure. A normal-looking, if possibly-oddly-colored cat from the tail forward, right up to just past the ears and then...that blue glow. No face to speak of. No glittering eyes, wet nose, or hungry mouth. Nothing to navigate the world with, no whiskers or teeth to rend food to pieces. Just a blue glow that shone at all times, even while sleeping. The Cat With No Face.

Not that The Cat responded to that name – or any name, of course, since she was a cat. The blue light annoyed her, but she'd long since decided it'd come from somewhere and she had been burdened by it and would have to simply make do – majestically, being a cat.

As for how The Cat could see, or eat, make sounds or sense things with no face: let's be very clear, here. The blue glow where The Cat's face should be is not *obscuring* a normal cat face, like some have chosen to believe. It is there *instead* of all the bits and bobs of a normal face. How does that even work? The problem is The Cat, being a cat and not a person, has never bothered to explain itself, and asking never got anywhere. Suffice to say it seems to do just fine, so people assume what they like and The Cat doesn't seem to care, and everything's good.

She hunted in the alley for her dinner, as she had a thousand-plus times before, and eventually found her prey. This time it was a squirrel, as she'd suspected, and she pounced, claws out, and killed it quickly, eating hungrily. Truth be told, the squirrel barley clung to life before The Cat With No Face hunted it, but even if it had been the healthiest squirrel to ever squirrel, The Cat would have, obviously, not had a problem with it, if you'd asked. Being a cat and all made her superior. This was clear, and it was ridiculous to consider anything other than fact.

The Cat ate the squirrel but didn't feel satisfied. As ever, she ate meat, as well as anything else that might smell decently interesting and found itself unattended, but the meals left her empty and distracted. The instinct felt strong, the results weak.

Angrily, The Cat stalked out of the alley and into the street. Seeing a bird starting to land nearby, The Cat yawned, then turned it into a hiss. The bird vanished. Not in some poetic sense where it flew into the sunlight. No, the bird had been there, landing, feet touching the ground, and then it was not there. At all. Poof. No one seemed to notice. The Cat walked on, feeling better.

Casey leaned back in her chair, having stuffed herself with a heavy breakfast. She reached down, then sighed as her hand hit her waist.

Jake laughed, "Did you just remember you're not wearing pants with a button to undo? Were you really going to—"

"It's the principle of the thing," she said, "undoing that button, it completes the meal – a meal like this, at least. But now, what? I can snap some elastic? Unsatisfying at best."

"Well, you didn't have to wear sweatpants to go out, did you?"

"So this is my fault?"

"A lack of preparation," he intoned, "loses many battles, as you like to say."

"When do I say that?" she asked, frowning.

"Every time you realize you forgot something for your set," he told her. "Then you make it work anyway, or, I guess," he laughed, "send me to grab whatever it is."

"You know what, jerkbutt," she said, laughing as well, "you weren't supposed to actually give me an example."

"What was I supposed to do?" Jake asked, setting his own fork down, his plate empty of food. He, too, felt bloated and satisfied with the condition.

"Sputter and admit I'm right, maybe?" Casey looked at the containers and plates on the table and considered clearing them, then decided it could wait another few minutes while she concentrated on happily regretting eating too much. "I'm too full to be witty with you. Let's try again after a nap."

"I wish," he said, "but if you want to get out the door on time, and still go over a few things—"

"Right, I have to teach you to kick ass," she said, stretching. "All right, give me maybe five minutes."

"Well, I can show you what I had in mind first, if you want," he offered.

Casey nodded. "I have to know what you have in mind, here," she admitted.

Jake got up, searched for a few minutes in a closet, and came back with a metal tin. Setting it down on the table, shoving aside some containers, he pried the lid off with some difficulty and sat back down.

Casey leaned forward and peered inside the box. A bunch of locks sat in the box, under a small leather tube tied with cord. Jake grabbed the tube and unwound the thin rope around it, unfurling the leather to reveal a set of old lockpicks.

"You want me to pick locks?" Casey asked, as Jake slid the old set of picks toward her.

"I want you to pick locks," he agreed. "This is the set I learned on. And here," he fished in the box and came back with an old lock, scarred with rust, but sliced to show a cutaway view of the mechanism itself, "is the training lock I used." He looked at her, turning the lock over in his hand again and again absently. "The thing is, from what you've told me about working with Grandmother—"

"Key, she's just Key, not some magical myth," Casey corrected.

"Sure, Key then," he acquiesced, "she seems to get you into odd situations. You had to pull a lift yesterday, right? And do some fast talk before that? That's where I live, Case. And I tell you right now you should know this stuff."

"I did fine," she said, lifting each tool out of its leather sheath and putting it back, one after the other.

"You did. And I did fine myself. And we should both be better prepared. I figure, I can show you this, and while you practice I can give you some tips on how to do more than fine, if the need arises." He set a hand on her arm gently, lovingly. "You got this – of course you do, shit, we both know it. But I also know that having it down better, and in different ways, can't be a bad thing."

Casey nodded, picking up the cutaway lock. "So, all right, I use those to poke at the tumblers?" she asked.

"Exactly," Jake said, grabbing one of the lock picks and using it to point out different parts of the lock's internal components.

They worked like that for a while, Jake explaining in detail how the lock worked, and how that applied to all tumbler-based locks, and then moved into each tool from tension wrench to short hook to jiggler.

Casey picked up the basics quickly and Jake cleared the table, moving better all the time, and kept up a light running commentary on lock picking while he did. Casey mm-hmm'd along, and kept picking and resetting the cutaway lock, watching the tumblers move. Then she grabbed a different lock at random from the box and tried that one. It took longer, of course, the tumblers hidden from view, but she got it and then reset it and picked it again, quicker.

Jake shifted his commentary to small-time confidence-game tricks. He discussed quick ways to get people to tell you things, ways to lie that left the mark feeling as if you already knew what they were telling you, so they didn't feel like they were sharing secrets, and so on.

He made tea after the first hour, Casey taking a break from working with the locks to ask questions about the various ways to convince someone to hand over whatever you needed them to.

Casey stood and stretched, went to the bathroom, came back with far less tea in her, and started stretching again, this time with purpose.

Jake smiled and stood as well, stretching the same as she did – or as much as he could, given the bruises.

She nodded at him and moved to stand facing him, roughly an arm length away. "All right. Punch me," she told him, shifting her feet.

"Just...punch you?" he asked.

"Take a swing," she agreed.

Jake did as asked, and Casey blocked it, turning the punch with her block to step inside his swing and come around, throwing an elbow that stopped just short of his chin. Jake jerked his head back – a few seconds late, after her elbow had stopped. "So, yeah, I have no clue what I'm doing, yup," he said, laughing.

"It's all simple stuff, in terms of seeing it and learning it," she said. "The problem is unless it becomes instinct, you won't reach for the movement in the moment. But it can still help, and if you keep your head clear, you'll remember it."

"So I'm screwed, you mean?" he said, taking a deep breath and thinking through what she had just done.

"Not at all, I've never seen you crumble under pressure. So let's break it down," she said. "Punch me again. Slowly this time – like slow motion."

Jake did as requested and Casey talked him through each step of what she did to counter him. Then she punched him in slow motion and he tried to replicate her movements, coming fairly close. They tried again, and again, until he could do it at speed.

She switched things up and showed Jake some holds, a few ways to get inside the swing of an opponent and what soft fleshy bits to hit first – different organs and how to make them bleed internally – and a few sweeps. These last she understood he couldn't really do, with his leg, but felt he should know, just in case, and for when his leg got stronger again. A few ankle hook-and-pulls to round things out, and they took a break to find lunch.

Jake wanted to go out, stretch his admittedly tired legs, and get fresh air, but Casey insisted they cook and stay inside. She knew she couldn't keep him in the loft forever – she even admitted to herself that once she went out to the party with Key there was a good chance he would decide to go out as well – but she tried her best, regardless.

They sat around together after lunch and just chatted, telling each other stories they were sure they'd told one another before. The day lengthened as the afternoon stretched itself thin and started to sag. Casey got up, took another shower, and found a dress to wear. Dark red, coming down to her ankles, and seemingly tight everywhere it should have been, the dress had a high neck and no sleeves. It also stretched and flared in a way that allowed Casey to move and not feel trapped, which was the real reason she'd bought it months ago. She considered, and rejected, jewelry, not wanting anything too flashy or too dull and finally settling on not bothering.

She fussed at her short hair, did nothing with it, and grabbed some lipstick. Deciding she'd done all she would in that department, Casey considered shoes. She wanted to just put on her boots and be done with it, but knew she couldn't get away with that. Heels would be appropriate for the long dress she wore, but she couldn't bring herself to strap on her one pair. She hated them. She grabbed some flats, nice purple ones that worked well with the dark red of her dress, and looked at her travel guitar, in its case, leaning against the bed.

She considered it, then sighed and left it where it was. A quick goodbye to Jake and she left the loft, heading down to meet Key.

Theresa Stanton sat on her bed and kicked her feet back and forth, enjoying the *thump-thump-thump* of her ankles against the wooden frame that extended to the floor. The mattress sat on that wooden platform, limiting her choice of bed size, and had annoyed her from the moment she'd first moved into the apartment. She'd been desperate then, and took the room even though she hated it. She could, however, afford it on her salary as a waitress, so it stood as something better than nothing, and since her alternative was exactly that – nothing – well, there she sat.

She looked over at her bag, a worn brown lump of waxed fabric she'd picked up somewhere ages ago. Stuffed full, she'd managed to tie it closed only barely. It looked, she decided, like she felt – crammed full of whatever fit, and resentful about it. Theresa stood, grabbed the bag, and slung it over her shoulder.

The room didn't rate a final glance, nor did the rest of the apartment. She'd liked her roommate all right, but by this point everything around her was lumped together in Theresa's annoyance and distaste.

Outside she started walking, heading wallward. Not that there remained that far to go. Still, far enough that by the time she got to the wall itself, Theresa felt out of breath, the bag weighing her down. She'd walked straight there, no stopping except for traffic and lights, and had never taken the bag off for a moment, not even when she could have used the moment. If the bag got set down, if she relaxed and let herself take a moment, she felt certain she'd lose her nerve. That was who Theresa was, in her own estimation. The woman who never got it right.

Born in Mur, to a happy family that lived a nice middle-class life, Theresa never fit in. Her parents told her that the problem was with herself, that she'd been given opportunity and chances but refused them. Theresa felt the city stood against her. It didn't want her there; Mur did not want Theresa, specifically, to thrive. She'd tried to fight back against it, she would explain to her friends, to her family, to people who asked what she meant at bars, but the city always won. It cheated, in the sense that Mur stood much larger than Theresa and held all the cards. She'd never stood a chance.

Not that, she'd add, she didn't try! Of course she did. She went to school, she learned things, tried to branch out and find her place, but nothing ever fit right. She continued to try. Cutting herself no slack, Theresa tried job after job, seeing if a career would bloom from one of them. They'd get hard, Theresa would struggle, and she'd eventually decide she'd been defeated.

She cut herself off from her family, after a while, ashamed of herself. She'd taken up a job as a waitress and been great at it, her boss eyeing her for manager. But Theresa didn't believe him. Obviously he only said stuff like that to keep her happy in her position. Mur wouldn't let her rise higher. The city would stop her, if nothing else did. She knew it.

She enjoyed being a waitress, the speed and chaos of it. Restaurants fit her brain perfectly. If it wasn't for the fact, as she saw it, that she always failed, she could really make something of herself there. Manager, then save up a bunch of money and open her own place – she could feel it. She could taste it. And she'd lay in bed at night considering it, laying out the path, and as she started to taste it again, it would turn to ashes on her tongue.

Which brought her to today. The city, she knew, wanted her gone. So she would go. She told her roommate that she'd planned a vacation – she felt her roommate barely listened anyway and just nodded at her constantly. Hire a Knocker, go on a small weekend out of the city – expensive, sure, but didn't she deserve it after working so hard? Her roommate had nodded, and shrugged, then nodded again, as Theresa remembered it. She promised to tell Theresa's mother where she'd gone when she called. See, Theresa cut her family off, but her family refused to cut her off. Someone called, every week, and hoped she would take the call that time. She wanted to, she just couldn't. There was no malice in it – Theresa simply couldn't do it. Her roommate fielded the calls and, against Theresa's desires, relayed bits of information back and forth – which was all her roommate could think to do to help. She knew Theresa dismissed her as yet another thing in her way, but she tried.

Theresa stood at the gate. People were allowed to leave Mur freely, of course, and most of the time the gates weren't even attended. People entered the city confused, and left the city alone if they so chose. Over the centuries the ideas of signs were floated, and had even been tried, as we've discussed, but the general feeling remained: you could leave as you wanted, and come as you pleased.

Finally, there, in front of the gate, Theresa put her bag down. She stared at the gate, people walking by her, and around her. Her bag leaned heavily against her leg and she thought about, seriously, what she wanted to do. Leaving Mur couldn't be done lightly, without a Knocker. A one-way trip, she'd known since childhood. Kids would threaten to leave – one of the big pushes for signs were scared parents worried their kids would run away too emotionally young to realize what they were doing. In reality, though, even kids understood, and the rate of runaways leaving town stood well below what anyone would have guessed.

Being in Mur carried its own gravity. Theresa understood that better than most, even if she'd never laid it out quite like that. She thought of it as the city being sadistic: it didn't want anyone around but also didn't want its playthings to leave.

All of it ran through her head as she stood there. Then, growing angry with herself, and not the city, she opened the gate and stepped through into somewhere else.

Key waved Casey over. Casey admired the woman's regal-looking golden gown, and noted that the messy bun of her hair sat tamed and straight. Key stuck her hand out to hail a cab and Casey shrugged; if someone else paid for it, she'd happily take one. They sat in silence for the ride, Casey still finding herself annoyed by the lack of guitar. Worse, she felt annoyed *that* she felt annoyed. She tried to not blame Key for it, and won and lost the fight again and again as their cab drove them windingly Spireward.

Key remained silent, watching the city speed by outside her window, for her own reasons. She let herself get lost in thought and memory, and rolled down the window just enough to feel a bit of wind on her face, but not enough to mess up her hair.

They arrived, after a time filled with traffic and not much else, close enough to the Spire to feel it loom over them. Still a few blocks away, the neighborhood sat full of brownstones and newer short glass-and-metal buildings, anything older having been torn down.

Key led Casey to a strange hybrid: a brownstone entrance with a smoked glass cube replacing the building from the second floor up.

"This is..." Casey trailed off, trying to find a way to describe the effect.

"Faintly hideous," Key suggested.

"Oh, yeah, that'd sum it. Who would do this to a perfectly nice building?"

"Someone trying to prove how much money they have," Key told her with a shrug, fishing in her purse for something. Sighing, she started up the steps to the door, Casey following. The door swung open to reveal two people, both in pristine black suits. The first, a large bald man, asked for their invites, while the other, a smaller woman with a clipboard, looked ready to check them off a list.

"You know, dear," Key told him, "I think I forgot ours at home." She turned to Casey, sneaking in a wink, and said, "I'm so sorry, honey, I'm just a doddering old fool, I guess."

Casey sighed, loudly, by mistake. Then, catching herself, she turned it to her advantage. "Well, there goes the night – and they were so looking forward to seeing you again, too."

Key looked at the woman with the clipboard. "Can you," she asked, advancing on the woman and pointing at the list, scanning it quickly, "just make sure we're there?"

The woman shot a glance at the man next to her and nodded, turning to talk to Key. "Just trying to get in to meet the fancy folk?" she asked in a low whisper. She snuck out a half smile and Key nodded.

"You know how it is, dear, my granddaughter and I thought we'd get dressed up but couldn't get tickets to the theatre." She laughed and pointed at the list, nodding at it as she said softly, "but thought we might..."

"I get it," the clipboard holder assured her. "Yeah," she told the man watching them, "they're on the list."

He shrugged. Casey walked past him, Key lagging behind to thank the woman.

"Normally," the woman said to Key, "I wouldn't, but I've been in a good mood. My roommate got her dog back, so she finally stopped crying all day and fussing about it and—"

"Well, whatever the reason," Key told her, "thank you."

Casey looked around the first floor as she waited for Key to catch up. Open except for a few support structures, the entire first floor seemed to work as a giant foyer. Warm wooden floors and soft cream walls, with an almost golden molding leading the transition between the two, defined the space, while two overly large but somehow never pretentious chandeliers hung from the ceiling to light the entire room softly and effortlessly. A staircase to either side led up, but Casey stood and watched people around her move. There was no surprise in how the people who worked in the house moved like clockwork, dodging and turning to carry and bustle things back and forth, all the while avoiding the guests who moved as if all the space in the world belonged to only them.

After a few seconds of watching the dance and taking in the space, Casey realized the floor did have rooms, in the back, but that no guests went back there. Only servers did, and she wondered if it hid a kitchen, on the bottom floor, or a coat room, and did it have its own staircase – thoughts all blown away when Key grabbed her elbow and whispered sharply at her, "Come on, then."

"We're in a hurry now?" Casey asked, as Key led her to a staircase and then up it.

"We always were, honey," Key admitted, "but who wants to come off that way at a party?"

Upstairs, as the building changed from brownstone to glass box, the inside of the house changed to suit. Gone were the wooden floors and cream walls, here exchanged for sharp black-and-grey marble flooring and light-grey, almost steel-colored walls, except for the one wall made of smoked glass. Large rooms ate up the space, all of it lit by recessed light from the flat black molding that ran around the walls. More guests milled around here, with tray-carrying people dotted between them, offering drinks and hors d'oeuvre in plentiful amounts. In the corner, a small string quartet played softly – so softly they were hard to hear over the general milling and conversation of the crowd.

Casey, of course, zeroed in on the sound of them anyway, listening and appreciating their skill. She stared into the small crowd of maybe fifty guests and let her eyes unfocus, following their movement as a whole and listening to the music. "What," she asked, as she enjoyed the sound a cello, "are we here for? A friend of yours works in the kitchen and needs some help?" she ventured.

"No," Key said, "not all my friends are the staff, you know. I wanted you to meet one of those friends tonight, and I knew he'd be here. Besides, our host serves good food," she insisted as she grabbed a small puff with mysterious filling from a server's tray as they went by.

"I know that you're lying," Casey said, turning to look at Key, "so let's just get to it."

"I am not lying," Key insisted, "I want you to meet him."

"All right, why?"

Key touched Casey's elbow again and started to move through the crowd. "I think he'd be good to know, for you, is all," she said.

Casey considered her options. She would go along with this, meet the stranger, and then stop being dragged around by an old woman. She didn't feel used – even though she knew she had been and should be annoyed by it – so much as she felt she could only see half a puzzle. Something in her needed to see the rest, so she kept playing along.

Key stopped in front of a short man with greying hair. He was talking to two people, a couple from their posture, Casey noticed, and seemed to be enjoying himself. Key coughed lightly and he turned, seeing her and smiling.

"Key," he said, the first person Casey had heard use her name so far besides herself. "How did you get in, I wonder?"

"No one stops an old woman," she told him. They shared a laugh, which spread to the couple he talked to, who obviously thought this was an old joke between them. "Anyway, Tom, I wanted you to meet Casey," Key said, tilting her head subtly toward her. "She's been helping me, and I thought maybe you two should get to know each other."

"Any friend of yours, Key," Tom said, and turning to the couple he nodded. "If you'll excuse me, I need to..." he trailed off and waved his hands slightly, "... old business, you understand I'm sure." He turned his back on the couple, who retreated into the party, confused but sated quickly by a passing tray of drinks.

"I'll let you two get to know each other while I find a restroom," Key said. "I'll be right back." She vanished into the crowd, Casey saw, in the general direction of one of the back rooms. Which was fine, except Casey had also noticed that the bathrooms were in a different direction, having heard a guest ask only seconds earlier. She didn't say anything, just braced herself internally for being tossed toward wolves again.

"So Key is dragging you around these days," Tom said, phrasing it like a question but making sure it came across as a statement of raw fact.

"Oh, I don't know," Casey told him, "I think it's more of an agree-to-go-along-with-her sort of thing. I'm just going along, helping her—"

"Friends," Tom finished, smiling. "She has a lot of them."

Casey laughed. "That she does. So, tell me," she asked him, "why didn't she ask you for an invite here?"

"I would've refused," he admitted. "Don't get me wrong – I like Key a lot and I've helped her...help friends a few times myself, but overall? It's never worth it."

"Why not?" Casey asked, turning her body subtly to point more toward Tom, shifting her body language to make him feel like the focus of her full attention while she kept half an eye and ear out for Key.

"Well, I like to feel I know what I'm doing," Tom said, "for a start. But she never really tells you, does she? It's always just going to help a friend, and so on, and she keeps so much to herself you have to wonder."

Casey agreed, of course. "I don't find that, at all," she said, however, to see what else Tom would tell her that she didn't actually know.

"Interesting," he said. "Well, I don't know that she ever really worked with me, I just helped her out after she helped me out once."

Casey nodded at him, but kept quiet.

"It wasn't anything big, you understand," he went on after a beat, "but you know how it is—" Casey stopped listening to him when her ears caught a name, almost floating to her: "Vink."

Refusing to turn and look, like she wanted to, Casey muttered an "oops" and bent down as if to pick up something she'd dropped. While she did, she glanced around and caught sight of two men only a few feet away as one of them said Vink's name again. Standing, acting like she was busying herself putting a fallen object back in her purse, she apologized to Tom and told him to go on. He did, but Casey wasn't listening. Not to him.

"—deal with Haimes," one of the men behind her said, "I don't know, I'm telling you, but it feels like they want to squeeze us out."

"Vink and Haimes?" the other man said, laughing softly, a mean tinge to it. "If you think they'd work together, that the Mayor would let himself...this is just ridiculous. You're working yourself up over nothing."

"Am I? Look at the permits, check the construction schedules. They're doing something and are in each other's pockets, I'm telling you."

"Well you should stop telling me here," he said, "you fucking idiot. Let's say you're right. You want to talk about it in this room, in the open? Is that a good idea? You fuck."

Casey heard them moving behind her and wanted to watch them go, to get a better look at them, but couldn't think of a good way to do it as Tom kept talking to her. "—which is when we—" he cut himself off, catching the ghost of a look on Casey's face. "Everything all right?"

"Those two men behind me, they sound familiar – I think one of them yelled at me in traffic the other day, maybe?" she said, still refusing to turn.

"Really?" Tom laughed. "Sergeant Flueval wouldn't yell at you from his car, and I can't imagine Bryce Hornshallar would either, really. I mean, maybe Bryce," Tom thought about it and laughed again, "no, he'd just glare, at best, if you cut him off, I'm sure of it. Did you want to—"

"No, no," Casey assured him, "I must be wrong, sorry, it's been a long day. I should find Key, but thanks for the information."

"Of course, of course. Let me know if you ever want to talk more, get a drink, or—"

"I will," Casey said, moving away from him quickly. She smiled as she left, feeling the hollowness of it in her cheeks, and let herself listen to the quartet play as she scanned the room, drifting around it counter-clockwise. Sighing, she went off in the direction Key had first left in, heading all the way back in the room until she hit a door.

Of course the old woman snuck around, Casey thought to herself, and of course she went in after her. No one guarded the door, after all, and testing it, it wasn't locked. No signs telling guests to stay out, nothing stopped her from opening the door, slipping inside, and shutting it again. A small, darkened hallway led to a much more lived-in space. The apartment behind the showroom, Casey figured. She didn't hear anyone moving around the small space, the rooms oddly tiny. She realized that she could hear, if she listened, the sounds of the kitchen going, and that whoever owned the place cared much more about looking majestic than their own personal living space. An interesting choice, to be sure.

Casey wandered the rooms, enjoying the sense of personality in them. Where the downstairs was grand and warm, and the upstairs cold and expansive, the apartment section of the building felt worn and settled. A mixture of design choices, it seemed comfortable and not worried with itself. A well-used recliner sat next to a highly polished steel side table, for example. The mash of looks coalesced into a view of someone who didn't care, out of the eye of their guests, what something looked like so long as it performed its function well.

Another small staircase sat in the back of one of the rooms, and from above it Casey could hear movement. She took the stairs cautiously, listening for signs of Key. She couldn't be sure but hoped the noises were Key, at least. Either way, it felt like the entire situation could go awkward any number of ways.

At the top of the stairs, a small hallway with three doors presented itself, lit in the same soft lighting as below. One of the doors stood open and, from it, Casey could hear muttering. Key, definitely.

"What are you—" Casey started to ask, but stopped as she entered the room and saw exactly what Key was doing. The woman sat on the floor in front of an old mahogany credenza, one of its doors open to show a safe nestled inside. Key worked at the safe door, mumbling to herself until Casey spoke, at which point she turned, almost lazily, and smiled.

"Just having a bit of difficulty, honey," Key said, as if trying to crack the safe remained the most obvious thing she could be doing. "Shouldn't be much longer."

"Key," Casey whispered with force, "we need to get out of here, we can't just—"

"I need to get in here, honey," Key said simply, "shouldn't take another minute."

"It's already taken too long," Casey insisted.

Key stood, slowly, and gestured at the safe. "Care to do me a favor, then?"

Casey sighed and looked at the safe. She knew, as certainly as she knew she hated the high neck of the dress she wore the longer she wore it, there would be no getting Key out of there until the safe stood open.

"If I had my guitar," she said, "sure, then sure I could probably get the safe open. Without it..." she shrugged at the old woman.

"When I first saw you in that alley, what you did with it, that guitar does it?"

"I do it," Casey admitted, "but I focus through the guitar. Without the music, it's not a thing I can just wave my arms about and make happen. The music, my intent, it's all a mix."

"But not that specific guitar?" Key asked.

"No." Casey shook her head for emphasis. Briefly she considered one of the quartet downstairs – a cello would do nicely, but how to get it up here, and away from everyone without notice – no, that wouldn't work.

"I could hum?" Key offered.

"That wouldn't work," Casey said, thinking now in military terms. She needed an instrument, from the surroundings at hand. She thought about the room and what it contained. Nothing musically oriented, and she felt sure she hadn't passed anything downstairs either. So, she chided herself, you make do.

The following back and forth in her head went from chiding to annoyed with herself to yelling and back again several times. Casey knew an answer lay somewhere in reach – she didn't give up on that front ever. Giving up meant death, she'd learned early, and even though in this case the stakes seemed much lower, that twitch in her brain that worked out strategy refused to deal with lower stakes. It started from the worst case and only worked up from there.

Casey considered the problem from a different angle. No strings. But the guitar wasn't the important part. The vibrations were, and you could make vibrations with anything if you needed to.

Combat Musicians came in a number of different types. String instrument types were by far the most common, and reed users the least. They'd joked about a combat tuba, until they'd met someone who kept one just in case. The bass from it could be used to do some spectacular things, and after that, no one joked anymore. But between the strings and reeds sat percussion. Percussion experts claimed they could make do with anything – they could drum on the surface of the object they wanted to effect and need far less influence because of resonant distances.

They weren't the most common, though many thought they should be, if only because their effects were far smaller. No one knew why, because combat music didn't get much study past 'oh this works and this doesn't' – but even with a good kick, percussionists landed with small-range effects and were often kept out of combat itself except when absolutely needed.

Casey took off her shoes – the flats didn't have much heel on them, but what there was felt solid – and held one in each hand. She sat in front of the safe and shrugged, then began tapping out a rhythm. Notes she couldn't do, but she could get one of her songs going, something simple. She considered it as she built a rhythm and settled on "Down by the Knife," a simple ballad she would kick the stage during to make a rhythm section for.

The rhythm built, the music flowed through her, and Casey put her intent behind it.

"Honey, we need to be able to close the safe and not have anyone know we were here," Key said suddenly. Her voice not only broke Case's concentration, it compounded the problem. She'd planned to melt part of the lock – simple enough to manage, she felt sure.

Actually picking the lock would be a different story. This wasn't one of the key padlocks Jake had showed her at all. But, she thought, it still did have tumblers, just attached to a whole wheel-dial system she didn't understand. Did she need to? Casey wasn't sure.

She started the song again, thumping the shoes' soles against the safe. Instead of pushing out raw intent to heat the metal quickly and try to melt it, she tried to ease her intent around to feel for the interior of the lock.

Vibrations from tapping shoes against a safe were minimal, but Casey's intent deepened them, so they penetrated the metal fully and gave her feedback. She could, so long as she kept the rhythm going, 'feel' the safe, in a sense. The structure floated just behind her closed eyelids, and slowly, carefully, she started to understand what she faced.

Wheels instead of straight tumblers were the first problem. She nudged one around and felt for how it interacted, and noticed notches that a bar would drop into place with if turned correctly. The first spun smooth, if slow, and she felt it drop into place.

The second wheel spun while she held the first in place, not sure if she could undo her own work somehow. She felt the notches and turned it but pushed too hard and felt the wheel start to warp, threatening to make the safe unopenable at all.

Sweat rolled down from Casey's temple in a slow drip. She couldn't wipe it, needing to keep the rhythm going strong. She just found herself too unfamiliar with using percussion as a weapon to get the second wheel to turn right.

Digging deep, Casey leaned her face against the safe as she continued to beat out her rhythm and started to hum along with it, trying to increase the vibrations. The wheel turned a little smoother, but she knew she wouldn't be able to get the final wheel, even as the second clicked into place.

In a last-ditch effort, Casey pushed hard with everything she had to work with and slammed the arm into place, bending the third wheel but opening the safe. She pulled the door open, dropping her shoes to the floor and leaned back, breathing hard.

"That's...why I bring...my guitar," she said through long, stuttering breaths.

"I'm sorry, honey, I won't force you to leave it again," Key told her. "So the safe is...?"

"Broken," Casey admitted, looking up at Key, "it'll close and probably lock again, but the dial won't turn correctly and I don't know if it'll be able to be opened again."

"Then again," Key said, leaning down to reach into the safe, "no one will think it was sabotage, a broken internal piece, will they?"

"Couldn't tell you," Casey said, standing slowly and slipping her shoes back on. "But won't they notice something's missing, either way?"

"Not for a while, I hope," Key said, and she pulled a small box out of the safe. She opened it, and nestled in soft velvet was an Exchanger's coin. Smiling, she fished the fake one she carried out of a pocket and swapped the two.

"You're..." Casey searched for the right word, "not serious," she landed on, starting to pace. "This is going too far, Key."

"Is it, though?" Key asked, closing the safe, box back inside, now carrying fake cargo. She spun the dial, stopped, and looked at it. "What are the chances the dial is always kept on the same number so any tampering—"

"Sixty-four," Casey said quickly.

"Thank you," Key replied, "but that's what it might have been when you first saw it." Smiling once more, she set the dial carefully. "Twenty-two when I got here, before I touched it, if I remember right. And now, we should make the rounds downstairs," she said, standing and smoothing her dress.

"We should get very far from here," Casey countered, "before you think of something else ludicrous to do."

"Now, now," Key said, talking Casey's arm and leading her back downstairs, "no need to be rude, is there?"

"There *so* is," Casey insisted, "and maybe there wouldn't be if you told me what we were actually doing. But you won't, will you?"

"Not right now," Key admitted.

"And why not?" Casey asked as they reached the door back to the main party area. Casey moved her arm and stood there. "Why should I keep...argh!"

"You angry at me, or you?" Key asked. "Nothing has changed, honey, but you seem to keep circling this particular drain. I know, you try to not feel it in front of me, but I can see it in how you pause, how you act. You keep agreeing to meet me, but you aren't sure why."

"I like helping people," Casey said.

"But you don't like that there seems to be something—"

"Bigger," Casey said, "and kept from me. If you want me to help, fine, but I can be a partner or not."

"I just need help these last few days," Key said. "Now if, later, you want *my* help in trying to help people, that's fine, too."

"So that's it," Casey asked, "you just wanted a bit of part-time work?"

"That's all I ever said, honey, and I'm glad you enjoy it—"

"Half of it," Casey said, shaking her head.

"But yes, for now, that's all this is. You talked to Tom, didn't you?"

"So this is how you do things, you use people?" Casey asked.

"That's unfair," Key insisted. "You make it sound like I trick people into helping me and then force them to go away. I asked for help with a few things. You agreed. The same with Tom. I needed some help, I hoped he would be able to. Now, in his case it didn't work out too well, but that's all right, too."

"Why didn't it work out?"

"He didn't tell you?" Key asked, shaking her head. "No, of course not – he wanted to help people but he wanted to profit from it. We had a different approach to things."

"So why did you want me to meet him? You knew he'd make it seem—"

Key shrugged. "You should be allowed to decide things for yourself, including if what I just told you lines up with the impression he gave you."

Casey didn't bother to mention she'd zoned out and hardly actually listened to Tom. That sat completely as her own fault. She sighed and reached for the doorknob. Casey knew she had to choose and not let herself get pulled every which way while dealing with Key. She couldn't trust the woman, not fully, but she wanted to.

It's never easy to trust someone when you know, flat out, that they're keeping things from you. Worse still when they've involved you in acts that could get you killed, or arrested, and still kept things from you. Doing dangerous favors for friends could be a normal part of life at times, and that was fine for Casey. But when those things had end goals you couldn't see, and you hardly knew the person asking, to boot, the cliff got too steep.

"Let's get out of here, and then I think we're done," Casey said.

"For real this time?" Key asked.

"You're asking me if I've decided to stop helping you? I think so. No," she stopped herself, "I know so."

"All right," Key said, a note of sadness in her voice, "I understand, honey. I really do. But," she pulled a slip on paper out of her sleeve, "if you change your mind, you can call me here."

"So you knew I'd be marking out?" Casey asked as she opened the door.

"What, no, of course not, honey," Key said, and smiled a smile that Casey filed away as her lying smile.

"You just happened to have your number on a paper up your sleeve? You always carry it there, do you?" Casey walked them out into the crowd.

"I may have given it a bit of thought," Key admitted.

"Thank you," Casey told her. "So you want to mingle a bit?"

"Less suspicious," Key said.

"Fine, lead the way."

∞

Casey got home an hour or so later to find Jake pacing around the loft – stalking, even, she thought – with hardly a limp.

"Looks better," she said, nodding toward his leg.

"Great, yeah, I need to go out," he said, hurriedly, before stopping to take a long breath. "Sorry, how was the party?"

Casey, in the process of kicking her shoes off and watching them slide toward the bed, shrugged. "Light crime, I guess?"

"Not bad, then," Jake said, "but not what you—"

"Signed up for, no – not at all, really. But I keep going over it, right? And then going back in."

"Not that often," Jake said, walking over to her and trailing a hand down her arm.

"Often *enough*," Casey insisted. "So I quit. For real. I'm done."

Jake pulled a chair out at the table for her and she sat gratefully. As he started to fill the kettle, he said, "If she is Grandmother, I don't know if that's how this works."

"She isn't," Casey said, "she's just—that's not a thing. And thinking it is, that may be the problem."

"All right," Jake conceded, grabbing down mugs and tea bags, "I haven't met her, you would know."

"Exactly, and she isn't."

"Then," Jake said, turning to lean on the counter while the water boiled, "she isn't."

"And if she isn't," Casey finished, "then there's no issue with quitting helping her endlessly."

"Agreed," Jake said, with a nod.

"So, in other news..."

"Does there have to be other news?" Jake asked.

"There does. I overheard some people, uhm what were their names? Bruce Hornswallow?"

"Do you mean Bryce Hornshallar?" Jake asked, pouring hot water into mugs. "What about him?"

"Yeah, that's - yeah, him and uhm, what was it, some Flueval guy—"

"Cop?"

"I think so? A Sergeant?"

"All right, what about them?" Jake sat down and passed one mug to Casey. She took it and warmed her hands on it.

"They were talking – well, one of them insisted that Vink and Haimes had some plans going." Casey stirred her tea by taking the teabag's string and dragging it around the cup, producing no real effect.

"That both makes no sense and perfect sense, though I still don't see how I fit into it," he said, sipping his tea and making a face as he realized it was still too hot.

"Maybe you don't – this could be totally unrelated," Casey pointed out.

"All right," Jake said, "then why is Vink going all guns-out for me?"

"No clue, but him and the Mayor?" she scraped her chair back, got up to grab her nearest guitar, the acoustic, and sat back down, fiddling with it.

"Would it surprise you to learn that many politicians are corrupt?" Jake asked, laughing.

Casey strummed a G chord hard and shrugged. "Yeah, yeah. Jerkbutt."

"Seriously though, I don't know why that's news," Jake said, sipping his tea.

"One of them was trying to convince the other it was true, and the other got mad at him," she said. "Which, it seemed odd. You're right, why would anyone care or be surprised."

"Only if the deals were so big or strange—"

"Something about construction?"

"Oh, that *is* interesting," Jake conceded, "Vink's never had an in to that end of the city. Who doesn't want it though, right? Big money there – big, generational levels of money if you can get the political end nailed down."

"But worthless, in terms of working out Vink's mad-on for you, right?" Casey asked.

"Maybe, maybe not. I could go to him and let him know I know. The threat might be enough to get him to back off, or at least tell me what he wants."

Casey got up, drained her mug, and set it in the sink before turning to look back at Jake. "That's a terrible idea, why wouldn't he just kill you there and then?"

"I—" Jake cut himself short and laughed. "Yeah, all right, good point."

"And yet," Casey said, sitting back down and playing a little flurry of notes as she spoke, "you still want to go out and you feel much better, and this is all silly, and you're sick of being stuck here after a whole day." She muted the strings and smiled. "Right?"

"When you say it all like that," Jake said, leaning back in his chair, "it sounds childish."

"There might just be a reason for that."

"I can't hide forever," Jake said, shrugging. "I figure—all right, how's this. I'll go out and get breakfast, with you, tomorrow morning."

"So...*we'll* go out?" Casey asked.

"I'll go out, with you," Jake repeated.

"You are such a child," she laughed, "but yes, fine."

While Casey and Jake chatted, rummaged for dessert and more tea, then went to bed, Ferdinand Vink walked the halls of his home. He kept his face calm and neutral, hands limp at his sides. He counted to ten, backwards, over and over again, trying to convince himself he felt calm. If he looked calm he could be calm. He repeated the mantra. If he looked calm he could be calm. If he looked calm he could be calm.

He could not be calm. Two days now and no one had killed Meyer. No one had even seen him in the last day, and Vink thought he could feel time slipping by, tightening around his neck and choking him.

Vink stopped moving and looked at the wall next to him. His hands itched to punch it, for no reason other than to do something, to feel something, to be in control. So he exerted that sense of control and did not hit anything.

Instead, Ferdinand made a choice. Tomorrow, he would go find Jake Meyer himself. His men didn't want to cause too much trouble at The Alibi, but Vink didn't care. They didn't want to burn bridges with a bar they enjoyed, or risk fallout that would linger, not even for the money Vink offered.

Ferdinand understood, to a point. Burning the city down for the goal of killing Meyer couldn't be worth it to anyone but him. Yet it remained his will that moved his men, like clockwork soldiers, he felt, and so a bit of that ought to have crept in: if the boss insisted so hard, it was worth anything. But they were human. A weakness not even Vink's threats could overcome all of the time. They weren't fighting for their lives; Vink was.

Tomorrow he would go down to The Alibi and torture every last person working there, if need be, until one of them told him where Meyer, or that singer he lived with, lived. Then the job would take care of itself with fire and blood.

The next morning, Jake rose early, as usual. He felt pretty good, to boot – the strange pills Casey supplied did the trick on everything but the soreness and stiffness in his leg. His arm stiches also still tugged at the skin and the wound itself still hurt. Less than it would've, he knew, but even so, with less to complain about, Jake zeroed in with focus and complained, only to himself, of course, about the last edges of the problem.

He got up, started coffee, grabbed a shower, and by the time he came back to get dressed, Casey was leaning on the counter drinking her first cup. She nudged another cup over for him, and he took a sip as he passed by, setting the mug down, grabbing her hand for a squeeze, and then finding clothes.

More mornings than not, Casey woke up and started writing in her notebook – she just woke up with song in her head. She didn't do it every day so Jake wouldn't have found her skipping it strange except he could see the tenseness in her shoulders, how she stood with the palm of one hand on the counter – not drumming or twitching her fingers, just feeling the countertop for reassurance of existence.

Jake didn't want to mention it; he knew she simply disapproved of going out to breakfast, she would be a string under tension the entire time, and he felt guilty about it. On the other hand, he couldn't sit in the loft and wither away the rest of his life. He needed to get out. He also needed to find out what Vink wanted, but one trip out with no incidents would lead to some level of acceptance. From there he could make a good case to just find Vink and discuss this with him.

Jake couldn't work out what Vink wanted. Nothing he did interfered with the other man's life, he made sure of it. He figured it would wait, though, until at least after breakfast. Casey, out of the shower, finished getting dressed and slipped on some boots. She grabbed her guitar, already nestled into the travel bag, and slung it over her shoulder. Jake joined her at the door, and he locked it behind them.

They went to the Square, because of course they did. Casey looked toward their favorite table and decided against it; the seating didn't give her a clean enough view of the door, or a great straight exit. She considered – while Jake stood and refused to shake his head, knowing what she was doing – an open table by the window, but dismissed it. Anyone walking by would see them, then. Jake waited patiently while Casey found them an open table with all of her current requirements.

They ate – well, Jake ate and Casey fussed with her food, spending most of her time scanning the room. Jake set his fork down with a clink, then cursed as it tipped off the edge of his plate and onto the floor. He picked it up, set it further away, and unwrapped another napkin-protected cluster of silverware for himself. "Hey, Case," he said softly.

"Hmm?" she asked, glancing toward him. "What's up?"

"Do you want to go?"

"No, let's eat," she said, and made a show of having a few bites.

"You've been a bit distracted, though," he said. "I noticed when I dropped my fork you didn't even twitch."

"I *saw* you drop the fork, jerkbutt," she said. "I'm sorry, but I don't like this. This is a setup waiting to happen."

"Or," he countered, "it isn't at all, and this is all just blown out of proportion."

"I will never understand how you can be so calm when it's obvious someone wants you dead," she said, reluctantly forking some eggs into her mouth.

"You get just as calm in a fight – I've seen it, remember?"

"That's different," she insisted, "that's when I have to act. You get calm and don't act."

Jake shook his head and waved down a waiter for their check, and a few boxes to scoop the remains of breakfast into. "We just act in different ways."

"Don't give me that," she said. "What have you done, then?" She fished in a pocket for some money.

Jake opened his mouth, closed it again, and silently got some money out of his pocket and added it to the pile. Then he picked the pile up, faced the bills, counted everything twice, and set the money under the tab.

"I thought so," Casey said, standing slowly and slinging her guitar over her shoulder again.

"It's not...we just have different ways of dealing with stuff like this. But really, I'm not ignoring it," Jake said as he stood. They walked out of the diner and started down the street.

"No, you're planning how to get me to agree to have you go talk to Vink," Casey said, "or was that supposed to not be obvious?"

"Hey," Jake said quickly, "did you hear that couple next to us inside?"

"The ones discussing a change of subject?"

Jake laughed. "That was them. No, they were talking about something crashing down from the sky last night, like a streak of fire."

"No," Casey shook her head, "I didn't catch... is that a thing? I thought, with no airplanes or anything, I mean the city is—"

"I know," Jake agreed, "stuff doesn't generally fall from the sky. I don't even know how it could, actually. I mean, I guess a meteor could? I suppose? I don't know! Never heard of it happening before."

"So they were just confused," Casey said, shrugging it off.

"Probably, but it sure did help change the subject," Jake told her, nudging her with his shoulder, and he grabbed her hand for a squeeze.

"Right up until you said that," she said, squeezing back.

Ferdinand Vick punched the back of the driver's seat hard. "Stop the fucking car," he said, managing to not shout, but only barely. The driver slid the car to a stop, pulling over to double park for a second.

Vink leaned over and looked out the tinted windows of his door. He could swear that right outside...it was. Meyer and that musician he lived with. Luck aligned itself for Vink, he felt. The universe wanted this. He was *meant* to kill Meyer with his own hands. It all made sense now.

"Follow them, but, like, circle the blocks a bunch so we don't get ahead of them or anything," he told the driver.

"Sir, with switchbacks it'll be hard to—"

"Just do it, and if you lose them..."

"But they could do anything while we're circling the block," the driver insisted.

"Just follow them," Vink said, his anger flowing freely again. "Somehow!"

The driver tried to drive as slowly as possible, hoping they wouldn't be noticed.

Jake and Casey walked, hand in hand. She'd stopped scanning behind them for the moment, just looking around the other three directions. She wanted to check behind them, but Jake had started to sigh each time she did. She snuck in a quick glance anyway, heard a sigh, and shrugged.

Jake stopped short, looking down an alley they passed. "Did you hear that?" he asked as he peered into the alley. A bit thinner than some, the alley contained the usual broken crates that somehow managed to spawn in urban alleys. Jake couldn't see anyone, or anything living, moving down there at first, but he kept looking.

"No," Casey said, glancing down the alley quickly before doing a sweep around them. She didn't like standing still.

"Sounded like a cat, maybe?" Jake said, taking as step toward the alley.

"Cats live in alleys," Casey agreed. "Why does this one rate investigation?"

"It sounded like it might be in trouble," Jake told her.

The noise repeated, Casey hearing it this time. "That I heard," she admitted.

"See? We should go make sure it's all right."

"Again?" Casey asked, remembering the last time they'd heard a cat in trouble a few months ago. Jake had insisted they take it to the vet and wait with it. Casey had nothing against cats, but once they'd paid for the vet bills, Jake didn't even want to keep the cat. Casey would've been fine with a cat around but Jake just wanted to help them out, not live with them.

When she'd pressed him on it, he'd laughed and told her it was because cats were in the same line of work as him. Tiny little cons, he called them. She thought it was sweet of him but also frustrating. That last cat went right back onto the streets – Jake hadn't wanted to leave it penned up in a shelter, either.

"Of course," Jake told her. "We don't leave our comrades in trouble."

"You just said that with a straight face," she said, and shook her head. But she also turned with him to head down the alley and find the cat in trouble. She heard the car door open behind her but didn't turn around, the street being busy enough to easily have a cab dropping someone off, or someone getting into their parked car.

She started to react even as the large hand hit her shoulder, shoving her hard to the side and away from Jake. She stumbled a few steps to the side, trying to not fall fully. By the time she recovered, mere seconds, Jake and Vink were already tangled and headed into the alley.

Casey reached for her guitar but even as she got it into her hands, elbow pressing the amp's switch at her hip, one of Vink's goons was on her, grabbing her from behind, arms tightening around her abdomen, pinning her arms.

She snapped her head back and felt his jaw take the impact. She could feel blood run freely down her scalp from the blow, and thought she could feel one of his teeth lodged in the skin there.

"You stay here," another goon, almost a twin to the first in size, said.

Casey smiled at him, a mean, cold look that made him doubt the force of his fists. "I'm going to melt your bones," she said, left hand pressing lightly against strings. "Literally."

He reached for her and she shrugged, kicking him right in the solar plexus.

Jake managed to get out a small "Awp!" awkwardly as Vink collided with him, carrying them both into the alley. Fists rained down on his face and chest as he hit the ground, a few steps into the alley. "Ferdi—ow!—nand!" he yelled, "Cut it out! What the hell do you even—"

"You won't kill me!" was all Vink would say. He shouted it once, then kept repeating it softer as he punched at Jake's body indiscriminately.

Jake started to fight back, utterly confused. He managed to fold his legs up between himself and Vink, the taller man on top of him still, and shoved as hard as he could. Vink stumbled back, hitting the wall of the alley with his back. Jake stood. "What the fuck are you even talking about?" he asked, then added, slowly, "I. Do. Not. Want. To. Kill. You," making sure to enunciate each word carefully.

"Don't lie to me, Meyer," Vink told him, rushing him again. As he did, Jake heard the cat noise again and turned to look without thinking. A dumb move that ended with Vink slamming into him and driving him back into the opposite wall.

"No, Vink, wait," Jake insisted. "Look!" Ferdinand Vink, against his better, unhinged judgment, looked where Meyer stared. A few feet away sat a cat, blue glow where its face should have been. "Vink, it's The Cat With No Face. We need to run, both of us. Now."

Casey stood over Vink's two guards, now both unconscious, but decidedly not possessing melted bones, and cranked up the volume on her amp. This would be tricky, getting just Vink and not Jake, but she had a plan.

She ran into the alley just as Jake and Vink stopped fighting, looking further down the alley. She saw the blue glow and the body of The Cat attached to it and felt reality slide away from her on some deep, personal level. But that didn't stop her from starting to play a solo.

Jake and Ferdinand froze as The Cat inched closer. It meowed, a perfectly fine, normal sound, and Jake felt betrayed. The Cat had lured him here, sought him out, and all he wanted to do was help. "Run," he whispered to Vink.

"We get out of here, I'm still gonna be the last thing you see, Meyer," Vink said.

"Sure, later." Jake agreed, and he tried to move. His body, frozen by confusion and shock, didn't work right. He heard guitar notes behind them and turned to warn Casey away, but before he could, The Cat's glow intensified, and as the blue glow swallowed Jake and Ferdinand, Jake thought that at least Vink would be wrong. The last thing he'd see was a blue glow.

Casey stood there as the light consumed the alley. She flung an arm up, then kept it going to join the other in covering her ears as her guitar started to squeal feedback loudly. The strings snapped, all of them, with a restless, deafening *twang*, and Casey simply sat down hard on the ground, her legs giving out from under her.

She scrambled to stand, looking down the alley at The Cat. And only The Cat; Jake and Vink having vanished. Casey didn't know what to do, but her instinct moved her body as she reached out, lunging to grab The Cat. No plan existed in her head after that – she just wanted her hands on The Cat. Maybe it spoke an understandable language. Maybe she could force it to give Jake back. Something. Anything.

Instead, The Cat meowed softly at her and then bolted. She started after it but within seconds couldn't see so much as a tail or strange blue glow. Casey stood there, lost in confusion. Home – she should go home and work out a plan. Sure, she told herself, that made sense. Sure. At the least it would get her away from Vink's thugs before they got to their feet again.

She turned and ran, feeling her life shatter behind her.

Sitting in the loft, alone, Casey tapped her feet on the floor as she sat at the table, staring at the empty chair next to her. She'd come home, taped up her head wound, and washed the blood out of her hair. That managed to be about as far as she could focus into the future. She had no plan, nothing close to an idea of what to possibly do. She couldn't even get revenge for him, with Vink having also vanished. That was, she thought, the one bright spot in the moment: Jake hadn't been taken from her alone. Knowing Vink, too, suffered the same fate didn't ease her pain so much as it helped contain it in a specific box.

She grabbed her acoustic guitar and sat and played, trying to think straight. She kept missing notes and fumbling transitions until she'd annoyed herself into setting the guitar down. Casey wished she could console herself by sinking into pure darkness. She honestly hoped she would lose herself in thoughts that this worked as a reason why she shouldn't be in relationships – that there stood a curse over her, anything of that sort – but that feeling never arrived.

Staring to pace, having kicked her chair out of the way to stand and knocking it over with a *thwack*, Casey tipped her head back and stared at the ceiling while her feet navigated her around the space. A knot in her stomach seemed to grow, and the unease filled her, her lungs starting to feel heavy and her hands beginning to shake. She sat down, heavily, on the floor and tried to breathe normally. A dim part of her recognized it as a panic attack, but the rest of her floated away on it, carried downstream in nervous confusion.

She laid down, on her back, forcing herself to take longer and slower breaths. Casey tried to take control of her body back and slowly, by tiny degrees, managed to ride out the panic. Looking over at the bed, from her vantage point on the floor, she noticed a slip of paper. She could see, from its curl, the writing on it, too. A phone number.

Key's.

The panic started back up. If The Cat With No Face stood revealed as a real...cat...thing...then that meant the rest of Jake's silly superstitions could also be true. And that meant, to Casey, that Key really could be The Grandmother of Keys. Everything added up to her then along that axis. An old woman, who seemed to know everyone and who seemed to align her plans perfectly in ways no one really should have been able.

Casey laughed a shuddering, panic-fueled laugh. Or she was just an old woman who got lucky. A combination of luck and planning, Jake would tell her, could also easily line up the facts as she knew them. Still, she could feel, the panic aside, that Key was the real thing, far more than she appeared. Or, at least, far more than Casey had allowed herself to see before now.

If that held true, she thought, sitting upright with a start, then Key might be able to help. She'd never given Casey a phone number before – why do it that one time, unless she knew what would happen? Unless she could help?

Casey grabbed at the paper, fumbling it, with twitchy fingers, before snarling and grabbing it in a fist, crumpling the paper tight. This would be her answer, her salvation. Key could help. She smoothed the paper out and grabbed the phone, dialing even as she tried again to calm her breathing.

The phone rang once, twice, three and four times. Casey started to put the phone back down when she heard a click and a voice on the other end of the line.

"Manchivas Deli," a male voice grumbled in her ear, "we deliver till eight. Whatcha want?"

She hung up quickly and looked at the number written down. She dialed again, sure she'd made a mistake the first time.

This time the phone answered on the first ring. "Manchivas Deli," the voice said again. "Listen, if this is you kids again, I know where you live and—"

Casey took as deep a breath as she could. "I'm looking for Key?"

"You're what now?" the voice asked.

"Looking for Key," Casey said again, feeling foolish. "She gave me this number."

"Looking for your keys?"

"Not *my* keys...an old woman. Named Key." Casey exhaled heavily, not meaning for it to sound exasperated but sure that it did, and considered hanging up. The old woman had obviously given her a fake number, and that was what she got for trusting her at all.

"Key? I don't know any...hold on," the voice said before muttering to someone else obviously in the room, "What? Yeah, here."

"You looking for Key?" a new voice asked.

"Yes!" Casey said, a mite too forcibly. She glanced back to her own doubts of a second ago and wanted to laugh at them. They stood there, though, warning her to not get her hopes too high up in only a few seconds.

"She's at the bookstore," the new voice told her.

"What bookstore?" Casey asked, tentative with herself more than the disaffected voice she spoke to.

"On Main," the voice said, and hung up.

Casey sat and stared at the phone receiver in her hand. She set it on the base slowly, carefully, as if it could shatter. She started to sit, then remembered her chair was on the floor, sideways, where she'd knocked it over before. She just stared at it.

Bookstore on Main. That narrowed her search down to a lot of Mur, but at least it narrowed it. There couldn't be that many bookstores along the one street, even if it covered miles of ground. She knew she just had to go find it. She could even ask around, find a guide to things like bookstores – there were any number of easy ways to find the store.

And then what, she asked herself. Confront an old woman about being some kind of capital-F Force controlling Mur, and demand she confront a cat, which had no face, and make it give back Jake from where it had vanished him? Even if there would be no coming back and Jake had been eaten by The Cat, somehow? The Cat eating Jake made no sense to her, but it also made the exact same amount of sense that a cat with a glowing blue light instead of a face made, so there was that.

Casey's brain felt like it kept skittering from one issue to the next, darting around the sides of those issues with abandon. She was, she reminded herself, the decisive one. Except she wasn't, was she? She laughed at herself, the sound feeling cold and echoey alone in the loft.

Given a mission, she could be on point. She could focus down and guide herself to target, according to plan and on time. She picked up the chair and set it back in place before walking to the sink and filling the kettle. Normally she did things, she made choices. But ever since running into Key, that had wavered.

Something tugged her in many directions and she couldn't tell what it was. She wanted to be the great person, the hero, who looked up at the sky and threatened to rip apart the universe in search of Jake, or justice, or whatever lay between those two points. Instead she stood at her sink and filled a kettle, trying to calm down and force herself to go confront an old woman.

There, kettle in hand, overflowing under the faucet, Casey felt the shift. She wasn't a big hero. She couldn't be that person who the military had tried to convince her she was. That was why she'd left, after all. What she *was*, however, was pissed the fuck off at the world.

This world, this *city* that she loved, took something from her. Took someone. Casey Harrison, she decided right there, loved too much to sit and drink tea. She left the kettle in the sink, shut off the water, and grabbed her guitar. She loved this stupid, impossible town, and she loved Jake Meyer, and those two things would see her through.

Because when the two things she loved fought, as they seemed to be in the process of doing just then, Casey knew she owed it to both to at least work out what'd actually happened. Then, if needed, if appropriate to the moment, she could finish having a breakdown and lie on the floor and drink tea. But until such a time, she needed to keep moving.

She locked the door behind her, reached back, and set her palm against it. She felt her love for the place swell in her chest. She remembered they needed a couch. Cursing and laughing in equal measure, Casey went out into Mur to find Key.

Rokendre Berkshire stood and stretched. He looked up at the sky and smiled. Rokendre watched the aurora borealis happily as he waited for his client to return. He'd been lounging on the ground for a while, but felt meeting your passenger standing gave off a more professional air. No one wanted to think they paid lazy people.

He happily admitted to himself, though, that he was lazy. As lazy as he could get away with. He still kept to his schedule, of course. A Knocker without a schedule might as well be giving money away. And this trip – out to Barrow, Alaska for twelve hours – crept toward its closing quickly.

The early twenty-fourth century treated Barrow fairly well, Rokendre decided. The place seemed to have a decent, if still small, amount of people in it. Buildings stood around as electric cars struggled to get down slush-filled streets. The place seemed alive, at least, and fairly happy. Rokendre's passenger wouldn't be happy if they didn't hurry up, however.

He checked his watch. Then he checked his other watch. The first watch told him the local time where he was, which he'd set when they arrived, and also the current local time in Mur, which never got unset. The other watch he only used as a countdown timer. He liked to give clients, on average, an extra minute from when they arrived before he started it, just out of kindness, though he never told them that.

The first entry could be strange, as strange as the first time you stepped into Mur, assuming you weren't born there. There was a dislocation to it, a sense of shifting that one didn't generally get by walking through most doors. Walking into an empty elevator shaft and expecting a car, but getting only empty air – that felt about right, if a bit harsher.

Rokendre remembered the first time he Knocked. Growing up in Mur, being a Knocker often landed as a dream job. You could leave the city and then return, and better still, get paid for it. A lot of kids considered the idea that maybe they could be Knockers when they got older, but it faded, as do most childhood career dreams. Except firefighter. People wanted to be firefighters even after they realized what the job actually looked like. This baffled many people, including many firefighters.

But Rokendre never wanted to run into burning buildings. The saving-people part could be cool, and important, but the on-fire part just didn't work for him. Also, it would be easier to become a firefighter. Which is not at all to say that firefighting was an easy career path, it really wasn't, but more to say that becoming a Knocker provided a few unique challenges.

Knockers will tell you, if pressed, that they can just always feel Mur, behind their eyes. That when they go to a door they can feel the city on the other side and align themselves with it. That's it – that's the job. Which, realistically, doesn't explain very much.

Doctor Rebecca Goldfeather advanced a theory that Knockers' brains contained enough neural quantum entanglement with the atoms of Mur itself that they could align themselves with the city and return.

A good theory, and many people repeated it, hoping you wouldn't ask the next question: then how did they choose where to go when they *left* Mur. At that question, Goldfeather would smile, shrug, and hope to get away with her doctorate intact.

No one knew how Knocking really worked. The only way to train a Knocker remained to take them outside of Mur and see if they could get back. Well, that's not true. You could also start by seeing whether they could leave Mur and pick a destination, but since the field worked on an apprentice basis, and most trained Knockers struggled with not choosing where they went, they would override people new to it.

When two Knockers tried to use the same gate to go to different places at the same time, one always won. The very rare Knocker Fight always ended up that way, seeing who had the stronger connection to Mur – assuming that the ability had any sort of link to a connection to Mur in the first place.

No one understood how any of it worked.

An apprentice would be taken out of the city and then left there, wherever 'there' happened to be. They would have to get back to the city to prove they could become a Knocker. Most teachers would go and collect their apprentices after a while, if they didn't return, and then fire them. A few left them alone for days, hoping that desperation would suffice where raw talent didn't. Some just forgot, and shrugged off the memory of some kid who wasn't up to the job.

Rokendre got back to Mur on his first try. After that, he spent a few years learning how to consistently get to where he wanted when leaving Mur, and how to take other people with him. Currently he worked for a client who needed, for a customer back in Mur, an authentic Barrow jacket. People had odd tastes, but this customer's family had originated there, generations ago, and he wanted the jacket – from a specific point far in the future – to take pride that his ancestral home still stood.

This sounded like a quick job, but the client, a Strange Artifacts vendor, said he knew better. Barrow wasn't the sort of town to have a ton of jackets proclaiming how great it was, how much you "hearted" it there or anything. This place was not Paris.

So he hired Rokendre for a bunch of hours longer than he should need, passing the expense on to the customer, and set out into Alaska. Rokendre didn't mind; he enjoyed just sitting around in the warm night air watching the sky.

Except the deadline loomed, and no client could be seen coming to meet him. This guy wasn't a long-time client, and Rokendre hadn't seen much paperwork for him using other Knockers (they kept good records of that sort of thing), which concerned him. A Strange Artifact dealer who didn't seem to go out of town much couldn't be great at what he did.

So, when Rokendre saw his client come running down the road, shouting "Quick! Quick! We have to go! Before they catch us!" Rokendre just sighed. This idiot had pissed off the local police and now they'd see Rokendre's face, which could close off a few years of this town to him.

He had exactly two moves open to him now: grab his client and go, then charge him double and hope he could pay, or ditch him here. Ditching him required far more paperwork than a lawsuit back home, and either way the town would be burned to him for a few years on either side of the event.

So he grabbed his client's arm, opened a door, and yanked him through. As the gate closed behind them, Rokendre punched the guy in the face and started explaining to him, in very precise words, what would happen next and how much it would end up costing him.

His client nodded and held out a jewel in his hand, obviously the stolen object in question. "They, uhhh, didn't have the jacket," he said, and smiled.

Rokendre hit him again and shook his head.
Idiot.

Casey slammed the door of the cab and took
the curb in one motion. She stood in front of Never
Spineless, the third bookstore along Main that
she'd found. The name made her want to smile but
she clamped down on the urge as it twitched the
corner of her mouth.

Striding inside, the swing of the door setting
off chimes above it, she took in the old shop: used
books from all over the planet, in terms of location
and time, filled seemingly endless shelves in a
pattern that appeared destined to collapse and kill
bystanders one day. She loved the place, or would
have if she'd stopped long enough to take it all in.

Instead she sought out the counter, no small
feat considering it sat buried under more stacks of
books, and faced the small man atop a stool behind
it. He set down his book slowly and smiled at her.

"Is Key here?" she asked before he could speak.

A frown, followed by a shrug, and then a point.
"If you're going to be rude, I shouldn't tell you," he
said, "but she's in the back, reading. Doesn't want to
be disturbed though."

"Me either," Casey said over her shoulder as she
tried to navigate an aisle and find the back of the
store.

A door sat between two bookcases, the floor
clear in front of it, and Casey opened it without
bothering to knock. On the other side she entered a
warm, burgundy-painted room, clear of distraction.
Thick grey carpet covered every inch of the floor,

and in each corner two plush armchairs sat, a side table with a lamp between each set. The far-right–corner lamp stood lit, a stack of books on the table near it, and in the chair, Key, sitting and reading.

"Honey," Key said, placing a slip of paper for a bookmark and setting her book down, "I didn't expect you, after the other night."

"Enough," Casey said, "Jake is dead, and you're some mystical expert, and I want answers now. Then I want to bring him back."

Key bit her knuckle in shock. "Your Jake died? Oh, honey, I'm sorry to hear that, but no one can bring the dead back to life."

"You don't deny the rest, then?" Casey asked, growing angry.

"Which rest, that I'm some mystical expert? Oh," Key shook her head, "no, I'm not that, honey. I just felt that accusations took a backseat to hearing your news."

"Are you," Casey asked slowly, "or are you *not* The Grandmother of Keys that people go on about?"

"Oh, *that*," Key said, laughing, "yes, yes I am."

"And you never thought to mention it?" Casey took a deep breath and walked toward Key, the anger, the panic, and the confusion all fighting for control.

"Would you have believed me? Do you even know what that means, now?" Key shrugged. "I'm not entirely sure I do."

"Don't give me that," Casey said, weariness flooding her system suddenly as the competing emotions dragged on and drained her adrenaline.

"I mean it," Key said, "everyone tells me what it's supposed to mean, but they never seem to agree with what I think it is, and I'm the one who should know, I would think. But I also can't say that they're wrong."

"I heard that you walk Mur eternally to protect it," Casey said, sitting down in the chair next to Key's.

"Some of that is true, I suppose. I wouldn't say *eternally*, for a start. And I'm not sure I protect anything. I do walk a lot, though, it's true."

"You're infuriating, is what you are," Casey muttered.

Key laughed. "That's true too, I suppose. But honey," she reached a hand out across the table, "tell me what happened to your Jake. How did he die?"

"He..." Casey trailed off, trying to find words that made sense to her, "this sounds...I know how it'll sound—"

"Just say it as plain as possible, honey."

"There was a cat, it had a blue light instead of a... The Cat With No Face, I guess, and the light flashed and Jake and Vink, they vanished. Then The Cat ran, and I didn't—"

Key nodded. "Well, honey," she said, smiling, "he isn't dead. Or at least, that didn't kill him."

Casey looked at Key and tried to remember how to breathe. Or blink.

Jake noticed four things in very short order: first, he realized he still lived; second, he saw Vink and that he lived as well; third, he caught sight of his hands and saw that they glowed faintly blue, the same color as The Cat's glow; and finally, it sunk in that they were not in Mur.

Looking around as he stood up, Jake saw multiple spires – tall gleaming buildings rising everywhere, and, rushing between them, small flying vehicles. Glancing at Vink between bouts of staring at the strange city around them, Jake wondered what to do.

He'd only been out of Mur once, with a Knocker. He'd found he didn't care for it. Mur remained his home, and other places just seemed too strange, too centered, to satisfy him. No, Jake only felt at home in a mash of cultures from across time and the ring of the globe. A normal city burst with history, of course, and influence from different times and cultures, but it still felt too plain for him. He couldn't explain it. Mur just had a sense about it that made perfect sense to his head. This place... didn't.

The glow around his hands started to fade slowly, but didn't rub off when he tried to wipe them off on his pants. Luckily, he thought as he realized what he'd done, it didn't spread, either. A glance at Vink – the large man was gaining his feet shakily. Jake sighed.

"Ferdinand," he said softly, "maybe we hold off on trying to kill each other."

"I'll kill you," Vink replied, swaying lightly.

"That's the opposite of what...look, Vink, we're *not in Mur*. We have much bigger problems than each other." Jake pointed to the buildings around them. He looked down as well, and saw they were in some small park. A newspaper rested on a bench and Jake went to go grab it, showing it to Vink.

"See? This is San Francisco, 2293," he said, jabbing the date printed on the paper. "We have no Knocker, Vink, we need to—"

"I'll kill you!" Vink screamed, lunging for Jake.

Jake threw the paper away and ran. None of this matched up with Jake's idea of a good time. He didn't want to fight Vink at the best of times, but right now he truly felt their only way through this would be to work together.

For the moment, though, he continued to run, Vink gaining on him. Stupid, long-legged fool, Jake thought, then tripped over an uneven crack in the pavement and hit the ground hard, scraping his hands as he tried to catch himself. His leg felt much better but still wasn't really up to running.

A run-in with The Cat With No Face survived, he reflected, and he would actually die from shoddy civic engineering. He got up, limping and running again. As he did, he and Vink both froze, crouching instinctively as a jet passed overhead. The roar startled them, making them both look up to find the source of what sounded like their incoming doom. Airplanes simply didn't fly over Mur, ever.

People nearby, having ignored two people running, stopped to gawk at two people frightened of the sky. They spoke to each other in a language that Jake could only make out glimmers of, but Jake caught the gist: "Stupid hicks."

Refusing to let himself feel too offended, or at least rejecting his instinct to take it personally, Jake started to move again. Vink did, too, leaping at Jake and landing hard on Meyer's back. They fell to the pavement and Vink started to slam his fists into whatever parts of Jake he could reach.

Jake punched back as best he could, noticing the glow around his hands flickered now. His hands hurt – not because of the glow, that didn't feel like anything – but punching people hurts, and Jake tried to treat his hands like valuable instruments. He didn't relish fighting, preferring instead to do a few card tricks, or pick a lock. He found himself distracted by thoughts of icing his hands later, then shook them off, chiding himself for assuming there would be a later for him.

Grabbing Vink's shoulders, Jake rolled them over, and then, on top of Vink, pushed off and landed on his ass. He kicked out, catching Vink in the face, and sat there to catch his breath. Jake still had zero idea why Vink wanted to kill him, but had accepted that the desire wouldn't go away, even for something as big as what they were dealing with currently.

Jake Meyer stood up, breathing hard, his face and chest hurting worse than his hands as the nerve endings came alive post-being-punched-a-lot. Fighting sucked, he reflected, allowing himself a laugh that hurt his ribs.

He started to run, squinting at a glow that hurt his eyes: his hands. The glow flickered and came back stronger than before, as strong as when The Cat had filled the alley. He felt the world slip, sliding in every direction at once, and tried to look back at Vink, seeing the man starting to get up again, even as he faded. He became ghost-like, a shimmering effect surrounding him, and Jake, looking down at his own body, saw he did the same.

They vanished, leaving people on the street to applaud, thinking they had seen a great bit of street performance art and waiting for either man to reappear with a collection plate. They left, disappointed, after a few minutes ticked by, the street still empty of the show they'd witnessed.

Key patted Casey's hand. "The Cat doesn't kill. Well, sure, The Cat *kills*, but generally mice. There's no point to it, though. The Cat can't eat mice – she doesn't eat food at all the way you and I know it. No, she eats *time*."

"What," Casey said, shaking her head, not sure how this had become her life so quickly, "does that even mean?"

"Exactly what it sounds like, I guess," Key said. She let go of Casey's hand and leaned forward, resting her elbows on her knees. "The Cat – and no, I don't know why, either – eats time. That's what she survives on. Mostly that means mice and squirrels and such will just vanish on occasion, who'd notice that?"

"But how does eating time lead to Jake vanishing?" Casey took her guitar out of the bag resting against her knee, ashamed to realize she hadn't restrung it yet. She pulled out a pack of strings from a pocket in the bag, along with a small string winder and cutter.

"When she eats time around objects they, well, lose that time," Key told her, moving her book on the table to give Casey space to set tools down. "After that, I don't know, really. No one does. The Walker before me—"

"Wait," Casey said as she pulled broken strings off the guitar, winding them as best she could so they wouldn't just poke people, "there was a Walker before—"

"Of course, honey," Key said, "I told you, I'm not immortal, just *very* old. But The Walker before me—"

"How old are you?"

"Does it really matter?" Key asked, watching with fascination as Casey slowly restrung the guitar.

"It so does," Casey insisted.

"I stopped paying attention, honestly," Key said, "but at least a thousand? Somewhere around that. Regardless, let me finish, honey. The Walker before me, he once told me that The Cat's victims, as it were, weren't hurt, just displaced in time. The time stolen around them, and from them, just shifted them around some."

"So Jake's alive?" Casey wound a string slowly, trying to not break it.

"He was when that flash happened. But honey, I don't see how he could come back. Time travel isn't possible."

"You just described time travel to me. Just now," Casey said. She felt frustration starting back up. She ignored the sliver of hope inside her, though. She couldn't afford to let it in yet.

"No, I described a terrible side effect of The Cat eating. It isn't a controllable thing."

"What if we got The Cat and—"

"Honey, she's a cat. She doesn't speak, or understand, human language. I'm sorry," Key leaned back and sighed.

Casey tightened another string, stretching it and adjusting the tension again, plucking it at intervals to listen for it coming into tune. "So that's it, then? Jake is gone? You want me to just accept that?"

"I want you," Key said, "to accept he isn't dead and that the world is stranger than you think—"

"Saying that to me, in *this* town—"

Key laughed, "Of course, but even so, you never know. But that doesn't mean there's anything you can do directly, either."

"That's about the same—I can't hold out false hope and just assume—"

Key clicked her tongue against the roof of her mouth loudly. "False hope? All hope is false, honey. That's why it's important. Hope is meaningless if you know a thing for certain. Then it's just a form of waiting. No, honey, no – hope is important *because* it might all be false."

"That's—"

"I know it is," Key agreed, "but it's also one of the most critical things there is. Hope is what this city runs on. It gets people up in the morning, it keeps people here when they feel lost – hope is—"

"Fine," Casey shook her head, "I'll see what I can do," she said, finishing tuning the last string and packing away her tools and broken strings.

"You already do hope for it," Key said, "even if you won't admit it to me and don't want to let yourself in on the fact."

Casey just sighed in response and leaned back in her chair again.

"While you sort *that* out," Key said, standing, "we have work to do."

"I quit, remember?" Casey told her, not moving.

"So you're willing to let all of Mur die?" Key asked, holding out her elbow for Casey to hook her arm through.

"I..." Casey stood. "This time you explain, in detail, what you know. No more half stories."

Jake looked around as the world came back into view. This time, at least, he stood when he showed up. On the other hand, he really wanted to fall down. These shifts, whatever they were, he thought, sucked.

Vink, too, swam into view near Jake. He saw Jake and started toward him, stumbling once. "Vink," Jake yelled, "just hold on!"

"No, I know this is all part of your plan, Meyer!" Vink yelled back.

"Oh, good," Jake said, standing his ground, "you've gone bye-bye. Come on, Ferd, think it through. If I could send us out of Mur to...where ever the hell we are, or were, would I have sat on that?"

"You gave me a drug, this is all a hallucination," Vink insisted. But he slowed as he approached Jake, no longer quite sure.

"If it was, I would be rich selling this stuff," Jake told him. "Think it through, I'm telling you. This was The Cat. I don't know what it was, or how it works, or worked, or...I got nothing. But if you keep trying to kill me for no reason—"

"No reason?" Vink laughed. "You killed me, Meyer! I saw it!"

Jake laughed in response. Not the unhinged, dangerous laugh Vink burst out with, but an honest, deep laugh at the ridiculousness of the universe. "I killed you, and you saw me do it. But here you are, Vink, so, uhm, no?"

"It was a future me, and I bet a future you," Vink said, starting to advance on Jake again, "so if I kill you *before* you kill me—"

"All of time unravels? Think about it, if you kill me before I – assuming you're right, which I truly doubt – kill you, then you would never have seen me kill you, so you wouldn't want to kill me, so you wouldn't have killed me, and round and round we go."

"And if I don't kill you now, then you *will* kill me. Nice try, Meyer, but no, I'm going to kill you. Now." Vink lunged, his hands outstretched to grab at Jake's throat.

Jake stepped back a few steps and tripped. He landed hard, dust rising up from the ground where he fell. Looking around, he realized the town they were in had just started to wake up around them: men and women in outfits he'd seen a few times from books and movies people brought with them into Mur.

Shabby and well worn, the villagers circled around Jake and Vink, staring at them. One of them, armed with a simple, handmade hoe, pointed the farming tool at Vink and asked a question that, of course, neither Jake nor Ferdinand could understand.

"Are they speaking...I want to say French? But I've heard French. This is older maybe?" Jake looked at Vink. "Whatever it is, they don't seem happy with us."

Hands grabbed for him and Vink from all directions and Jake yelped loudly, grabbing his keys from his pocket and holding them high, jingling them.

While they held Vink tight, the villagers took a half step back from Jake, watching him carefully. He lowered his hand, held out the keys, then shifted them to the other hand, palming them expertly. He half turned as he did to drop them in a pocket without anyone noticing, because he held up the first hand to show it was now empty. His other hand opened as well, and the crowd gasped.

"See, magic always confuses them," Jake said to Vink, "now they'll fear us and let—well, they'll let *me* go, at least."

The villagers started to shout and grabbed Jake, dragging him to the ground.

Vink laughed. "Maybe I won't kill you, Meyer – maybe they will."

"They were *supposed* to worship me. They're ancient, right? I should be a god to them!" Jake insisted.

"Or a demon," Vink said, still laughing.

"Oh, come on!" Jake fumed, wrestling and trying to get free.

Jake kicked and flexed, bucking his whole body as the villagers lifted him. He noticed Vink didn't fight, acting meek and limp in their grasp. Jake cursed, loudly and often, even though he knew the sounds would further convince the natives he did, in fact, work for the devil. Why did he have to try a smart-ass trick, he thought to himself. He'd showed off when what had been needed was to simply do what Vink had done: out-docile the other man. But no, Jake couldn't turn it off. Now he would die at the hands of...or would he, he wondered.

He tried to stretch his neck to see his own hands. His arms were being pulled behind him, and the jostling of being carried by angry people who were, at the same time, terrified of him, made it difficult. Nor could he see Vink's hands; he could, however, hear the man's fake simpering, which only served to make Jake rage more.

No, he yelled silently at himself, calm is the only way to go. He went limp, the sudden change in weight distribution causing the men carrying him to drop him for a moment. Jake didn't try to escape, he just used the time to glimpse his hands. The blue light flickered. Jake smiled.

There were only two ways this could go: the flickering would repeat the previous pattern and Jake and Vink would find themselves shifted again, or it would simply vanish and he would be killed by a group of superstitious, angry people.

If the flickering and vanishing happened, then great, he was saved. If it didn't, then he'd need a plan. Which is, oddly, why Jake smiled. He didn't assume a blue glow would save him yet again. He smiled because of his new plan. Jake quickly slapped his hands together – clapping once, loudly – startling the people around him. They let go of him again, but as they hadn't lifted him too high the drop didn't hurt as much.

Jake didn't care. He rolled up onto his knees quickly, before they could grab him, and kneeled there, hands clasped together tightly, raising them to the sky. This they understood. It confused them further, making them stop and consider their actions. Vink said nothing, being led by a pack of villagers, allowed to walk calmly, but they watched him warily regardless.

Meyer started to speak gibberish, whispering at first but letting his voice rise every few breaths. He shook his hands, raising them higher then lowering them again. Then as they started to come for him again he began to shake, his whole body spasming, twitching, and shuddering frantically.

Jake kept his eyes open wide, trying to convey fear and shock, but really just to be able to see if they were buying into it. The smart early play would have been to shrink in on himself, but now he had to go big as a last resort. And big he went. Jake threw everything he could think of into his faked fit, eventually dropping fully to the ground and laying prone in the dirt.

As he slowly made a show of struggling to get back up, he kept looking at the sky, smiling, then down toward the residents, over and over in a slow cycle. They were, he thought, starting to buy it. His conversion, his casting off the chains of the devil act, seemed to, hopefully, tide them over and confuse them from their plans involving possible death.

He stood, slowly, smiling and reaching out to touch villagers on the shoulder or head with all the fake benediction he could muster. They flinched, the first two times, and then started to go with it. Jake came to a crossroads in his plan, though: he could save Vink, easily, right now, or he could leave him.

Leaving Ferdinand, when Jake knew the man intended to kill him, would be the smart move, he told himself. You don't help people who want you dead. You leave them to their own solutions and hope they can't find any. But Casey's voice floated in his head, and he knew that she wouldn't leave Vink, even with the threat he posed. Casey wasn't here in the moment, though.

But Jake found himself burning time considering the move, anyway. He didn't have much time to waste, either, he knew. Soon the natives would get restless, as the saying promised, and the choice would be out of his hands. Stalling too long was making a choice as much as anything else would be. Jake looked at Vink, catching his eye. They stared at each other, and Jake shrugged. Then he pointed at the man and waved him over. The locals smiled, cheering as Jake blessed Vink and embraced him.

"I'm still going to kill you," Vink whispered.

"I know, but I'm gonna hope you change your mind," Jake whispered back.

Jake's hands started to glow again and grew brighter by the second. He rolled his eyes as the flash engulfed them both.

Key and Casey walked toward the Spire. Casey, her guitar bag slung over her shoulder as always, gripped the strap tightly in a fist. She'd never been inside the Spire, like most residents of Mur. "This is a bad idea," she said, refusing to glance at Key as she did.

"It's the only idea," Key replied as they waited for the light to change. "Mayor Haimes is planning something, and we need to know exactly what it is. I have an idea, but it's too loose to work off of."

"And no more little jaunts helping people to disguise your plans?" Casey asked, crossing the street with the old woman.

"They were legitimate things to help people. But I needed you to be there, to hear, and to see other angles."

"You could have told me that, though."

"Not without poisoning the well. If you knew what to listen for, all sorts of bad data would have leapt out at you. I needed you where you could just listen and counted on you hearing something worth hearing. Which you did."

Casey laughed. "I'm not sure if you're feeding me a line or not. I genuinely cannot tell at this point. Either you're an amazing mastermind, planning for totally random events perfectly, or you're just making it sound like you are. I can't tell which it is."

"If it gets results," Key said with a shrug, "does it matter which it is?"

"You are never allowed to meet Ja—" Casey stopped, cutting herself off and gulping air. Knowing that she wouldn't see Jake again, trying to hope for it but still not holding it close enough to be comfortable, hurt. She hadn't gotten used to using a past tense for him, and speaking of him snuck up on her the way a hammer sneaks up on a nail.

"Honey, it's OK to hurt," Key said, patting Casey's arm. "I know—"

"I know it's OK to hurt," Casey said bitterly, "I don't need permission. I...no, I don't mean to snap at you, I'm sorry."

"I understand," Key said, "and I'm sorry, I should have been more straightforward with you." They stood and looked at the Spire, together. It rose into the sky, brick and stone with wide windows spaced throughout.

"There's still time. What do you *think* is happening, and why did you need an Exchanger's coin?" Casey asked, not ready to go in just yet.

Key nodded. "I think Haimes and Ferdinand Vink are, or were, working together to take control of Mur."

"Don't they already?" Casey asked, pointing at a street vendor's cart. They weren't common in a lot of Mur, but near the Spire they served the workers generously. The two women went over, walking slowly. They both knew they were in a hurry but had to seem slow and unaware of what they were walking into.

"Not like this," Key said. "I think they're plan something involving The Silent Heart. There are so many myths around, but I know that Haimes believes them, and even if he didn't, Vink would have gone along for the sake of influence. Haimes believes The Silent Heart is something he can control. He can't, of course, but damaging The Heart would kill the city. For good."

"Wait, so The Silent Heart is real, too?" Casey bought them both pretzels and bottles of water and they wandered back along the side of the building, eating half-heartedly.

"Of course," Key laughed, "but it isn't what you think – or at least, I doubt it. We don't have time for that though, so I'll ask: can you trust me there for now?"

Casey nodded. "Sure, so Haimes wants to control The Heart, but how does that kill the city?"

"Mmm," Key said, swallowing, "assuming he could find The Silent Heart, and I sadly think he might be able to, and then actually get to him—"

"The Heart is a him?"

"Not now, remember? But if he did, I think his attempts at control would kill The Heart. Without The Heart...it's hard to explain, but the city is a reflection of the current Heart. And yes, like me, there were Hearts previous, all of their own names, and all influencing the city in their own ways."

"So The Heart, this one, The Silent Heart, reflects what the city is—"

"And vice versa," Key put in.

"Sure," Casey agreed, "and The Walker, you...do The Heart's bidding out here?"

"I wouldn't say I do anyone's bidding, except my own," Key told Casey, wadding up the napkin her pretzel came in. "But I listen to him, The Heart, and try my best to help shape the city the way he feels it, to keep everything going."

"And The Cat—"

"Is a cat that eats time. That's all."

"That's *enough*."

"You're telling me," Key admitted, laughing. "We should go in."

"I need to know why The Heart is so important to the life of the city, Key," Casey insisted, even though she followed Key to one of the doors into the Spire.

"Not in here," Key insisted.

"But the coin—" Casey started asking. She shook her head as they came to the building's metal detectors and security. Key only nodded. They both emptied their pockets of anything that might set off the detectors, Casey watching, fearfully, for appearance of the Exchanger coin, but Key seemed to have left it elsewhere. Security questioned Casey over her guitar and portable amp, and she gave them short, brusque answers, trying and failing to hide her annoyance.

Key, meanwhile, explained to the guards that they were there to see her nephew, who worked in the Mayor's office, on his PR team. They called up and confirmed her story, seeming to resent doing so, and eventually let them both through.

They took an elevator and were met by a cheerful Hispanic man in his early twenties. He smiled and embraced Key. "Grandma, so good to see you," he said, "and this must be—"

"Case," Casey told him, raising an eyebrow. "Heard all about me, huh?"

"No," he admitted, laughing in return, "but manners matter to Grandma, so I thought—"

"We don't have time for that, Franklin," Key said. "And I know, you'll mock me with that forever, but it is true. Can we talk in your office?"

"Of course," he said, leading them there. He tried to exchange pleasantries again, but Key frowned and Casey just shrugged, so he let the matter rest. Franklin Garcia had never seen Key agitated before. Disappointed, sure, but never antsy the way she seemed now. He wondered if it had to do with her companion.

"I'm sorry for rushing us, Franklin," Key said as Franklin closed his office door, "but I fear we may be on a clock. I'd love to be wrong, though. Can you get us access to Haimes' office?"

Franklin's gut reaction was a sharp outburst of laughter that died quickly when he realized Key was not joking. "No, of course not," he said.

"Well that's...unfortunate," Key muttered.

"Key," Casey said, "do you need Haimes, or just some time in his office?"

"Just some time, alone, in his office."

"How much?" Casey asked, thinking.

"I don't really know," Key admitted, "and if he has a locked drawer or—"

"So you want me to go into his office, without him there, and see if I can find anything?"

Key shrugged. "It wasn't my first option, but I fear it may be the best choice. Why?"

Casey stood up and smiled at Franklin. "You can't get either of us into Haimes' office, I get that, but can you get him out of his office? Not to see us, or anything, just the opposite."

"I mean..." Franklin thought about it. "Possibly, but Grandma, Haimes isn't known for writing things down. He keeps it all in his head – he doesn't trust anyone."

"Like most people in power, haven't I told you that?" she asked Franklin, who nodded in return. "But I think in this case we're going to have to risk it."

"Even if we get part of the picture, Key, I have a plan to get the rest," Casey added.

"Already?"

"What else am I doing?" Casey asked, shrugging.

"Working on your plan to get into Haimes' office," Key replied. "You really were the right choice."

"Franklin," Casey said, "can you get Haimes to go downstairs, and – this is important – get me into the stairwell next to the elevators?"

"The second is easy," Franklin told her, "but getting Haimes downstairs...out of his office for a minute I could do. But..."

"If you can get him out of his office," Key said, "I can get him into an elevator." She looked at Casey. "You don't have anything dangerous planned, do you? Nothing that would hurt him?"

"No," Casey reassured her, "but it may be scary for a bit, if you're there with him."

Key nodded and stood. "Franklin, go get our Mayor, would you?"

Franklin walked Mayor Haimes out to the main reception desk. Haimes, Casey thought, would be a large, barrel-shaped man. She'd never seen him, only heard him on the radio a few times. His voice seemed to fill the space, with a profound bass to it, and she'd just drawn her own mental picture. Instead, he stood barely five foot two and was wire thin. He favored, at least on this day, pinstripes and suspenders, which matched more of Casey's expectations – except they were all made of some slick, strange fabric she'd never seen instead of the old, worn cottons she'd assumed.

"What is this about an appointment?" he asked the receptionist. She shrugged, and Franklin insisted, and soon the three of them were going around this mythical appointment that the Mayor was supposedly late for. Before it could be chalked up to a simple error on Franklin's part, as it would be of course, Key hurried up to Haimes and grabbed his arm tightly. Casey nodded at Franklin, who then led her to the emergency stairs near the elevator bank.

"I need you to tell me which elevator they get in," she told him, "just kick the door gently once for A and twice for B." Franklin nodded and tried to look busy as he loitered by the elevators.

Key was well into her act by then. "...and Mister Mayor, your honor, if you can just...he's right downstairs..."

"Madame," Haimes said, exasperation clear in his voice, "I do *not* have time to go downstairs and talk to your nephew."

"But you must, he came all this way, all the way to Mur to meet you," she said, pleadingly.

"Wait, he *came to Mur*? I thought he was your nephew?" Haimes tried to work it through.

"Well, he's a natural Knocker, Your Honor, and I just thought..."

"No, I see, I see, and he isn't in the guild yet?" Haimes smiled. "Well, we should get him signed up. But surely you don't need me for that. There are procedures, there is protocol for this sort of thing, and—"

"Of course," Key agreed, "but still, Mister Mayor, it would mean so much to him."

"I can't just—" Haimes cut himself off and did the sort of internal math that politicians everywhere could do while sleeping. To wit: if the time spent talking someone out of a simple need could be cut down by just doing what they wanted, and it helped ensure a vote and/or favor later for something – bonus points for it being something technically, but not provably, illegal – you did the thing. "Very well, dear lady, let us go and meet this nephew of yours."

"Oh thank you, sir," Key said, and she took the Mayor's arm, leading him to the elevators.

Ferdinand kicked the door to the stairwell once before heading back to his office. Casey turned on her portable amp and set it on the floor. Pressing the box hard against the wall with her foot, she took a deep breath and started to play.

She had the amp dialed down, hoping that no one would be able to hear her from the office outside. She glanced around her, but saw no one on the stairs, either. The first part of her plan would be the simplest. A few harsh, discordant notes and the wall crumbled in a small circle right over the amp's speaker.

Now she'd just have to hope they couldn't hear her in the elevator car itself. The second part of her plan remained a bit trickier, and she considered her fingering carefully. Too sudden a build and she could kill both Key and Haimes. Too slow and the elevator cables would resonate and throw the car around in the shaft but not do much else. At best that would engage the brakes, but a simple reset would allow the car to resume its travel, and that wouldn't be enough time.

She focused her will into the quiet solo she played and closed her eyes. Vibrations rebounded and she shifted, feeling the information start to flow both ways. She could use the notes as a sort of sonar, rough but accurate enough for light sabotage.

Casey tilted her head unconsciously, making sense of what she could 'see.'

She kept playing, trying to make sure she would target the right spot, but sped up, knowing her time to pull this off would be short. A few chords, a flurry of notes up the fret board, and she targeted the elevator car's brakes themselves.

First they clamped down, shuddering the car to a short, jarring stop. But Casey didn't stop there. She kept playing, heating the brake mechanisms until they start to melt. Just enough to make it believable that a strange, friction-based accident could have happened, but more than enough to require a rescue mission that building security wouldn't want to perform themselves and would have to call for assistance with. That would eat enough time for Casey to check out Haimes' office. She hoped the Mayor liked making idle chitchat with Key.

Stowing guitar and amp where they belonged, Casey left the stairwell quickly, hoping to go unnoticed. She hoped in vain, as a security guard walked right up to her as she tried to get past the receptionist. He turned her away, having seen her enter the stairwell earlier, but she couldn't take an elevator as the alarm from the stopped car rang loudly and people busied themselves with trying to find out what happened.

The guard told her to stay put and she stood stock still as he walked away. The receptionist decided the elevator panic bored her when nothing new happened after an entire thirty seconds, so she turned her gaze to Casey instead, making sure she didn't try and sneak off again.

Casey smiled and nodded at her, counting in her head. Her count reached zero and...nothing. She forced herself to not sigh and was starting to work out a different plan when an alarm went off. Casey didn't let herself smile, either, forcing a fake look of shock along with everyone else's real ones. The fire alarm flashed and cried out and, after a few seconds, the sprinklers turned on. People started to run, while the guard, who had been helping see what could be done about the elevator, found the garbage can fire and tried to get everyone to remain calm and settle down.

Casey knew the small fire would have dislodged her tiny fire-starter kit: a small spare battery from the amp with some old guitar string connecting the negative to the positive and secured. The battery had been low enough in charge for the effect to take a bit to kick in, as planned, from when she'd dropped it in the can as she went to the staircase in the first place. Casey allowed herself a prideful smile as she hurried to Haimes' office.

The large corner office proved her last guess right, as there were no sprinklers raining down in it. Illegal, but who would call him on it, and he didn't want to risk ruining his paperwork in a false alarm such as the one going off now.

She dug through papers quickly, careful to make sure they went back where she found them, but saw nothing that might be of interest. Franklin was, of course, right. Haimes wouldn't leave something this big to risk an assistant finding it. A locked drawer, the lock easily picked even by Casey's early abilities, showed her more of the same, along with a gun and a bottle of rum. She shook her head – locking the gun away sounded like a smart idea right up until you needed it. Then you suddenly had to find your keys and manage to unlock the drawer all without the person who needed shooting working out your plan.

Locking up the rum she understood.

Casey felt she was out of time, and was considering leaving when she noticed a stack of papers she'd already flipped through. Her first glance had showed her nothing, but this time she noticed an invoice sticking out at an odd angle. She pulled it and confirmed what the partial bit of header meant – Haimes had hired nine Knockers, all for the same day. No one could possibly need that many Knockers on one day. The reason on the invoice itself was for 'FV Transport,' which made Casey laugh at how blind she'd been earlier in her initial rush. FV for Ferdinand Vink, of course. Subtle enough to pass unnoticed, she was sure, unless you went looking for it.

It felt right, it added up for her, but it did mean they'd have to go talk to Vink's men next. Before that, however, Casey straightened the office back up and hurried out, the sprinklers still going as she walked back down the hall.

They shut off just as she got back to the receptionist's desk, who glared at her angrily. "Where did *you* go?" she asked.

"Like running water's never made you have to pee?" Casey asked her. The guard came back, wet and frustrated, ushered Casey into the stairwell, and, along with another guard who met them on a lower floor, made sure she left the building.

About an hour later, Key walked into the diner near the bookstore Casey'd found her in earlier. She looked none the worse for wear and smiled as Casey waved her over. Sitting in a quiet corner, alone and undisturbed, they caught each other up. Key told Casey all about how she'd endlessly annoyed Haimes on principle, apologizing by the time they got out of the elevator that 'her nephew' must have gone home but promising to bring him around in a few days. Haimes had shaken his head, disenchanted against his better judgment, and waffled on agreeing to make a time to meet.

Casey explained the only information she'd found, and Key agreed Vink's office would have to be their next stop. Key wanted to ask a few people she knew and see if they could get information for them, but Casey favored going in there angry. After all, she had cause – no one would suspect her of having an ulterior motive past bringing the whole place down.

Truthfully, she wanted to. She wanted to hurt what Vink had left behind, the way she hurt. If she could do so and feel she also was going in with a good reason beyond that, even better. Key worried they would cause too much of a scene, but Casey pointed out that Vink, like Jake, wasn't exactly going to come back and hold it over either of them. Without him there, his entire organization would be in disarray and probably squabble its way to an early grave in the next few months.

"Actually," Casey said, "given that, do we even need to bother with any of this? Vink isn't here to push through the plan. So maybe it's worry over nothing."

"Unless Haimes has enough in motion to finish the plan. If he can get enough going, he doesn't need Vink, and it may even be worse without him – Haimes finding and destroying The Silent Heart by himself...honey, we can't take the chance."

"Then I think tomorrow we go through the front door and say hi."

Jake fell through bright-blue nothingness.

Well. No, he didn't. Not really.

First of all, not even Jake could really say he fell. Falling denotes both an up and a down to work properly, and Jake possessed neither at the moment. He didn't feel like he fell through anything, either. And yet, he had to admit there definitely seemed to be a motion, of some indiscernible sort. If pressed on the matter, Jake would demand that as far as direction remained concerning his falling, he fell in. Into what, and out of what, he could not articulate.

Blue nothingness also didn't quite mean what it seemed like at first. The blue light that had surrounded both Jake and Vink's hands in prior stops seemed to fill the space around them, now. Enlarged, however, Jake noticed the blue wasn't pure. Instead, the light was shot through with various colors. Streaks too small to notice along his hands could be seen in the wider field he moved through.

He squinted at the space around him, wondering if he breathed in air while he did. He didn't feel air moving, and yet his lungs worked. He exhaled and remained fairly confident that nothing happened when he did, except muscles moving from memory and expectation, but he felt fine.

The patterns, though – those Jake tried to see. He could have sworn – would have, if asked, in fact – that if he squinted just right, unfocused his eyes a bit, he could see people in the colored lines that shimmered around him. Whole cities' worth of people.

Which is when Jake thought of something else. The first times they'd traveled through this bright-blue nothingness that wasn't, Jake didn't have the capacity for rational thought. A third time though and he had started, in the way of many sentient beings, to simply get used to it. So he worked out what he could feel and see. He tried to shout but heard nothing, so there went that experiment quickly. He blamed the apparent lack of air, and tried to not let that acceptance trouble him.

And then Jake stuck out his tongue. Jake licked at the nothingness. And he tasted it. Worse yet, for him, he realized he could, somehow, taste it. After trying to gag, Jake licked at nothingness a second time and tried to catalog the taste. He knew the human tongue can only taste five basic tastes and the combinations were what made things taste like – well, like the things they were. Bitter, salty, sour, sweet, and savory were all he had to work with.

Except this nothingness tasted like a sixth thing, a thing without a proper name. Jake decided to name it blech, but then reconsidered, figuring blech was already a perfectly good name for quite a few combinations of the five he knew. He settled on plort, feeling secure that no one else had ever thought to think that something tasted very plort in the history of tasting.

Jake wanted to share this with Vink, though he couldn't speak, since no sounds seemed to work. He waved his arms, but Vink's eyes were closed tightly. Jake thought that silly; you might as well try and enjoy whatever you're in the middle of, even when it isn't enjoyable. That's how you found new things to appreciate. Vink's loss, Jake considered with a shrug. If he didn't want to be the second person to know the taste sensation plort then that would be his loss.

What Jake called plort was, he didn't realize, time. Jake was the first human being to lick, taste, and catalog the flavor of time.

"Where's Vink?" Casey demanded, pressing her boot down on the man's chest. She knew he wouldn't – hell, couldn't – have an answer. None of them did. They knew, word spread from Vink's driver, about Ferdinand and Jake vanishing.

Better still for Casey's purposes, word had also spread about her. She looked around Vink's office while the rest of his men decided what they wanted to do. Moving her foot, she nudged the guy on the floor with a toe. "Go, tell the rest of them I want five minutes, then I'll be gone. But if any of you come after me? I'll bring this building down, and you know I can." She jerked a thumb at the hallway leading to the office they were in: the plaster crumbled, shattered, the wood floor running, almost liquid. She held her guitar in one hand, by the neck, and waved it a bit. "We agreed?" she asked as he rose.

"Y-yeah," he said, backing out of the room and standing just past the door. "I'll, hey, I'll make sure no one bothers you, OK?"

"You're sweet," she said with a slight shrug. She tossed the desk and kicked open the locked drawers. Stealth wasn't exactly a priority. She moved slow enough to take in what she saw, but fast enough to come off as someone just looking to trash the place.

She found a folder with a copy of the same invoice she'd found in Haimes' office and flipped through the other pages. It looked confusing, but that felt about right. Cramming the entire folder into her guitar bag, she walked out of the office, trying to not laugh when the guy at the doorway flinched as she passed him.

Key waited outside, looking at purses in a nearby second hand store. Casey tapped her on the shoulder and they went into the back room, the owner being an old friend of Key's – like everyone else in town, Casey thought.

Casey spread out the contents of the folder on a table in the small back room. She and Key sat across from one another looking them over.

"So, doesn't being The Walker help at all? I mean, you tell me The Cat eats time, and The Silent Heart reflects the city and influences it...and you?" Casey asked as she read though a memo she realized had ended up shoved into the wrong folder.

Key set the paper she was studying down and looked at Casey. "Honey, I just try and make sure this is a good place to live, as best I can. I protect The Heart, of course, and I like to do right by the people – I love helping people, it makes you just feel good, knowing they pass it down."

"You protect The Heart, sure, but shouldn't you have some sort of ability, to help you?" Casey set a paper aside for further thought and grabbed another.

"Do I need one?" Key asked. "I seem to be doing all right so far," she said with a smirk.

"I didn't mean you weren't," Casey insisted, "just that it makes no sense to me."

Key nodded. "Does much in this town make sense to you, then? Because I find, honey, it's best to just live and let the rest sort itself out."

"I suppose, but even so—" Casey fell silent and slid a paper across the table to Key. Key took it, looked at it, and set it back down. "I don't get it," Casey said, "but—"

"I do get it, I think," Key told her, "and it's worse than I thought. Look here," she laid the paper between them and pointed, "the seven dots, connecting back to each other. But there're also lines outward that seem—"

"Those lines would converge too, if they went on for a while, yeah, I see it. But Haimes hired nine Knockers, not seven. So are we sure this is it? And if it is, hell, Key, *what* is it?"

"Seven Knockers for seven gates, honey," Key said softly, "two more for backup, if I had to guess. I mean, I do have to guess, so yeah, you want two more for back-up in case someone gets sick, or...or anything, really. Oh, honey, we have to stop this. This is bad. I'd bet this was Vink's part of the plan, and is probably still in motion. Yes," she said, considering, "this would let them...remember what I said before about their plan being able to destroy Mur?"

"Of course."

"This is worse."

"How can it be worse?" Casey asked. She studied the paper and tried to put the pieces together, but came up short.

"I'm pretty sure they intend to open all seven gates at the same time," Key said, tracing the links between dots inward.

"That happens all the time," Casey said. She looked at the other papers again, searching for more information. "So what's the problem?"

"They want to open them—see the outer lines, how they would link?" Key asked, tracing a finger along one. "This has to be it. They want to open them all to the same place and time."

"Wait, is that...is that a thing? What would that do?" Casey tipped her head back and looked at the cream-colored ceiling above, trying to imagine it. "Wouldn't that—"

"Collapse Mur in on itself? I think so, yes," Key told her.

"So how do we stop it?" Casey asked, then stopped herself. "Duh, we just stop them from doing it."

"Well, yes," Key agreed, "but I'm not sure how many we would have to stop. Would six Knockers doing it be enough? Five? Do you need all seven, or is that a precaution? The only thing I'm certain of here is that Haimes and Vink didn't know, either. This isn't something that's ever been done."

"The Exchanger coin," Casey said suddenly.

"I think so, yes," Key agreed, standing. "Let's not wait, the invoice says they've been hired for tomorrow night."

Casey and Key got out of the cab outside of the Knocker's office. Vink and Haimes used a firm popular among the rich; they tried to never ask questions and offered multiple Knockers under one roof for multiple trade-route use. Relay Knocking wasn't common, given the cost, but the shuttle of goods from an old time and place to a much later one could bring in big money if you could absorb the start-up costs.

Key flashed the Exchanger coin and asked to see the shift boss in reference to the invoice number they'd noted. Getting in to see her happened quickly, the Knockers happy to work with an Exchanger on their biggest contract in years.

"So Haimes needs adjustments?" the shift manager, Karla Ortega, asked. She looked over the paperwork they'd hastily filled out when they'd arrived. "The time isn't good, now? He expects us to reschedule everyone?"

"Well, just half of them," Key said. "For the next day. Delivery problems, you know how it is."

"I really don't," Ortega told her. She glared her way through the forms and pulled the schedules. "And you're here instead of Haimes' normal man, why?"

"We were in the area," Casey said, smiling, "offered to take care of this on our way. Always good to be owed a favor."

Ortega sighed. "Let me see that coin again."

Key passed it over and Ortega looked at it carefully, inspecting it from a few angles.

"It's real," Casey said, testily.

"Yeah, I got that," Ortega replied, "but here's the thing, it's also not yours."

"Excuse me?" Key said, leaning on the counter and smiling.

"Owner of this coin, I know him. You're not him. You don't work for him, either, and even if you did, before you try and tell me you're new or whatever," she said, sliding, Casey noticed, a hand along the underside of the counter between them, "he wouldn't give you the coin to use. Stealing an Exchanger coin is a serious crime."

She came up with a gun, pointing it at Casey, having decided Key was too old to worry about being a runner.

"Now, dear," Key said, "let's not do anything foolish."

"Like steal a coin?" Ortega replied. "No, you stay where you are and we'll let the cops sort this out."

"How have you done this for so long?" Casey asked Key, annoyed.

Key reached out, far faster than Ortega thought her age would allow, and slammed the woman's head against the counter. "I normally have more time," she said. "Leave the coin, we have what we wanted."

They left, quickly but calmly, and hailed another cab. "I saw the time, too, but won't she tell them and arrange for more security?"

Key shrugged. "Of course, and Haimes will call Vink, but one of his men will answer and cover for the boss. They'll claim to set it up and not have the details, most likely. I'd say we have a good chance at not running into too much security."

"And if we do?" Casey asked, then told the driver to get them to the nearest gate.

"Then we hope they'll listen to reason," Key said.

Jake and Ferdinand sat up in a field of grass. The grass itself was a small plot of dirt, just about big enough for them to lay down in, and dangerous next to the curb of a busy street. Jake rolled away and stood up, realizing they easily could have landed right in traffic and died before they'd known what happened.

"Vink, look, before you even get up," Jake said quickly, "if you don't try to kill me, we can work a way out of this. I know it. We're being tossed through time, sure, but there's something else, I'm positive."

"And what would that be?" Vink asked, standing and brushing his suit off. It'd seen better days.

"If I knew *that*..." Jake said, shaking his head. "But can we at least agree to not try and kill each other, for a little while?"

"Sure," Ferdinand told him, holding out a hand, "sure thing. Peace."

Jake reached out a hand to shake and felt no surprise as Vink yanked him forward and punched him right on the cut in his arm. Pain, annoyance, frustration—those things Jake felt, but not surprise. He doubled over, and then, as he started to straighten, before Vink could come around for a second blow, kicked out, catching Vink in the knee.

Vink dropped but punched out as he did, catching Jake in the side. Jake dropped to his knees and the two of them laid there in the grass and dirt a minute. By this time they were both covered in dirt from their various stops, and a little more wouldn't hurt. Vink's suit had a few tears in it, as did Jake's shirt and pants.

People passing by took a few steps around them, no one offering to help. Jake wanted to laugh. The indifference of people in cities seemed eternal, unless they were hoping to burn you alive for being a demon.

Jake and Vink fought, scrabbling and jabbing at each other with as much force as they could muster and all the discipline and training of schoolyard children. Jake rolled on top of Vink and started slapping, not punching, him. "If we don't," he said between slaps, "try to solve this, we'll just keep doing this bullshit!" He stood and looked at Vink, already getting to his feet, anger on his face. "Or worse, we won't, and we'll be stuck somewhere stupid!"

"I told you," Ferdinand said slowly, "I know how this ends, if I just ignore it. I die. This is my only play, Meyer – you won't talk me out of it."

"I don't want to kill you, Ferd," Jake said, his shoulders slumping as he said it. It was true. He really didn't want to. He saw no gain in it. Vink was an annoyance, and prone to stupid outbursts, but that didn't call for death. Jake just wanted to go home, hug Casey, make some tea, and relax. That was all. Instead, he thought ruefully, he was here, dealing with this.

"You're gonna have to, though," Vink said, "if you want to live. I'm fine if you don't, of course."

They stood, a few feet apart, for a minute, and then Jake turned and ran. He ran into traffic, looking around and realizing he recognized a few buildings. The revelation startled him enough that he almost got sideswiped by a car, the driver leaning on the horn until he'd driven well past Jake.

He tried to place the buildings. This wasn't Mur, the air just felt wrong – no, he knew they hadn't landed home. He glanced behind him to see Vink giving chase – not unexpected – and ran right into a woman on a bicycle, sending them both tumbling and scaping along the street.

"Fucker," the woman yelled, picking her bike up, "watch where you're going!"

"Sorry, avoiding death!" Jake yelled back as he started to run again. Mostly run. A limping run, at best, but his head start still held for the time. Looking around, trying to pick a good direction to run to, Jake placed the city. Provo, Utah – had to be. A friend, Richard Torbon, had showed Jake a picture of the giant, hundred-story–tall history museum they'd built there in the early 2200s. He'd wanted a mural of it in his living room and, stranger, wanted Jake to agree that the idea was a sound one.

Torbon didn't even come from Provo; he'd been born in Mur, just like Jake. Unlike Jake, he'd found himself obsessed with various other cities and times. Jake never did find out what the finished mural looked like. Supposedly the art would include other notable things Provo, like its new subway.

Jake smiled and looked for an entrance to the underground system. He couldn't remember if construction had finished before or after the giant museum. Nothing looked right for an entrance, though, and the smile started to fade.

It vanished completely when Vink landed on Jake's back and sent them through the glass of a bus shelter. Jake felt shards rip into him and his clothing, and he hit the ground hard. His knee slid along the pavement and torqued badly, forcing him to bite back a scream. Using the metal supports of the shelter, Jake got up, watching Vink putting shards of glass in his inner jacket pocket. In his other hand he held a single shard, wrapped in a cut piece of his shirt.

He lunged at Jake, slashing in a wide arc. Jake let himself stumble backwards, bringing his right leg up to kick at Ferdinand, keeping him away. Jake waited until Vink came across for another slice and dove in close, inside the arc of the swing. He punched out several times, as fast as he could, hitting Vink in the gut and solar plexus. Ferdinand doubled over and dropped the shard of glass. Jake crushed it under his heel and tried for an uppercut to Vink's jaw.

Vink took the blow square and leaned his mass forward, cutting off Jake's small window. He wrapped his arms around Jake's body and lifted, then shook him side to side. The move didn't hurt, or disorient much, but it confused Jake just enough so that when Vink suddenly dropped him, Jake hit the ground and crumpled before he knew what had happened.

Vink's shoe came down toward Jake's head quick enough that Jake wondered what the shape was right before it stomped into his forehead. Black flashed in front of his eyes, and he rolled onto his back.

As he did, he felt the world slip away, but couldn't be sure if it was a return to the nothingness or just blacking out. Right then, they were the same thing. He only hoped he would wake up from it.

Key and Casey stayed near a gate for a few hours, waiting for Vink's men to arrive with a Knocker. The Knocker pulled out a walkie-talkie and put an earbud in, so he could listen to it without broadcasting what was being said. Casey walked right up to the security detail, two meatheads looking unsure about what they were supposed to even be doing, and smiled at them.

They tried to wave her off, but she kept walking toward them, and as the mook in charge reached for something at his belt, Casey's foot connected with his kneecap, sending him to the ground.

"Keep to schedule," the other guard told the Knocker, who nodded, listening to his headset and looking at his watch. Key came around to try and talk to the Knocker, even as Casey tangled with the second guard.

He swung a fist she blocked, grabbing his wrist as it went past and yanking him forward, face-first into her elbow. Staggering only slightly, he grabbed her upper arm and pulled her close, wrapping his foot around her ankle to shove her off balance.

"Please," Key said to the Knocker, "don't do this."

"It's just a job, lady," he said, looking at his watch.

"It's worse than you think – this isn't a normal job."

Casey hit the ground ass-first, bruising her tailbone and scowling as the guard kicked out, thinking her that easy a target. "Now I'm just offended, you get me?" she asked him. He laughed, but only up until her legs scissored around his waist, her body flipping over and contorting as she came up on her elbows.

She threw her weight sideways and twisted her hips, flipping the guard as she threw him. Curling back into herself, Casey got up and axe-kicked him, dropping low to let her heel slam into his head as hard as possible.

Key reached for the Knocker, intending to hold him back, but he shook her off as his watch beeped, an alarm going off.

He reached for the gate.

Casey and Key yelled for him to stop, simultaneously, Key reaching out again to yank him away. She was too late.

He pulled open the gate.

Mur shook.

Jake woke up and felt his mouth full of grit. He spat a few times, wondering what had happened, and, most of all, why he hadn't died. After a few seconds he attributed the lack of death to the hill he'd fallen down. Vink had too, he noted, as the larger man lay there, on his side. They were both covered in dirt and torn clothes by now, and Jake, at least, felt it.

The air smelled fresher than he'd ever smelled it, and Jake took a second to look around. The area crept toward desert, sand underfoot and all around, but with the occasional scrub brush here and there. A stream ran nearby, but it seemed thin and sickly. There was a herd of animals drinking from it some distance away. Not far from them stood a wall. New and rising roughly twenty feet, the wall stretched in both directions, curving away in the shimmering sunlight.

Jake felt his heart beat faster. He'd never seen the wall from this side, but Jake knew it deep in his being. Mur. The wall fresh: constructed recently, he guessed. But no one saw the wall from outside because you could only enter through the gates, and those doors shifted. The outside of the wall remained a legend. Regardless, Jake knew it on sight.

He looked around more. The herd of animals crept closer, whether slightly domesticated or what, Jake had no way of knowing. They were small antelope, and they seemed underfed. Jake knew how they felt. He went to the stream and laid down on his stomach. Sticking his face directly into the cool, fresh stream, he drank slowly.

This was, he knew, wrong. Up until now, every jump had placed them square inside a city. Now they were not only outside a city, but outside Mur. Jake knew that looking for sense in a series of sporadic trips through nothingness wouldn't help, but the way they traveled – it remained slower, certainly, but still reminiscent of Mur itself. Well, evocative, to Jake, of how he felt Mur must travel. So why the change? Why now?

He sat up and watched the antelope, having forgotten, in his confusion and excitement about being near Mur, about Vink. He remembered when the larger man came growling up to him at speed, knocking into him. They tussled, Jake trying to make Vink see where they were.

"Damn it, this is Mur!" he shouted as he blocked a slow punch from Vink. They'd been chasing each other through time and space and neither had eaten, nor slept.

Ferdinand didn't care what Jake had to say, and didn't believe him, in any event. He kicked Jake in the ribs and laughed. "Mur, huh? Doesn't look like home to me. Maybe your apartment is this shitty, Meyer, but—"

"You asshole, look behind you," Jake said. He held his ribs and backed away from Vink, standing up and pointing.

"It *is*," Vink said, seeing the wall. "But that means..." He grabbed Jake and picked him up, bodily throwing him as far as he could. That turned out to not be too far, but Jake rolled and skidded on the sand, knocking into one of the antelope and causing the others to scatter. Then Vink turned and ran for the wall, looking for a gate.

Jake knew he needed to follow him, but the antelope he'd slammed into grunted in pain, and Jake took a deep breath. He looked at the animal and helped it to try and stand. Nothing seemed broken, but the antelope was obviously in pain. Jake glanced behind him, watching Vink find a gate and run through it.

One thing at a time. He helped the antelope to the stream, using his hands to cup up some water and offer it to the beast. His hands still glowed blue, and the antelope licked at the water and his hands, letting the kindness overwhelm instinct for a moment. Water wasn't the only thing the antelope drank in, licking at Jake's hands. Jake watched as the blue glow seemed to vanish from his hands and start to coat the antelope's face.

A word about this particular antelope. It had never felt like an antelope. Deep down, the others in the herd knew there was something different about it. First of all, it seemed to be fine with humans. The others would stray close, but never as much as this one did. This antelope only knew that the world was a thing for it to play with and explore. Still, its body always felt wrong for the job. Fast and sleek, to be sure, but it couldn't understand why the other antelopes never seemed to want to hang out with humans, forcing affection from them. The antelope liked the silly creatures, all gangly and wobbly. She felt sure they would give her food if she hung around enough.

The blue glow made the water taste strange to the antelope, but in a good way. It wanted more. Licking at Jake's hands, the antelope felt a change begin to grow inside it. It felt stronger and stranger, at the same time.

Jake didn't really notice, assuming the blue glow was just starting the normal blinking phase as it had every other trip. Seeing the antelope looked better, he patted its head and ran toward the gate Vink had used.

The antelope followed. Jake heard the movement and held the gate for it, shrugging. If an antelope wanted in, well, why not? Who was he to say no? Once inside Jake laughed, seeing Mur. No Spire at full size – the center of the town could be still seen as the biggest building, but it was only a large temple. These were, Jake knew, the earliest days of Mur.

He saw Vink not too far away, confused and in awe himself. Jake went toward him with an idea. They just had to find The Cat. Jake couldn't explain why, but he was sure The Cat already lived in the city. He was both right and wrong.

The antelope wandered away from Jake, then broke up into a run, exploring the city quickly as the energy it'd drank coursed through its body. The first wave hit hard, and the antelope disintegrated into glowing blue dust.

Seconds later it reformed itself, into a small cat. This felt right; for the first time in her life, the antelope, not a cat, felt its body and shook it, feeling at home. Then the energy hit again. It exploded out and The Cat's face got lost, now only a glowing blue focal point for the energies contained inside it. But the burst, digested and vomited by a reshaped Cat, spread through Mur and unhinged it. The city broke free of time and space as The Cat meowed happily, becoming itself.

Mur shook.

Casey held onto Key as the gate opened and the city trembled. "We have to close it!" Key shouted.

"No, really?" Casey shot back. The Knocker had vanished in a spray of red mist that drifted around the open gate. "What happened?" "Opening all seven gates to the same moment and place, the Knockers suddenly all occupied the same spot at the same time," Key said. "That doesn't end well."

Casey struggled to move forward, the forces whipping through the gate pushing against her. "Well, all we have to do is close—"

"Don't touch the door!" Key shouted. "They're all still connected."

Casey let the force push her back to where Key stood, sheltering the old woman from the waves of wind and energy spilling from the gate. "If we can't touch the gates we can't close them," she said, "so what do we do?"

"I don't know," Key admitted. "Right now Mur is stable," she said as the ground shook again.

"This is *stable*?"

"In maybe an hour max I'm pretty sure the entire city will collapse into a singular point," Key said. "But for now the city is anchored in one spot. It isn't moving, but the energy, it's built to move the city constantly. Plus the—"

"Explain later, fix now. How?" Casey asked. She hit her amp on, with an elbow, and grabbed her guitar. "I could generate some force and push them closed, maybe."

"You'd need a lot of force," Key said, "and that much counterforce could shatter the gate, and right now that gate is all gates."

"Great," Casey said, squinting against the winds that were picking up even more speed. "So then *what*?"

"We find you a really big speaker, and hope," Key told her.

Casey opened and closed her mouth a few times, and then thought about where to get a big enough speaker. The Alibi, sure, but there would be no way to get it, lug it back to a gate, find a way to power it...not in the time they seemed to have.

Key struggled to walk, the constant winds still growing. Around them Mur trembled and wheezed, the wind tearing through the entire city with raw anger. She struggled to get to the curb and held onto a car. She fished a flat, folded bit of metal out of her bag and clicked it into place, shoving it between the window and the seal of the car she held.

"We're stealing cars, now?" Casey asked, going over to help.

"Don't help, get into the car behind this one," Key said.

"I can't jimmy—"

"Then break the glass!" Key yelled, wrenching the door to the car open and cramming the refolded metal back in her bag.

Casey shrugged and put a foot through the driver's side window of the car. "Why are we—"

"Cars have speaker systems, right?" Key asked. "So if we—"

"We don't have time to crosswire a bunch of cars, much less the wire to do it," Casey said, reaching in and popping the hood of the car. "But I have an idea – pop the hood on that thing, will you?"

Key did, and she watched as Casey also popped open the trunk and went rooting around in it. She came back around with a small toolbox, "Thankfully these people think ahead," she said loudly, and ducked under the hood. A few minutes – and much grunting – later, the hood dropped, hitting Casey on the back. She seemed to expect it, however, and reached out to grab either side of it with a hand, lifting it and walking it a few feet before dropping it on the sidewalk.

"Now for yours," she said, coming over to Key and ducking under the hood of that car. Key watched her sweat and pull to loosen and undo the bolts holding the hood on and repeat her surgery, dropping the second hood near the first.

"All right, Key, this is gonna suck but I need your help," Casey said. "I'll soften them, but I need you to stand on each hood in turn and pull it, bend it. Crescent."

Key nodded, stepping onto one of the hoods and reaching down to grab an edge along the longer side of it. Casey grabbed her guitar again, amp already primed, and walked around the hood, facing Key, and started to play.

Melting the metal would have been easy, but was impractical for her needs. It also would've melted Key, so that was right out. Casey focused her will into the guitar and played a slow, steady set of notes, choosing a minor scale to work in. The wind, the chaos, and the shaking around them made it harder and harder to keep playing both soft and slow, but Casey closed her eyes and felt the notes as they left the amp on her hip.

Key strained, pulling at the hood. She ducked her head against the onslaught of the guitar's energy hitting, as well as everything else around her. Slowly the metal started to bend, feeling soft but not hot.

Casey took a deep breath and opened her eyes. She saw Key standing, mostly blocked by the bent hood. "Now the other one," she said, feeling the effort she'd spent deep in her bones and knowing that it was nothing compared to what she would be trying soon.

Manny Harper tried to not cry. His mom told him to be strong, and brave, and he intended to do what she said. But the building shook, and outside the wind howled, rattling the glass of the windows. He curled into a ball under the kitchen table, his favorite hiding spot.

His mother crawled under the table with him, after a few minutes, and held him close. She whispered to him, kind, gentle things to try and calm him, but Manny knew the score. The city was angry. It hurt: the sound of the wind and the building itself groaning was a sound of pain.

Manny wanted to be brave. He wanted to help the city. So he tried to leave the safety of the kitchen table and make his way to the window. His mother reached for him, missing by inches. She called after him, following quickly to scoop him up, but Manny fought back. "We have to make the city not hurt," he insisted.

His head started to hurt, and he would have sworn he felt something pressing against his eyes. The gates, his mother had explained to him, just a few weeks ago, let people pass in and out of the city. She'd talked about other places, and of being careful to never go without permission or he wouldn't be able to come home. Manny could feel it, though. He would. He would be able to come back whenever he wanted, if he needed to. He could feel, from his kitchen, the gates, crying in pain.

He thought hard about calming them, not knowing he was a Knocker, linking to the city far too early.

Other Knockers, more experienced than Manny, felt the same pain and worse as Mur locked itself down to one location, with all the gates connecting back to themselves. The city shuddered not only physically, but spiritually and emotionally as well. Knockers fell to the ground writhing in pain; ordinary citizens were hit by debris knocked loose by the shaking and sent spinning by the winds. Somewhere, a Heart normally Silent became Loud, screaming its pain back into Mur and amplifying it, unable to contain itself.

Key bent the second car hood back while Casey played. They worked as fast as they could, sweating and feeling every second tick by as if death itself worked as their step counter. The two hoods curved, Casey ran over to them and rolled them until they sat together, touching and overlapping as best they could. She took a deep breath. She started to play again.

This time the hoods both heated, melting at their contact points and merging into one. She rolled them over and did it again at the other seam. Casey wanted to throw up, or curl into a ball on the side of the street and sleep. She, instead, continued to play. Every note ripped energy from her, forced her will down a wire, converted it, and drained her.

She stopped playing and swayed on the spot. Key came over, resting a hand on her arm. "Honey, we can't stop yet."

"I know," Casey said, "and I'm not. Just thinking it through."

"What's next, then?" Key asked. The Walker also felt near the point of dropping. Normally, though Casey might not know it, Key drew energy from the city to keep going. She refused right now, given the fragile state of things, and was feeling older by the second. If she had to give her life to the city, she would, without hesitation, but she refused to go quietly and without a fight.

Casey tried to roll the metal structure until the wider end pointed at the open city gate. Key helped as best she could, and they got it there, wind whistling through to the small end and coming out stronger.

Shaking her head, Casey wedged the tiny portable amp into the smaller mouth and hoped the wind wouldn't dislodge it. She stood away from it and looked upon her craftwork. The bent metal horn she'd built should, she hoped, amplify the volume of her amp by enough to affect the gate against the forces keeping it open.

Casey also hoped the device, if it could be called that – maybe the scrap heap in the shape of hope would be better – could survive the forces coursing through it in both directions long enough to get the job done.

"Get back," Casey told Key, "I mean, maybe the next block over."

"Oh no, honey, I don't think your energy can do this alone," Key replied, standing next to Casey.

Casey nodded and began to play, one foot up to brace the amp and hold it in place. She could feel the thing quiver as the wind thumped against it, and she had a sudden, fearful image of it blowing out of place and tearing her foot clean off.

The makeshift metal amplifier worked, and Casey's music ripped through it, coming out painfully loud. She played faster, willing everything she had into it, trying to push the gate closed.

Swallowing hard, Casey struggled, playing and feeling the energy of the ripped hole in everything fight back. Key put her hand on Casey's shoulder, fighting to stay upright herself, and concentrated. Pushing the energy of Mur through herself and into Casey didn't come easy. That energy kept her alive, after all, as well as Mur itself. Spending it might mean killing the city faster even as they saved it, but she couldn't think of a better option.

The door started to budge, pushing aback against the forces keeping it open. Casey could see it shimmer, all seven doors overlapping and changing places as they still occupied the same space. Beyond the doors she thought she saw movement, possibly a group of people. She tried to make out details, straining against the wind and swirl of doors occupying the same space, and could swear they were a group, armed.

"Don't break the gate!" Key yelled, trying to be heard over the noise. Casey heard her but didn't bother to reply. She figured Key wouldn't know how much force that would take, so the advice only served to make her paranoid.

She kept playing, feeling the guitar get hot in her hands as she focused down into it, willing the notes of her solo to shift into physical, aimed force. The gate twitched, the physical mass of the door creaking loudly enough that Casey could hear it. She wanted to back down the force for fear of shattering it but knew more force would be needed to close it. The group she saw moved closer. She wanted to yell at them to back off, but they kept coming. She realized they intended to cross through, not understanding what would happen.

Shifting her solo to chords, she played the bridge of a song she hadn't finished yet and tried to widen the area of her push to take in the entire gate. If she could press against all of it at once, like a giant hand, maybe everything would stay in one piece.

The group on the other side kept getting closer. They approached the door.

And then: red mist.

Casey winced at the sight and ducked her head to focus. The guitar continued to heat, something Casey hadn't had happen before. Her hands hurt, holding it, and where it rested against her body she only wanted to fling the thing away from her but instead leaned in, curling her body about the guitar further.

Notes started to shift, and Casey realized the strings felt loose, becoming slack. The heat, she cursed to herself, was messing with them. She didn't have much time – not that there were oodles left laying around *before*, but now she felt the pressure in whole new ways.

She played harder, letting notes ring and using the time to retune strings not in use. It shifted the solo, sending her out of sync with intent, and the force coming through the makeshift speaker dipped.

One deep breath, then a second. Casey centered herself, took everything she was, everything Key added to the mix, and her own love of Mur, and she sent it down her arms to her fingers, playing one last, desperate flurry of notes.

The notes rang out, and Casey felt the vibrations pour out into the world. Through the pain, and the love, she sent, she also felt it all return. Mur sang back to her, in ways she couldn't articulate, and for a moment everything was connected through her. Gathering it up, everything she offered, and the energy and spirit Mur gave in return, Casey felt the shift of power, and released it.

The gate slammed shut.

The wind and noise stopped.

Mur stood still and calm.

"Casey?"

She heard the voice and tried to respond but couldn't. Her hands hurt, her chest and abdomen felt cold, and she realized she was laying on the ground. Opening her eyes took effort. She did it anyway.

Her head lay in Key's lap, the older woman cradling her gently. Casey shifted, feeling embarrassed, and sat up. The wave of dizziness made her reconsider, but she held the line against the forces of inner-ear wobbling. "So," she said thickly, "that sucked."

"You're not going to ask if it's all OK, or if you did it?" Key asked.

"We're alive, city's not destroyed, I worked it out," Casey said.

"Just, I feel like people normally ask those things," Key said, shrugging and standing. She helped Casey up, grabbing her upper arm, and being careful of her hands.

"People with no sense of perspective or ability to look around, I guess," Casey said. "Though, we are sitting here discussing this all *far* too calmly."

"I wanted to distract you," Key admitted.

Casey looked around, now worried. She spotted it quickly. Her guitar. Melted, already cooled, but run along the street, twisted out of shape for good. She looked for the amp in her makeshift cone. She could see where it had exploded, leaving scorch marks along the metal of the cone. The cone itself had split its hasty seams.

But the guitar. Casey reached for it gingerly and stopped when she saw her left hand. The fingers seemed to jut out at strangle angles, though they only ached. She could see much of the skin blistered, and checked her right. Similar burn marks, but the fingers at least worked.

"I think only two of the fingers are broken – you were twitching the others while you were out. They're probably just dislocated," Key said quickly.

"Great," Casey said. She felt the cold pit of fear about broken fretting fingers, but pushed it deep as she stared at her guitar instead. The instrument had been her closest, oldest friend. It'd seen wars, and helped her learn to convert anger into music in a healing way as well. The guitar was one of the only things she'd kept from her time outside Mur, the others being her notebooks.

She refused to cry. She laughed at herself, internally, instead, for refusing to show normal human weakness out of an expectation that it would make her seem less capable to people around her.

"Know how to set fingers?" she asked Key after a while.

"I don't make a habit of it, but yes." They walked over to one of the cars that now stood without a hood.

Casey set her hand down and closed her eyes tightly. "Just do it quick, huh?"

Key started with the fingers she felt fairly certain were unbroken, grabbing and jamming them back into place one by one. Casey only turned her head to vomit once, and managed to not scream at all until Key set the broken fingers, ring and pinky.

Casey wasn't even sure if she did scream, at first. She felt the memory of screaming, could feel the burn of it in the back of her throat, along with the acid of vomit, but didn't remember the scream itself.

Leaning heavily against the car, Casey unslung her guitar bag, now useless to her, and cut part of the strap off with her string trimmer. Key wrapped the broken fingers for her as best she could. "So what really happened?" Casey asked.

"The broken fingers were—"

"Not to me, to Mur."

"The connected gates, the doors, they stabilize the city, but the energy that keeps it drifting needs to keep moving or it will pool. And that's—"

"Bad, yeah, I noticed. So how could that be a good plan, destroying the city, if they wanted to control it?"

"I don't think," Key said, chewing on the idea, "either Haimes or Vink actually knew what would happen. They probably assumed it would simply stop the city, and weaken The Heart. For all I know, Vink had another part of the plan in there."

"I'll bet – I think I saw it," Casey said.

"Really?" Key asked. "What did—"

"On the other side of the gate, I could see a bunch of people. I think they tried to come through. Vink may have wanted to bring in a small army of his own to take control of the city."

"And they..." Key shook her head sadly.

"Reduced to a bloody mist, like the Knockers," Casey confirmed. "No one thought this through."

"There was no way to," Key said.

"Let's not find excuses for the bastards, let's just go stop Haimes. If The Heart was weakened by this—"

"He was."

"Then we need to stop Haimes still," Casey said, pushing off the car with her forearms.

"Not yet," Key said.

"What? Why not?" Casey looked at the wreckage around them.

"Well, for one thing," Key said, looking at Casey's hands, "you need medical attention. We can't stop Haimes if you can't use your hands at all. You couldn't tie a shoe, right now."

Casey didn't want to agree, but she had to. "And for another?" she asked, hoping her own injuries weren't going to cause the city to die.

"Haimes still has to find The Heart. If Vink did have an army ready to invade – a dumb plan, sure, but still, if they were counting on it—"

"Then Haimes will wonder where it is. He still thinks Vink is *alive*," Casey said. "But shouldn't we move now to stop him? Why let him plan, and get closer?"

Key held an arm out to hail a cab. "I need to check in with The Heart myself," she admitted. "See how bad the damage is already. Start the healing process, if possible."

"If possible?" Casey asked as a cab stopped. "So you mean..."

"I mean I hope, honey, we're not looking at worst case. Take a few hours. Bandage yourself, some ointment maybe—"

"I have things, don't worry," Casey told her, getting in the cab alone.

"Good, I'll call you in a few hours, then."

"If I don't answer, call The Alibi," she said as Key closed the door for her. "I might need help, at first."

"That's not a bad thing, honey," Key said, "help is a goodness in this world."

Mur began its wandering through space and time as Jake watched. Vink, he could still see, leaned heavily on a small building that still shook. Most of the town still shook. The rocking came and went in waves, the city being gently tossed around like an egg rolling along a counter. Jake only hoped they didn't tip over the edge. Then he laughed; he knew they didn't. Mur would survive, because it already had.

He stopped and considered, though: were there stories of quakes and collapses from the start of the city? He thought possibly, but also knew the city stood some sixteen thousand years old. Not all history survived correctly. Well, no time to worry about being hit by a falling building, Jake decided. You just couldn't worry about everything, every time. Pick and choose. Right then, he chose Vink.

He raced for the man, leading with his shoulder. Slamming into Vink, Jake pinned him against the wall of the small stone building Vink'd been leaning against. Calling it a building was generous, though – really it was a single room, ringed by stones stacked and sealed with mud. Nothing in its construction came with designs of withstanding the force of two grown men falling into it with force, so they went through the wall easily.

They tumbled over each other, a jumble of limbs that helped no one. Jake's foot ended up in a cooking fire, and he yanked it out, yelping. Vink took the opportunity to slam an elbow into Jake's face.

He'd had enough. "That's it, Vink, you want me to kill you? Fine, I'll kill you!" Jake raged. He snapped. Something in him broke then and he knew, even as it did, it wasn't a thing that could be fixed or replaced.

So be it, he decided.

"No, Meyer," Vink said, struggling to get on top of Jake, "I want you to die."

"Whatever," Jake snarled, headbutting Vink after he said it. The two men continued to fight, earnestly, for their lives, not noticing that around them, Mur settled. Blue flashes still swept through the city but they grew dimmer, and the shaking stooped.

They vanished.

They both landed from a small drop onto a street. Jake looked around and inhaled sharply. Mur. He could feel it. Close enough to his own time to make his heart ache. But first he had to deal with Vink.

"We could've done this right. We didn't have to fight," he said, calmly. He felt the cold, calm certainty now. It scared a corner of him, but that small part sat and waited, knowing it wasn't in charge now.

"One of us has to die," Vink said. He realized, seeing Jake on top of him, how he looked, where they were. He craned his head back and saw himself, watching. He knew, then, how it would end and gave in, playing his part. He struggled to get up and stood facing Jake.

Vink reached in his jacket for the largest remaining shard of glass in there. How it could have remained in one piece he didn't know. Terrible, ugly luck, he supposed. He stabbed out with it, knowing what came next.

Jake grabbed his wrist, exhaling as he did, remembering what Casey had showed him. He wrenched the wrist sharply, twisting, and picked the glass up. He held it in his hand, feeling it bite, sliding apart skin. Jake Meyer thought about it and knew Vink had been right. One of them had to die, and he didn't want it to be him. He stabbed down, once, hard, sliding the shard between Vink's ribs and into his heart.

"You win, Vink. We're both dead, now. You bastard," Jake said softly, leaning over the man as he started to fall to the sidewalk.

"Boys, get him!" Vink roared in the distance. Jake looked up. Cursing to himself, he dropped the part of the glass that'd broken off in his hand and ran. Some of Vink's men gave chase, but Jake knew the city better than they did, and he remembered a small basement entrance that the shop owner above never locked. He slid inside, closing the door quickly, but carefully, behind him.

As Jake stood there, in the darkness of the basement, everything clicked. Why Vink had been after him, why he'd remained so certain of his need to kill Meyer, all of it. And he hated it, even as he wanted to laugh. The problem, he thought, now, was how he would get back home. Home in time, not only space, he corrected. Only one thing to do.

He waited another few minutes and left the basement. He went in search of The Cat.

Casey sat with Oscar in the loft. She'd gone right to The Alibi, knowing Oscar's shift wouldn't start for another half hour, and grabbed the man to help her. She couldn't, just then, even get her own keys out of her pocket to open the door.

Oscar got her the ointments she directed him to. He laughed at the field box Casey kept medical supplies in and she went cold and stiff, hearing only echoes of Jake. She tried to hide it, but Oscar caught the note and asked what'd happened.

That was when Casey broke down laughing for a solid three minutes and change. Eventually she told him, leaving out ninety percent of it, focusing only on the Jake-and-Vink-vanishing part. Oscar doubted it, at first, but could see that Jake was very much gone and Casey believed it with everything she had. It was enough to convince him. Belief, like guilt and some moister forms of cake, could be contagious.

As he coated her hands with a strangely scented lotion, then wrapped them in cloth bandages, they talked. Oscar helped resplint her fingers with actual splints as she talked about how much she just missed Jake. The hole he'd left. How she thought she could feel him, still, but not in a way that made any sense to her.

"How long until you can use your hands?" he asked after a while.

"I already can," she said, "except the broken bits. The burns, those will fade in a few days, but the pain's gone and should stay that way. That ointment, where I come from, is Gov issue. Field medic stuff, meant to return you to active duty with severe burns, worse than these, within a few hours. Why?"

"Can you drink while it's working?" he asked.

"Good idea, I'll get my coat – and you have to work anyway, huh?"

"Exactly. Always gotta mess up my hours. Pain in my ass."

Casey shrugged on a jacket, trying to move her hands as little as possible. Oscar opened the door and stepped over the threshold into the hallway. Casey looked for where he'd tossed her keys and then started to look around for her guitar bag before remembering she'd lost that, too, today. "Love you, too, Oscar."

"Let's get you and whiskey reunited," he said as she locked the door behind them.

"I'm still working," she said, "so only one."

"Working at that job you can't explain?"

"Oh, I could," she told him, shaking her head, "I just won't. Not yet. Only one crazy thing a day and I think we're up to seven so far, all right?"

"All right," he agreed.

Jake wandered around Mur, confused. He'd lost the guys following him, but his hands, he noticed, had stopped glowing. No other leaps seemed likely. He'd served his purpose, if that was actually a thing, and helped create Mur, he guessed? Or maybe that was a knock-on effect. For all he knew The Cat just really disliked Vink. Or the entire thing had been some big cosmic fuckery that he'd ended up tangled up in for no good reason.

None of the why mattered to Jake. What mattered would be getting back to where he belonged. He could, he supposed, just wait it out – hide until the day he knew he vanished then walk back and yell surprise, or whatever it was people who had been time-tossed did when they returned. Wandering around, waiting, seemed like the wrong move, however.

From Jake's point of view, sitting around in hiding would just be a waste of time. Finding The Cat and getting sent back, hopefully ending his brief fling with being tossed through time, made sense. He took a deep breath and thought it through from the top again.

Find The Cat. Not easy, but, sure, move ahead with the plan from there. Convince The Cat to zap him again. Doable, he figured. But how to get zapped to the right place and not flicker around again? Why wouldn't The Cat just send him somewhere random? The idea had more holes in it than a pegboard. Jake still thought it would work. He couldn't even explain to himself why, outside of one core glimmer of bad logic: he believed it would.

Step one remained finding The Cat. Jake wandered, refusing to call out for The Cat. That didn't work too well with cats in general, but one without a name would leave Jake just yelling the word 'Cat!" over and over. He laughed at the idea but didn't give in.

Instead, he did what many people of faith had done before him in the history of the planet: he sat down and waited for faith to reward him, blindly. He crossed his legs, cleared his mind, and closed his eyes. Sitting in an alley, Jake waited, patiently, for the universe to reward him. After only a few minutes, it did.

Well. Sort of. If you squint.

Someone kicked him in the leg, cursed him out, and told him to move. He took it as a sign. He got up and moved. He started to wander, realizing how much he missed Casey. He could go see her, but then he'd also see himself, and he knew he hadn't done that. Even if he managed to catch her without himself around, she would've mentioned.

He imagined how it would go. He would show up, explain what happened, and tell her to not tell the other him who hadn't left yet. She would tell him anyway because that's not the sort of thing anyone actually keeps to themselves, and then everything fell apart. He knew he hadn't been warned. So he couldn't go see her now.

Jake possessed no good idea of what would happen if he did create a paradox like that. The only ideas he could summon up about it were all bad, in fact. So he stayed away. But he could, nevertheless, feel the ache from knowing Casey was out there and had – or rather, relative to where he stood right then, would soon – see him vanish.

He hated the idea. Hated that she probably thought him dead. The anger he felt at how she must hurt, and at how he hurt, built. He turned it inward for a minute or two, and then back out, toward Mur itself. Mur the Eternal, as street proclaimers would shout. Mur the everlasting, the city he loved and had grown up in and that caused as much heartache for him as it did joy. More, possibly.

Would it have been true of anywhere, or anywhen, he could have lived? Possibly. Probably, even. But, Jake knew, the facts involved would have at least made more sense to the rational mind. Jake Meyer wanted to hate Mur but couldn't, quite. Or, sure, he could be angry at the city in short bursts, but even then he came back around. Jake found himself excusing and forgiving the town for its sins.

He sighed.

Then he sighed again, liking the feeling. Expelling the anger and sadness and confusion. He tried to rid himself of all of it and find the faith that, he could swear, had coursed through him only seconds ago.

He could feel it, that shine of faith, at the edges of his mind. He focused on it and just leaned against a wall, staring at nothing, while he thought about it. Which is when he heard the meow.

Mur, like any urban environment, found itself infested with cats. Millions of them, literally, skulking around the streets and fending for themselves. You learned, fairly fast, to ignore the occasional cat noise. Sure, Jake listened for cats in trouble, but a perfectly normal meow – nothing to care about. He stayed there, staring at nothing for a good minute.

Then he looked around for the source of the noise, giving in to hope against his better judgment. That kernel of faith lit up and he reluctantly followed it. And saw a blue glow. He hurried to the corner where The Cat sat, licking its own ass.

Jake stopped himself from getting too close, choosing instead to sit on the street, close enough that he knew The Cat could hear him and walk over if it wanted, but far enough that he didn't come off like a threat.

"Hey," he said softly, patting the sidewalk next to him, "you and me, we should talk. I don't know if you remember me, from any of this – or care, either way." Jake took a deep breath as The Cat looked up at his words, the blue glow of its face shining on him, but not doing anything insofar as moving him around in time went.

"You took me from someone," Jake told The Cat, "and hey, you had your reasons – or not, I suppose, since you're a cat and all – but either way, I want to go back. Back to her, back to my life. I know you *can* send me there. That much is obvious, I think, to both of us."

Jake reached a hand out for The Cat to sniff. He held utterly still while The Cat made up its mind and slowly, so painfully slowly, inched over to sniff at him. If it sniffed him at all, since it didn't seem to have a face. Jake marveled that the glow didn't seem to secretly obscure The Cat's face, but actually replace it. The more he knew, the less he understood, he thought, and wanted to laugh but held still and silent.

The Cat sat down next to him, not inviting attention, but not shunning it, either. Jake slowly moved his hand, running it down The Cat's back. A purr, then more of the same, only louder. "So," Jake asked, "can we work this out?"

The Cat turned its face toward him and yowled briefly, causing Jake to yank his hand back and go ridged once more. The blue light of The Cat's face glowed brighter, and Jake squinted. "I mean," he said, trying to hide his nervousness, "if you ever need anything, you let me know. Seems fair, right?"

As he faded out of time, Jake closed his eyes tight and hoped he would land somewhere even close to where he belonged, and most importantly with Casey, in Mur. He took notice, as he thought it, of the order of those two, and smiled to himself as he went.

Casey sat at The Alibi's bar as Oscar started his shift. She nursed a whiskey, taking small sips of it between thoughts. Rhona came up to her, clipboard in hand.

"Case, you playing tonight?" Rhona ran a finger down the page on the clipboard quickly, double-checking something. "Feels like you haven't signed on for a night in a bit."

"I just did a night," Casey told her.

"Yeah, but you didn't sign on for any more, did you?" Rhona checked again, flipping a few pages down in the stack trapped by the clipboard, huddled together in fear of over-administration of their contents.

"It's been hectic," Casey said, "and it'll be a few before I can again," she added, holding up her bandaged hands.

"Oh shit, what happened?"

"Long story," Casey said, taking a sip of her drink, "but I'll be back in form soon, promise."

"I am holding you to that," Rhona said, "but also, can you do me a favor?"

Casey nodded, "Of course."

"Stop pulling my floor manager and bartender out of the place whenever you or Jake feel like it? He has a job, I swear."

Oscar laughed, turning toward the women. "Boss, I don't miss shifts."

"You vanish during them, and always for these two," Rhona said.

Casey bit her tongue, almost hard enough to draw blood, to stop from going into her need to use Jake in the past tense now. She glanced at Oscar and he picked up on it. There'd be time later.

"It's called taking a break. I'm allowed breaks," Oscar insisted.

Rhona shrugged. "Could you at least try to take these breaks close to the bar?"

"I'll stop pulling him away," Casey said.

"See, Oscar, she gets it," Rhona said.

"No, she just wants you to go away," Oscar shot back.

"Hey now, I'm not getting in the middle here," Casey said, holding up her hands. "Injured woman here, begging out of the fight."

"Your hands aren't the problem—" Rhona started.

"They are to me," Casey told her.

"You know what I meant."

"We both know what you meant," Oscar said, trying to keep his tone light, "but fine, Boss, I'll try to stay close to home base – when I'm not hunting food, at least. Deal?"

"So you're saying," Rhona said, seeing how she was losing the fight, "you'll take your lunches by eating at their place?"

They all laughed, feeling the argument diffuse around them. "You just gave me an idea," Oscar said.

"You're bad for business," she told Casey. "And you," she looked at Oscar, "are a terrible employee."

"Yup," Casey agreed lifting her drink in salute.

Oscar laughed again and chimed in, "We try, Boss."

Hezekiah Eccles wiped the blood from his hands onto his apron. The amount of washing it took to clean the aprons to something resembling white annoyed Hezekiah pretty much daily. He wiped his hands a second time and put on a new pair of disposable gloves. What he could never work out, and he thought about it a lot, was exactly how so much blood got under the gloves, no matter what he did. Shaking his head at the stupidity of it all, he grabbed his cleaver and went back to separating ribs.

He'd worked as a butcher his entire adult life, taking the shop over from his mother when she got too old to keep working. He supported her, happily he might add, and still made enough to keep the place open.

Working as a butcher in Mur presented interesting challenges. No good, wide land for raising animals existed in the city anymore, so butchers had to pay Knockers for a constant stream of fuel for the mill. Twice a week Hezekiah accepted deliveries of entire sides of beef, chickens by the crate, and pigs by the dozen. It drove up the price, to be sure, but while many markets paid Knockers to bring in pre-butchered meats along with vegetables and other necessities, there were still enough people who wanted fresher cuts in town.

So Hezekiah got up at the crack of dawn every day, as his mother had before him, and accepted deliveries when they came, and cut meat taken from the large cold-storage room in the back of the shop.

He'd learned to change into a slightly cleaner apron by the time he opened fully for business. Customers liked to see a little blood on his apron – it made them feel he really worked for their money and that the cuts were truly fresh. Too much blood, though, and they nervously ordered a bit less, and left faster. Too much blood felt like a crime scene, his mother said.

She would also point out that the customers who seemed to prefer it when the aprons carried too much blood were the customers no one wanted. They were either criminals or just had a thing for a lot of blood, and, either way, you wanted them out of the shop. Hezekiah felt that might be unfair to lump them all that way, but he found he'd taken it to heart regardless.

He looked at the counter and realized he'd need another set of roasts to put out for the day. He took off his gloves, threw them away, wiped his hands reflexively on his apron, and headed to the back room.

Oscar poured Casey another drink. She sipped it and stared at the phone. They'd fallen into silence not long after Rhona left them, Casey trying to get the memory of Jake out of her head. Oscar left her to her silence, knowing she would talk when ready and not wanting to push his friend.

He could feel the dark days ahead of her and aimed for winning the long game, helping her as needed out the other side of grief. Not that, he knew, this sort of sorrow ever faded fully. So he stood around, serving other regulars and making sure to drift by her field of vision every few minutes, just in case.

The door to The Alibi opened, no one paying attention to it. The bar had never been the sort of place where, when a stranger opens the door everyone looks up expectantly, baited breath and the music pausing, to see who revealed themselves. No one gave a shit who showed up, in general.

"Uhm, hey," Jake said as the door closed behind him, "Casey?"

Casey closed her eyes and didn't turn around. She wanted to look, to react in some way, but couldn't bring herself to. She felt certain, a cold-stone-sitting-in-her-gut type of certain, that she'd imagined Jake's voice. A mix of one of the pain meds and the rum, maybe.

"Casey?" Jake asked again. He started to walk toward the bar but stopped. She didn't move, didn't turn toward him, and Jake was at a loss for what to do. He took a deep breath and spotted Oscar just *staring*. "Oscar," Jake said, "I, uhh..."

Oscar just waved him over, not wanting to speak, either, waiting for Casey to react. Jake walked over to the bar, slowly, mentally counting his footsteps as he went. Two, three, four, five, maybe he should run, eight, nine, and he stood next to Casey.

"It's me, Case, I promise," he said softly.

Casey turned, opening her eyes as she did, and saw him standing there. She blinked a few times, then reached out, tentatively, to touch his shoulder.

"Your hands, what—" Jake started to ask.

"Shut up, jerkbutt," Casey said quietly, "where the fuck have you *been*?"

Jake sat on a stool next to her, and Oscar poured him a shot of dark spiced rum. Jake took it, lifted it in salute, and downed it quick. "That is a story both long and improbable," he told her. "But I fought my way back," he said, "literally, for once."

She looked him up and down, "And you come back and you think your first move is to go to the bar?"

Jake laughed, shaking his head. "I came back inside a meat locker. The butcher, he was really surprised when the thing opened from the inside. I'm - you know that butcher on twelfth we like? I don't think we can go back for a while. But no, from there I went home but didn't find you. So I thought—"

"Key said no one had come back from—"

"So she *is*—"

"She is, but then how? How did you—"

"Could we," Jake suggested, "discuss this back—" he got cut off by the phone under the bar ringing loudly. Oscar snatched it up and spoke into it for a second, then listened and handed the receiver to Casey. "All yours, Chica."

"I'm not...thanks, Oscar." Casey took the phone but didn't take her eyes off Jake. "Yeah? Oh, hey," she said into the receiver. "Sure, I can do that – where? Right. Do I have time to go and change?" She smiled at Jake. "Figure an hour. Do we have an...all right, I'll speed it up. Any equipment I should....right." She handed the phone back to Oscar and leaned over to kiss Jake hard. When they broke apart, she stood up and tilted her head toward the door. "We need to go – well, I do. You can explain at home, while I change."

"Can I explain while I'm taking a shower? Fuck, I need a shower," Jake said, standing.

Casey put a handful of money on the bar and patted the surface gently, smiling at Oscar before turning back to Jake. "Sure thing."

Jake showered back at the loft and explained his trip through time as best he could. His explanation contained a lot of conjecture, and a lot of accidental truth. Coming out of the shower, he helped Casey change her bandages and reapply ointment to her hands. She'd given him, in-between his explanation, her own story. Like his, her tale contained a bunch of holes, saved for a later time, and a lot of confusion.

They fell back into habit quickly, listening and accepting the stories of the other. The relief they each felt they each kept inside some, not out of shame or embarrassment but simply not wanting to put more on the other, given they'd both dealt with a bunch while apart. A bit more communication would have solved that, certainly, but for all they cared for one another and all they relied on each other, they still kept distances based off their own pasts.

They still found incredible joy being near each other, hearing the other speak, and knowing things might be back on track for them. Casey still held back a bit, afraid of what was still to be done, but Jake felt certain they could pass through this, too.

Casey's hands were already much more usable, and she changed, pulling out black pants and a black dress shirt to go with it. She got dressed and pulled out her black combat boots – from her old life, beaten and worn – slipping them on and tying them tight.

"Where are we going?" Jake asked, digging through clothes himself. "Is the all-black look necessary? Is it crime?" he asked, smiling. "Crime would be nice right now. I could go for some crime."

"It's not crime," Casey said, "and you're staying here."

"The hell I am," Jake told her, pulling on a black shirt himself and grabbing some dark grey jeans. "I'm not leaving you alone again for quite some time if I can manage it. Sorry if that's clingy, but after all this? I'm feeling a bit clingy."

Casey sorted through a box at the table and pulled out some old lockpicks, rolling them back in their case. "This isn't going to be good, I think. I'll be a lot happier if you stay here and safe."

"All right, so," Jake said, taking the lockpicks from her and going over to a drawer to pull out a much newer set, then shoving them in a pocket, "I don't want you going off into dangerous things by yourself, not because you can't deal with it, but because I am sick of not seeing your face. Plus!" he said, feeling triumphant, "you need lockpicks? You're *totally* doing crime, and I want in."

"You're a needy baby," she said. "And this isn't crime."

"I am," he agreed happily. "So let's go do some crime, or whatever it is. Together."

"No," Casey said. "Please? I'll just worry the whole time. I just got you back."

"And now you want to leave. See how that's not great? We go, I'll help, we'll kick whatever asses need kicking, pick some locks maybe," Jake grabbed a few other small tools, shoving them in his pockets, and then, as an afterthought, shoved a pack of cards in as well, "have a good time, and circle back to... you know what we should do after this?"

"What should we do after this?" Casey asked, seeming to give in to Jake's idea.

"Buy a new couch."

Jake smiled as Casey processed what he'd said, staring at him. They both broke up laughing and had to sit down at the table for a minute to recover. When they had, Casey stood and gestured toward the door. "If we're going, let's go. We're already late."

"Late for crime? Perish the thought."

"Will you *stop* referring to this as crime?"

"Probably not," he said, closing the door after her and locking it.

Casey pushed the door to the Never Spineless bookstore open and waved Jake inside. The same small man sat behind the crowded, piled-on counter. She smiled at him and tried to be nice this time. "Excuse me," she said, "but—"

"Back room," he said, shrugging, "but hey, thanks for the politeness."

She nodded at him and walked through the store, Jake right behind her. He hadn't said anything – unusual for him, he would admit, but he felt lost and confused that in such a short time, this had become Casey's world. A world he knew nothing about outside of a few fairy tales he'd learned as a child and held close to his heart. Not that they were fairy tales, he remembered. He'd always wanted to believe and now, the closer he got to dealing directly with them, the more he worried. Faith is a wonderful thing when it doesn't have tangible proof. Once it does: duck.

Key sat in a chair, waiting for them – or at least for Casey. As Jake closed the door, he noticed the older woman staring at him, looking shocked. "Oh, honey, is this..."

"Jake, yeah," Casey said, "he found his way back."

Key stood up and walked over to Jake, inspecting him as if he were a confusing new lawn ornament when she didn't own a lawn. "Now, you, I understand," she said to him, still circling and considering him, "were taken by The Cat. That isn't a thing people come home from."

"Well, Ma'am....Grandmoth...I'm sorry," Jake said biting back a laugh, "what *should* I call you?"

"Oh, whatever you like is fine. Key will do, no need to stand on any sort of ceremony." She poked his arm with a finger and hmm'd.

"If you *say* so. Key, The Cat took me and Ferdinand Vink, he was a—"

"I know who Vink was, go on," she said.

"Well, we kept bouncing throughout time, and also sort of space but not really. I think we ended up in places Mur had been occupying, sort of, at the times we arrived, but it wasn't there when we did. I don't know how to sort that, but it—"

"Local frame time," Key said, smiling. "All right, I always wondered where people went. So if you move in time, you're moving in time relative to your own personal timeline and spatial location, not to Mur's. So if Mur was on a spot ten minutes ago, all right, you were in Mur, but if it was in a location hundreds of years ago and you go there, your own frame of reference might put you where it was, but not where it is, even though it's technically in all those places at once."

"If you say so, Ma'a...Key," Jake said. "I'm not actually sure what you even said, really, but I'll take your word for it."

"Oh, honey," Key said to Casey, "this town is dreadful for making sense. I'd say someone should make sense of it, but then I worry it would just vanish and reappear even more confusingly." She patted Jake's shoulder. "I'm sorry, go on."

"Right, well, at the end there I found The Cat again – one of my stops was back in Mur, see, and I asked."

"You...asked? That was the whole trick? You asked The Cat, and somehow she understood and sent you back here. That's...different."

"Well, she isn't a cat, not really. She's an antelope. I think knowing that made a difference. I don't know how or why that *would* make a difference, but—"

"She's a..." Key shook her head. "Well, we're going to have to circle back because I have a lot of questions now, young man."

"*You* have questions?" Jake asked. "But you're The Grandm—"

"I know good and well who I am, but it's never meant knowing everything. Regardless, we're on the clock now. I really should've listened, honey," she said to Casey, "moving sooner might've been to our benefit. Nothing for it now, though, except we have a much stranger problem."

"Stranger?" Casey said. "I'm afraid to ask."

"Vink's men have amassed outside the Spire, according to Franklin, intending to storm it and take over the city if Haimes doesn't produce Vink for them, since they're now sure the reason their end of the plan failed was due to Haimes double-crossing them. Haimes, I hear – also thanks to Franklin – thinks this is a ruse by Vink. Which makes sense since he doesn't know where Vink went, either."

"Oh no," Casey said, softly.

"Exactly. So Haimes thinks this is a power play by Vink. The whole thing is a mess, and liable to become deadly for a whole host of innocents very quickly."

Key picked up her bag from where it sat and looped it over her shoulder. She smiled at Casey, who nodded and opened the door. Then they were moving, right for the street, where Casey hailed a cab.

"I get why we need to stop this, but do we need to stop this?" Jake asked as they waited for a cab to stop for them. Key and Casey both gave him a look and he nodded, then shrugged. "Like I said, I get it."

A cab slowed down and pulled over to the curb as Casey asked, "How's The Heart, then?"

"Not great," Key admitted as she slid into the car. "This is sort of a reflection of that. As his pain grows, it'll show through the city."

"So shouldn't we deal with the root cause?" Jake asked. "Again, not saying we shouldn't deal with this, but if the cause is elsewhere..."

"Young man," Key said, "we do what we can. I admit, this is a bit outside the normal realm for me as well, but those of us here also had a hand in causing it."

"I think what he meant to say," Casey said, "was along the lines of, if we fix The Heart, will this go away then?"

"Sure," Jake said. "That."

"No, not at all," Key said, waiting for Casey to give the driver their destination, a few blocks from the Spire. "Yes, The Heart's damage pushed this over the edge a bit, but it would've happened in some form regardless. Either way—"

"Yeah, the City Heart, man," their driver said suddenly, "you gotta listen to it. My mother—"

"This is official city business, sir," Jake said, staring into the driver's rearview mirror to catch his eye, "no offense, but if you could—"

"Oh, yeah, sorry officer," the driver said.

Jake smiled at Key. "Go on?"

"We can't help The Heart by fixing this, any more then the reverse would be true."

"Then shouldn't we focus on the bigger picture?" Casey asked, lowering her voice some. "Then circle back?"

"Oh no," Key said, "by then the Spire would be a disaster and the May—" she looked toward the driver quickly, "the Boss would be gone."

"That's bad?" Jake asked. "He's not exactly high on anyone's list."

"Better than having full-on war," Key said, chiding him. "We stop that first, then tend to The Heart." She looked at Casey. "He's a little dismissive, isn't he?" she asked, nodding her head toward Jake.

"I'm right here," he said.

"He's had a day or two of it, just like us," Casey told Key. "But he's *my* Heart, all right?"

Key nodded and Jake reached for Casey's hand. He started to squeeze it, then remembered her injuries, her bandages under his hand feeling cold. She winced lightly but smiled at him.

The cab pulled over to a curb and Casey paid the driver, giving him a bigger-than-normal tip and thanking him for 'his discretion.' They stood on the corner, a few blocks away, and realized they could already hear the mob outside the Spire. "You see the problem," Key said. "Franklin told me they're in a panic upstairs. They don't have enough guards up there to deal with this, and even if they did, they do not relish a massive firefight."

"And the cops?" Casey asked.

"Warned away for the same reason," Key said.

"Worse," Jake added, "there could be enough cops on the take that for this sort of war, they can't be called in and are praying they won't be – no one knows who would respond and who would turn – and the war would engulf the city. All right, yes, we need to stop this."

They walked slowly forward, taking a switchback and creeping up on the sounds of unrest and trouble. As they turned another corner they could see fifty or sixty armed people crowded around the front entrances of the Spire. A few guards nervously blocked the entrance, but anyone could see from their faces they knew they wouldn't actually be holding anyone back who truly wanted in.

"If I could *play* I could hold them back," Casey muttered, holding up her bandaged hands.

"That wouldn't stop them," Jake said, "only force them to try and push forward. It'd be the fuse. No," he said, reaching into his pocket and taking out the fresh deck of cards, "I have an idea."

"No," Casey said, watching him unwrap the deck, shuffle the cards a few times, and put them back in the box. "You can't use cards to stop this."

"Watch me," he said, dropping the deck back in his pocket. "But stay close, this'll need you, too," he said.

"And me?" Key asked.

"Get upstairs when I wave you past," Jake said, "and go talk to your man inside. Tell him they need to trust you and—"

"Franklin will, but the rest have no reason to trust me. I can talk to them, but, young man, this isn't something I can just force on people. Getting Haimes to listen won't be easy."

"Explain that trusting you is a condition for this not turning into a bloodbath. By the time you get there he'll understand. Have them make sure one of their guards has an open radio they can hear upstairs in Haimes' office, if they don't already have audio up there."

Jake smiled at both women and walked around the corner right into the crowd, and up the steps so he could be seen. At first no one noticed him, but soon enough there were murmurs of confusion as the various people assembled nudged their friends and explained who he was. Jake waved at them, making Casey wince, and turned to the security behind him, standing in front of the Spire's entrances. "Hey guys, strange day, huh?" he asked them, and turned away without bothering to wait for a reply.

"Did you come here to die, Meyer?" a woman in the crowd shouted. Jake waved at her and shrugged.

"See, here's my thing," he said to the crowd, acting as if he'd somehow been invited to be their special keynote speaker, "I get why you're all mad. But I have to say, you're all also pretty stupid."

The crowd yelled, cursed, and spat in no particular order. Casey stood to Jake's side, a step behind him, and started trying to work out how she could get them out of this alive by force, if needed. Jake kept his arms at his sides but, glancing at Key, started to wave her behind him and into the building.

She started to, and was stopped by security. "Let her through," Jake said over his shoulder, in a low voice, "or I'll rile these guys instead and we'll all regret it." The guards looked at each other and let Key through, though Jake couldn't see them. He just decided they would listen as he started to address the crowd again.

"You all think," he said, "that Haimes betrayed your boss. That Ferd...I'm sorry, that Mister Vink would be taken in by some clever ruse or another. It shows a certain lack of respect, don't you think? Do you really think Vink is *less* capable than Haimes?"

The crowd roared with laughter, finding themselves agreeing with Jake.

"But more than that, what's your big plan, here? Raid the Spire itself? Burn the place down? Take out the Mayor? Come on. No, no, you need to think bigger."

"Why should we listen to you?" a man in the front asked Jake. He clenched and unclenched his fists, anger showing in every line of his body.

"How many of you," Jake asked, "know who I am?"

The crowd responded with more curses and shouting.

"Thought so. And yet here I still am. Your boss wanted me dead. None of you could do it. That's why you should listen to me."

"I could kill you right now," the guy in front said, stepping forward slowly.

Jake smiled at him and reached in his pocket. "All right, you want to do this? Let's get this out of the way. You want to kill me – chances are a lot of you want the opportunity, right? Then you could show Vink how great you are, maybe even take over this mob. I get it. I do. But I say you should listen to me. So let's decide this."

"No way!" shouted someone in the crowd. "Vink wanted you dead. For all we know you're working for Haimes on this!"

"You think I would work for Haimes to get rid of Vink and then come stand here like a sacrificial pigeon?" Jake asked.

"Maybe!" the voice replied.

"Maybe the two of you killed Vink and this is your cover-up!" another voice added.

"Then wouldn't I want to be far away from here?" Jake asked. "No, I have an idea. And I want you to listen. But fair is fair. This guy in the front, he wants to kill me right now. So, I don't know..." He shook the cards out of their box and started to shuffle them quickly, his fingers grazing them on all sides as he went. "Let's cut cards for it!" he shouted.

There was silence for a moment as they processed this new and strange offer. A woman stepped out of the crowd, laughing. "No way, Meyer, there are enough of us who know you and cards."

"Oh fine," Jake said, holding out the deck, "you shuffle. Me and this guy, what's your name?" he asked the large, angry man.

"Roadkill," he replied.

"Your parents adored you, I can tell. Me and Roadkill will cut. Highest card wins, aces high. Fair?"

The woman nodded and took the cards from Jake, shuffling them quickly. "But then how do you know I won't—"

"Trust," Jake told her quickly, "has to start somewhere. Just shuffle."

Casey took a breath to calm herself. This sort of patter, the ease with which Jake worked – she knew he had a plan, an angle she couldn't see. She just didn't like it. She made a mental note to smack him upside his head if they got through this.

The woman with the deck of cards finished shuffling and held the deck out in her open palm to Roadkill. He grabbed part of the deck and held up the bottom of the stack, a five of clubs.

As he put the deck back, Jake looked at him. "Did you want to do best out of three maybe? That's not…it just doesn't look good for you."

"Are you *serious*?" Casey asked, not meaning to speak out loud.

Jake turned to her quickly and nodded. "Why not, give them a fair chance – this is just too easy so far."

Roadkill smiled, "Sure thing, Meyer, you idiot."

"Thanks," Jake said, as he reached for the deck and cut the cards. He held up the ace of hearts and shrugged, "but I think you need the luck more, yeah?"

The woman shuffled her deck again and this time held the deck out to Jake, who reached for it, then stopped and snatched his hand away. He shook his hand out quickly, then grabbed part of the deck, holding up the seven of diamonds. The crowd laughed, and Jake just shrugged. "I never said I would win," he told them, to even more laughter.

Roadkill cut the cards next and held up the ten of spades. The crowd cheered for him and he smiled at Jake. "I'm going to enjoy killing you, you know that?"

"One cut left, Roadkill," he said, looking at the woman shuffling. "If you want to do me a favor here, I'd be thankful, uhhh—I don't know your name."

"Leslie," she said, "not that it matters, in about a minute you'll be dead."

"But Leslie," Jake told her, "I'll be dead knowing I was polite, and that makes a difference."

She shook her head and held the deck out to Roadkill, who cut it fast, holding up the jack of hearts. The crowd went wild and Jake made a show of cracking his neck and looking nervous. He reached for the cards slowly, his hand shaking slightly.

"We're not doing best of five, Meyer," Roadkill said. "You cut these cards, then I kill you."

Jake cut the cards, looked at the card on the bottom and then at Roadkill. He held up the king of clubs. The crowd went silent, and Jake smiled out at them. "So, look, like I was saying earlier," he started, taking his cards back and putting them into the box and then his pocket with a show of care, "this makes no sense. You won't get what you want this way. I mean, well – all right, I'll be honest, you've already gotten part of what you want. You just don't even see that yet, do you?"

"What the fuck do you mean, Meyer?" a familiar voice said. Jake laughed.

"Baozhai Lane!'" he said loudly, "what are *you* doing here? You have no love for Vink."

"I have less love for the Mayor screwing us all over. There are lines, Meyer. And you're on the wrong side of one."

"Right, right," Jake mused to the crowd, "the wrong side of a large-scale criminal uprising.

That's a new one. All right, Lane – and everyone else – let me break it down for you." Jake pointed up and behind him toward the Spire. "You think the details of Vink working in Haimes' pocket can *possibly* go ignored at this point? Haimes is finished in Mur, and you all know it. So really, I figure, if the guys upstairs bring Haimes out and arrest him, this is over. Otherwise this turns into a full-scale war."

Jake looked at his feet in silence for a moment, noticing the crowd had gone silent with him. Then he looked back at them. "And yes, you could win, but then what? Then you become the law, and I don't think a single one of us got into crime in order to go political meetings. This town won't turn into some big crime playground, I'm sorry. Cities don't work like that. All that would be left is mass bloodshed and fighting. And then what?" He looked at Casey. She looked back at him and stepped forward when he reached a hand out for her. "If I hand this to you, can you make them see it?" he whispered.

She thought about it. This was Jake's game—but then she ran through what he'd said. No game, he was *right*, and it needed heart, not quick thinking. She nodded at him.

"So look, you all feel I'm maybe, just a little bit, giving you the business—am I right?"

The crowd laughed but agreed.

"Right, sure – I'm not, but I get it. That's my problem. But here, Casey Harrison, she's not me. She's not one of *us* even – she's just a citizen, that's all. So maybe you'll listen to her."

The crowd muttered amongst itself, unsure of their stance on an outsider coming forward.

But they'd been swayed enough by Jake that they decided to let Casey speak. She took a breath.

"We all have families," Casey said. "A giant war, I don't even know what it would look like, I can't imagine – but I *can* imagine it would end up with a lot of people dead, injured, and otherwise attacked. People I care about, sure, but people you all care about, too. I've fought wars, real ones. No one comes out unscathed. The idea of that happening in Mur, even a small, strange war like this – it terrifies me."

Jake moved out of sight and took one of the security guards' radios. "Key, did you guys hear all that?"

"We did, young man, and thank you," she replied after a minute. Jake fiddled with the volume, lowering it and hoping the crowd couldn't hear.

"You have to get Haimes down here. That'll close this."

"I'm not sure that's—"

"I'll send someone up," he said quickly, and handed the radio back.

"We need," Casey continued to the crowd, "to avoid this. I'm not pretending to know what it is you all do—" the crowd laughed, "—but I know we all live here, we *choose* to live here. And I don't think any of us want to ruin it, not in a major, life-changing way." She knelt and touched the ground she stood on with her hand, pressing down, ignoring the pain. "This city is ours, and we need to keep it that way. A war," she said, standing, "of this scale, you hurt *everyone*."

Behind her, Jake spoke quickly and quietly to two of the guards. "Look at the crowd. This will end now if you go get Haimes and arrest him. You know you can get him to a jail, safely, if you act *now*. If you wait, this will only flare up worse, and you'll be the first to get trampled."

They looked at each other and turned without a word to go into the Spire.

"It isn't the kind of thing," Casey continued, "a city recovers from in a few years, or even generations. I've seen it. I've seen the scars across the land, the breaking of social norms and contracts, the desperate attempts to put that particular genie back in the bottle. It doesn't work."

The crowd remained silent as she stopped speaking, and Jake touched her shoulder lightly. They smiled at each other, and Jake addressed the crowd. "They're bringing Haimes out soon. This is over. He's done, let the law have him. Let Mur continue to be Mur, and let's just all go and stop standing here like idiots."

A few people in the crowd considered clapping but quickly gave the idea up when they saw the looks their neighbors gave them. There would be no applause, no ovation or cheers for what had just happened. But there would be a calming. And that was enough, for all of them.

Haimes came out of the Spire, handcuffed, led by two guards, and even then the crowd stayed oddly silent. They parted to let the procession go by as the guards handed Haimes off to the cops, who took him away. He'd be charged with conspiracy, and he already knew his time as Mayor had crashed to a sudden stop.

Key slipped away to join Jake and Casey as they considered the silence, wondering how long it could possibly go on for. Then, the crowd started to disperse. The cops didn't bother them; no one tried to get to them leave, and it was that, finally, that convinced them they could go. Jake took Casey's hand, but stopped before squeezing. Key nudged Casey's other arm and whispered, "We need to get going."

Casey nodded and tugged at Jake's hand. He shrugged but turned away and left with them.

"So," Jake asked as they got a block away from the Spire, "*where* are we going? Isn't The Heart under the Spire?"

Key laughed. "Of course not. Though Haimes thought there could be a passage in the basement that would lead him on the road. But no, it's...well, it's not a straight line."

"Nothing in Mur is," Jake said. They continued to walk further from the Spire, taking a switchback as they worked wallward.

"I need to know," Casey said after another block, "the cards. How?"

"Well, the high card," Jake said, smirking, "is the winner, and—"

"I will end you," Casey said, laughing.

"No, when I shuffled the deck before I handed it over, I nicked a few cards really carefully at different points along the edge, and once each along a side I chose as top to orient myself. Then it was just a matter of feeling for the top mark and sliding till I felt the side mark to tell me what card."

"And you didn't worry that woman could tell?" Casey shook her head. "Seems like you left too much to chance."

Jake clapped his hands together and showed Casey both palms. "I left *nothing* to chance. I needed them to go best of three. One shot and they would've all assumed I cheated, just like they would have done. So I made sure he would cut first, so I could be sure I would know what card to grab on the *third* cut. He cut low the first round, so I went for the ace I marked. Anyone smart would've gone for something lower to just nudge him out of the way, but going full-bore first, it *looks* like maybe you're cheating, so going as high as possible first cut," Jake smiled, resting a hand on Casey's back, "that just looks too stupid to do on purpose. That set the hook."

"So then you draw second and it's sheer luck," Casey said.

"Oh, no," Jake told her, "I needed to lose the second – this had to look good, good-to-a-criminal good. So lose the second, then win the third and look nervous doing it – that's why they bought it. It was the whole game, played out before she finished shuffling, just no one but me knew it."

"What if he'd pulled an ace out for his last cut— you marked two?"

"Couldn't, that would look too strange," Jake said.

"So if he *had* pulled an ace on his last cut? What would you have done?"

"Accused him of cheating. And I would've gotten away with it, too."

"No way," Casey said, starting to laugh, "they wouldn't have bought it."

"Sure they would've," Jake insisted. "He loses the first, badly, then wins the second fairly close, and then pulls out an ace for the final? That *looks* like cheating. Unlike what I was doing, which looked real, but actually *was* cheating."

"Some days I think you might be a terrible human being," Casey said warmly.

"But I'm really *good* at it," he insisted. They both laughed.

"If you two can stop discussing crime for a second—" Key started.

"See, she calls it crime, too," Jake said happily.

"—we're almost at the start."

Key stopped walking and Jake and Casey came up short, managing to not bump into her just barely. Key nodded to the old wrought-iron gate in front of them, wedged between two buildings. Without the gate, it would have just been another alley. With it, however, the space became hidden, unremarked on, subtle. Key pushed the gate open, shaking it a bit to get the hinges to cooperate. Jake and Casey followed her through.

"The Heart is in the back of...what is it with you people and alleys?" Casey said.

"I tell you," Jake said, "alleyways are nature's way of sending us a sign. It's like warehouses."

"The Heart isn't in an alley," Key said, fishing a small silver key on an old worn string out of her bag and stopping in front of a door along the alley.

"Wait, what about warehouses?" Casey asked.

"They seem to exist mostly to do money exchanges in," Jake said, "but that's not really important, sorry."

Key let them in the door, and they followed her into darkness. Jake kept waiting for her to turn on a light as they walked further and further from the door behind them, but she didn't. Casey trailed a fingertip along the left-hand wall as they went, counting her steps, just to be safe.

They heard Key start down a flight of stairs. Partway down she flipped a switch, throwing the staircase into yellowing, weak relief. Casey went first, Jake taking up the rear. She didn't want him to – the rear would let her protect them if something came after them – but she couldn't hear anything else moving. Besides, they weren't going into a fight, not that she knew of.

The three of them walked down, seeing a landing with no opening, only a continuation of the staircase.

Caroline von Strauss laughed and fixed her necklace, twisting at it until it lay flat against her throat. She looked out over the party and smiled. A man caught her eye and smiled back. Caroline looked away – not meaning, or wanting, to engage him – and shifted her shoulders slightly, back and forth, wishing the bra she'd chosen didn't bite into her collarbone. She wished she could afford something nicer, something better built, with fabric and elastic that didn't fray and pinch, but what money she had had gone into her dress and jewelry.

Her friends had laughed when she showed them the dress, telling her what a waste it had been. She'd never get into the party, they told her – and even if she did, what of it? What was there to gain from being at a party? Was she, they wondered out loud, trying to embarrass herself, trying to find a wife?

Caroline shook her head at them. The point of going to a party like the one she intended to sneak into remained the thrill of it. Also, you could make friends. Friends who could help you out of scrapes that her current friends, also poor, simply couldn't. Oh sure, she happily admitted, Louise and Qi would both help her move, or hide a body. But neither of them could pay to deal with her back rent.

Rich friends came in handy. And yes, she told herself, she knew how cruel and cold that sounded, making friends with people just because they might help you. She buffered the guilt with her own self-knowledge that she'd never actually used any sort of friend that way for herself. Instead, she gathered favors from people of all stripes and used them to help her other friends when they were in need.

The practice had become a favorite game of hers over the years, and her friends didn't seem to understand it, but they always accepted the help when they were well and truly in need, either way.

The party was a bust that night, though. Boring people, with no interest in anything but their own silly lives – consumed with using money to make money, and using that money to make even more of it. Caroline couldn't think of a more boring way to spend her life.

She left early and used the fact that she was already dressed up to talk her way into the Spire. She liked to – when she could bluff her way in at night, posing as someone who worked there, or who had to make a delivery for her fictional spouse or family member – stand on the upper levels of some office and stare into the city.

She stood there now, in a random, empty office near the top floor, when she heard a noise behind her. She turned, ready to explain herself to a janitor and was greeted, instead, by a man in a shabby leather jacket, jeans, and sandals. He waved as if he knew her and walked over toward her.

"Can I help you? I'm just here to grab a—" she started.

"Oh come on now," the man said, "you're here to look out the window and admire the city."

Caroline winced at being caught out. "I'm sorry," she said, "I'll go."

"Why?" he asked. "Is there some reason we both can't use this window? Is there," he wondered aloud, "a better view you think we should be looking at?"

"Uhm...who are...I mean, what—"

"Tor," he said, and held out a hand.

She shook it. "Caroline." She chewed the name he'd given her over and over in her head. Something about it felt familiar.

"Well, Caroline," he said, after a few minutes of silence where they both stared at the view, "I'll see you around, maybe."

She watched him walk away and decided she should get out of there herself. Qi and Rustev, two of her good friends, came over when she called them, and they all drank cheap vodka while she told them about her boring evening and strange capper.

"So he said his name was Tor," she told them, laughing as she refilled her cup for the third time.

"Tor?" Qi asked, brushing her hair out of her eyes as she, for the thousandth time, decided she hated her overlong bangs. "Wait, what did he look like?"

"I told you, some crappy jacket, it might have been leather, maybe," Caroline said, "if it was a hundred years old, and sandals, if you can believe it. In this weather!"

"You met The Translator!" Qi insisted.

Rustev coughed, swallowing wrong, as Qi said it. "That's a myth," he said, recovering.

"Shows you what you know," Qi insisted. "He's The Walker. So cool, Key!"

Caroline sighed. "Can we stop with the nickname?"

"You earned it," Rustev told her, "walking into parties, buildings, like you own them."

"Like you're some sort of human—"

"Yes, Qi," Caroline said, "I get it. I don't hate it because I don't understand it. I hate it because I *do*." The three friends laughed and debated the reality of The Translator until the sun came back up and they gave in to the urges of sleep.

A week later, Caroline met the stranger again. He looked shabbier, somehow, something Caroline hadn't thought possible. "Can I help you?" she asked, kindly. "I mean, do you *need* help?"

"I do," Tor said, "but it's a big favor to ask. It's not for me, though."

"Doesn't matter," Caroline told him, "who it's *for*. What can I do?"

Tor laughed warmly. "I *like* you. Let's talk." And talk they did, as Tor explained what Walkers were, and what they did. He also explained that his time was near an end, and that he wanted Caroline to take over for him.

She scoffed. She dismissed it. She listed reasons why it would be a terrible idea. But even as she did all of that, they both knew she would say yes, and that she loved the idea of being able to help people full time.

Tor explained that most Walkers chose a new name, something that would let them sound mythical, to help keep the people of Mur convinced they weren't real so that no one would become dependent on them. It served only to help The Walker work. Sighing and laughing in equal amounts, she told him about her friends' nickname for her.

They laughed together, and Tor explained more.

The bottom of the stairwell opened into a small tunnel, two-people wide. A thin stream of water ran along center of the floor, and regularly spaced lights gave a dim, if serviceable, glow to the place.

"This is...pleasant," Jake said. Casey shushed him, but also shot him a glance of agreement.

Key walked on, just ahead of them. "The oldest parts of Mur are a bit lower than the new, as is the case with anywhere that can't spread outwardly," she said over her shoulder. "And we have a while to go yet. The path isn't straight."

"Never are," Casey said, shrugging. Jake nudged her shoulder with his own as they walked. "So where are we going, anyway?" she asked.

"The Heart's location is kept," Key said as they walked, "secret. Only The Walker knows the way, and only they can pass without trial. We're walking the path there now, the same place that the very first Heart was born."

"Wait, can we back up to the part about trial?" Jake asked.

"The Walker, me," Key said, "can get there without issue, of course," she said, "but anyone else...there will come a point where we will be separated. I don't know when, or what, you will face. But I'm sure you'll be able to get through. That's all it is. You just have to get through."

They kept walking. Every nine-hundred-or-so feet, the tunnel widened into a junction chamber half the size of their loft. Not all the junctions even had other tunnels leading off of them, but they occurred regularly, each junction having doors that opened outward back into tunnels.

"So it isn't dangerous," Jake said.

"Oh, it most certainly *is*," Key corrected. "I just have faith in both of you, is all. That was fine, fine, work before with the crowd, young man. You and Casey here avoided a riot, if not a war."

"Casey avoided a war, I just set the stage for her," Jake said, nudging Casey with his shoulder again.

"And you had faith in her to do so," Key said. "Just as I do in you both."

"So," Casey said quickly, feeling embarrassed, "we're going to where the first Heart lived?"

"It's where all The Hearts stay, but yes, it is where the first blossomed. Not much is known about him, truth be told. He was, as far as I know, a man who loved the city so much that, when it fell out of normal space and time, he gave himself to protect it. He became The Heart, his connection was so strong, in fact. But that's...it's been millennia, you understand. The details are lost. But I do know that he sat on the floor of his house and told stories to calm the people of Mur, right up until he became The Heart."

Urshananti sat on the floor of his home and counted his blessings. The city had stopped quaking, and the strange blue energies had stopped flooding the area days ago as well. The Gods, he thought, must have released their anger. The city gates would no longer open, of course, and the people started to starve, fields and crops having been laid outside of the gates. New crops, from the seed stores within the walls, were being planted, but no one knew if they would grow fast enough.

He stood and stretched, feeling the years in his bones. At the doorway, the sun bright overhead, he called out to all who would or could hear him, inviting them in. Many came, wondering what Urshananti wanted.

When enough had gathered, he sat in the center of the floor once more and began, slowly, to speak. He told them their own history, and the reasons they would survive. He believed every word he spoke, and the force of that belief flooded into each of his listeners. They left long after the sun had set, and Urshananti boiled some of the meager grain he had left.

The next day he did the same, and the day after. Different groups came, many coming more than once, and soon, the daily trek to Urshananti's house became a staple of life in Mur. The gates would not open. The walls could not be climbed over. They were trapped, and, as their fear rose, so his calm grew.

One day a cat came to see him, glowing blue, the same as the lights that had swept the city. Urshananti took The Cat as a sign and welcomed her into his home, where she sat and slept near his fire. The chill at night caused Urshananti to sleep near the fire as well, and he and The Cat became companions of happenstance in the way of cats and humans everywhere.

The Cat hid when others came into Urshananti's house, however, and they laughed at his stories of The Cat With No Face. They marveled at his ability to find new and surprising ways to lighten the slow decline of their lives. Life moved on, as crops grew just enough to keep the people alive, if not happy, for a season. Still, people came daily to hear stories and be reminded they would get through this.

Then, one day, as the sun rose, Urshananti woke up to find he could not move freely. He could walk, he could stretch and bend, but he could not pass the threshold of his own home. He refused to panic. Everything would be fine, he told himself. The Cat came and left, as did visitors, so he knew it was something that affected him, and not the house or city overall. That was all right. So long as others did not suffer. He hid his condition and considered it at night, lying next to the fire with The Cat, consigned to unhappiness.

A few mornings later, when Urshananti woke up, he felt a sharp stab of despair in his heart. Calling out for someone to come to him, he asked them how they felt. Fine, came the too-quick reply, and Urshananti considered. Slowly he teased out the truth.

The crops had started to die, the food animals were scarce and could not be fed any longer, and the slow depression of death had settled over the city. Urshananti fought against it, and as he felt better, he noticed the others did as well, without him even having to tell stories. Soon, people could not enter his home. They tried, but, except for The Cat, none could not pass the entrance. Urshananti didn't even notice their attempts, lost as he was in feeling what the city felt, and knowing the city would feel what he felt in return.

Realizing this, deeper and deeper within himself, he focused on feeling hope and love for his city. He knew, though, that he needed to check up on his friends and family, and on strangers and their families as well. He reached out with the core of his being and felt his connection to Mur, and he focused it.

Samaqin, a mason, looked up from his work. He set down his tools and hurried to Urshananti's home. He passed freely over the threshold and sat next to the man. They talked long into the night, about everything and nothing, and by the time night fell, Samaqin rose and left. He headed for one of the city gates and stood, considering it. Turning, he noticed a woman walking past and asked her to open the gate for him.

Laughing, she reminded him the gates did not open. He asked her to try anyway, and Delondra pulled open the gate, stepped through, and found herself in Paris, 1605, though of course she had no way of knowing that then. She came back and laughed, recounting her short adventure and the strange world outside.

Urshananti stayed in his home, feeling Mur and talking to Samaqin, who walked the city for him, helping the people work out the foundations of their new reality. Though, at first, many were lost to the gates and their inability to return, Delondra worked and founded the Knockers.

The Cat With No Face didn't care about any of this.

It was the third start of everything, for Mur.

Key felt the air around her change as she led them down the tunnel toward the ground of Urshananti's home. Not that she knew that name for it – no one did, or had, for literal ages. The air thickened, it seemed to her, in a way it didn't normally when she would walk down here. Not that she did so often. She feared being followed, even with the trials others would face in their crossing. She'd been warned by Tor about people discovering where The Heart lay.

"I'm not sure what—" she stopped as she looked back and noticed that neither Jake nor Casey walked behind her. They'd been going through a junction, as they had many times already, but this time the door behind Key had closed – silently, since she couldn't remember hearing it. She tried to open it, prepared to scold her two charges, but the door wouldn't budge.

On the other side of the door, Casey and Jake stared at the closed door together.

"That door," Jake said, pointing at it accusingly, "was open a second ago."

"We almost walked into it, I was here," Casey said, agreeing. She reached for the door, but Jake grabbed the handle first and tried to turn it to work the latch. No joy. He tried again, cursing at the handle as he tried to turn it. No luck at all.

"Cursing didn't change its mind?" Casey asked.

"Not at all, which is plenty rude, if you ask me."

"I'll go ahead and say it," Casey said, looking around the junction. The door behind them had also closed.

"You think it's—"

"Trial."

Jake sighed and kicked the door gently, not wanting to break a toe. "Oh no, will we survive the trial of the sticky door handle?"

"That can't be it, right?" Casey asked.

"Well if nothing else, the thing has a lock. Maybe it's just locked," Jake said, kneeling in front of the door and grabbing his lockpicks from his pocket. "In which case, this trial picked the wrong person to...trial."

"You lost that at the very end," Casey said, laughing.

"But I won it in terms of style," Jake insisted, unrolling his tools. He looked at the lock and tilted his head to the side. "This thing is ancient, or at least it *looks* ancient. But I can—hold on," he worked a thin metal probe into the lock, "this thing is really complex. Oh, fine, be that way, lock. You won't stop me, just make me look foolish for a moment, but what you don't know is I am *fine* with looking foolish!"

"You're talking to a door," Casey told him.

"I'm talking to a *lock*," Jake said. "The door is just an innocent bystander, I'm pretty sure."

"It really is a good thing you're fine with the whole looking foolish thing," she said, laughing.

"I know, it's great," Jake told her, working his probe in the lock. "Anyway, give me a few minutes and we'll be clear of this mess."

"You might want to hurry that up," Casey said, the edge in her voice enough to make Jake turn around, worried.

"All right," he said, looking at the four large, wood-and-stone-looking, human-shaped figures walking, oddly silently, across the junction at them. "First I need to know: who invited these guys?"

"The trial, I think. It seems rude," Casey said, dropping to a crouch.

"Very. But secondly, how did *they* get in, and can we get out that way?"

"I doubt it," Casey told him, "one second they weren't here, the next they were. You work the lock, I'll deal with them."

Jake nodded and turned back to the lock and then stopped, standing. "No, you can't hit these guys with your hands like that," he said. "Change of plans, you get the lock, I'll get these four."

"Jerkbutt," Casey said, "that seems like a terrible plan."

"It's a terrific plan. It's a plan that doesn't end up with you crippled. I love it," Jake told her, pointing back to the lock picks on the ground near the door. "You'll be fine, I'll be fine. Besides, this sort of stupidity is the *last* thing the trial will expect."

"Are we committed to talking about the trial as if it were a person?" she asked as she backed away from the creatures and made her way to the door.

"I think so, sadly. Sorry about that."

"Kick these things' collective ass and consider it forgiven."

"Just get the lock open, will you, slowpoke?" he asked, grinning. Jake turned and considered the four creatures advancing across the junction. Each stood about six feet tall and seemed to be made from wood and/or stone, but the surfaces reflected light wrong for either material. They were silent, and hairless. The silence fascinated Jake, as they not only didn't talk, but their footfalls seemed to make no noise, either.

He waved his arms at them and then backed off, trying to draw them away from the door where Casey was working on the lock. They turned, as a unit, and followed him. Jake smiled. One of the four got close and Jake swung a foot out to kick at it, not wanting to risk his hands against the possible stone of its leg.

Jake's foot made contact, but what he hit didn't feel like stone at all; it gave, and reacted like flesh. Very toned and muscular flesh, sure, but still a lot softer than he'd worried about. "Hey, Case, what looks like stone but feels like flesh?" he asked as he, just barely, dodged a punch from the second creature.

"This isn't the time for riddles," Casey said, "what?"

"Oh, sorry," he said, "these guys."

"Then there you go," she said over her shoulder. The lockpicks were hard to hold in hands coated in ointment and covered in bandages. She cursed at the lack of firm feedback from the probe as she worked in inside the lock, trying to feel, and twitch, the pins. She heard the sounds of the scuffle behind her but fought to stay focused, concentrating on the lock.

Jake, meanwhile, had leapt at one of the creatures and tried to repeatedly punch it in the face. He grappled with it, but the thing threw him against a wall easily, far stronger than it first looked. Picking himself up from the ground, feeling the aches of his time fighting Vink still, Jake reconsidered his plan.

"It feels like the pins are resetting after I get them to the shear," Casey said, "and that's not possible, right?"

"Uhm," Jake started, then got caught by a blow to the shoulder that sent him spinning. "Crap, yeah, if you keep pressure on the tension wrench, they should turn enough to trap them at the shear."

"That's what I'm doing," Casey said, "but..."

"You might be letting the pressure wobble, try and keep it constant," he said, "but while we're asking questions..."

Casey refused to look, hearing flesh hit flesh. "Go for it," she said.

"Best joints to just take someone out of play?" Jake asked. He circled two of the creatures, trying to make sure the other two were still in sight, not getting behind him.

"Knees, ankles, hips, in that order," she said, "if you're trying to not kill."

"I don't even know if these things are alive," he said, ducking a punch.

"Don't go for big neck twists, takes too much skill. Just cripple from the waist down," she said, resetting the tension wrench in the lock and taking a deep breath.

Jake dropped to the ground as one of the creatures got behind him and reached out to grab him in a bear hug. He caught the motion out of the corner of his eye and managed to, ungracefully, get under it.

Kicking out as hard as he could, Jake felt the knee of the creature shift out of socket and watched it drop to the ground without making a sound. Even as it hit, it somehow absorbed the noise of its own impact.

Casey felt a pin lock properly and smiled. Only far too many to go, she reasoned, but progress was progress, and if she could hold them, this shouldn't be too bad at all. A yelp from Jake made her turn her head, and she saw him dangling by the arm, being held up by one of the creatures.

"Keep working," he said when he caught her glancing at him, "I got this." To prove it, he swung his legs up and braced them against the creature's chest, pushing with all his strength. It let go and Jake dropped back to the ground, hard, but tangled his legs in its and twisted, toppling it to the ground with him.

Casey turned back to the lock and cursed, realizing she'd let go of the tension wrench when she'd turned. She worked it back into the lock and put pressure on it, working the pick in to nudge the pins again.

Jake grabbed the leg of the creature he'd toppled and twisted until he felt a series of pops as cartilage gave way. The two now crippled lay on the ground, dragging themselves on their elbows toward Jake. He got up, backing away from the two remaining and made sure to step on the necks of the ground-stuck one he passed on the way. He felt a crunch and it stopped moving.

Jake frowned, pretty sure these things weren't alive but, even so, finding that he truly disliked the feeling of killing another thing, more so now than ever before. Which made sense, when he closed his eyes and remembered killing Vink. That act felt like a stain he couldn't get clear of, certain he never would or could. Caught while looking down at the thing he'd just stopped for good, Jake found himself thrown hard across the junction. He slid down the wall and found himself next to Casey. She hadn't even flinched at the impact near her, and Jake smiled despite the pain.

"You can not be flapped, can you?" he asked her.

"I'm unflappable, under the right conditions, it's true," she said. "I think we're doing this wrong, though."

"How so?" Jake asked as he got up, resting his hands on his knees and catching his breath.

"Key said we just have to get through," Casey said, "she didn't say we had to defeat things, or kick a lot of ass. Just: get through."

"So through the door is getting through, and the rest—"

"Might just be a distraction."

Jake nodded and rolled his shoulders. "I'll distract, then. Easier than beating them. You get the door."

"No, you missed it," Casey said, standing and dropping the tools into Jake's hand. He caught them by reflex. "If it's a game of keep-away, tag me in, I'm fresh. And dry hands, not in slightly damp bandages, will work faster."

"You call the play," he said, turning and sitting in front of the door.

"Just get the lock open, will you, slowpoke?" she asked.

"Fine. Kick these things' collective ass...wait, no, just don't get tagged," Jake said, as they both started laughing.

Casey faced the three remaining creatures, one crawling toward Jake, and felt her world go still. She watched how they moved, and when, and started working out her openings. Then she ran a few steps right at one of the creatures. It swung at her, just after she dropped to her knees and skidded past it, bowling into the other creature and knocking it over. She sprang to her feet and watched to see how they would react, gathering information the entire time.

Jakes set his tension wrench and slid the lock pick home with ease born of a thousand practice runs. Yes, he knew, the lock had more pins than it should, and some of them felt like they could be at strange angles, but it was still a tumbler lock, and those were just asking to be opened, in his opinion.

He flipped the first two pins into place, twisting the tension wrench to hold them there, in a few seconds. "Two minutes out," he said.

"I can do two minutes," Casey said, as she grabbed the wrist of one of the creatures and, knowing it was far stronger than her, used it to swing herself over, then planted her feet, shifting the remaining momentum into its arm to flip the strange and silent foe. Casey watched it and the other one she'd knocked over get up again and stayed out of the way of the third, crawling toward her. She saw it turn and start slinking along the ground toward Jake.

She moved quickly, knowing she was supposed to just keep away and not really try and take them out. Regardless, she wasn't going to let it grab Jake. He was hunched over the lock, working the problem, and, given the creature made no noise, had no way to know it was bearing down on him slowly but surely.

Casey reached down and grabbed its ankles, tugging it backward, but couldn't budge it once it dug hands onto the ground. She sighed at herself and then walked up alongside it and put a foot on one shoulder, then the other, twisting as she pressed down just enough to dislocate both joints and leave the thing unable to crawl. She looked at Jake, who hadn't noticed. Casey turned back to face the other two again and ran at them, brushing against one as she moved past it to ensure they turned to follow her.

Jake and Casey were on opposite sides of the junction now, with two creatures between them, both headed for Casey. A loud *CLICK* and Jake stood, turning to locate Casey, who saw him around the creatures. "Got it," he said, "want some help getting clear?"

Casey laughed and ran right at the creatures. She dropped and spun, sweeping their legs out from under them and dropping them both, then stood up and walked over to Jake. "I think I got it, but thanks," she said, smiling at him.

"All right, show off," he said. Shaking his head at her, he grabbed the door handle and leaned hard, turning it. The door started to swing open and all four creatures vanished. No smoke, no noise, no light – nothing to show their passing, They simply ceased to be.

"You have to wonder," Casey said, "who—"

"Thought these things up? Yeah," Jake agreed.

"I mean, why make them look like wood and rock? What was the point of that?"

"Intimidation, I guess," Jake said, "but the silence thing, that was a nice, creepy touch."

"Oh, yeah," Casey agreed as they walked out of the junction to join Key, who had waited for them. "Hey Key, so now what?"

"You two are in fine spirits," Key said, looking them over. "I take it the trial wasn't anything to worry about?"

Jake held up an open hand palm down and tipped it from side to side. "Eh, seen better, seen worse. Can see how it might've stopped either of us alone, or anyone alone, but if that was the only thing keeping us out, The Heart needs to talk to the head of security."

"Different times," Key said. "No one goes looking for The Heart, or has in quite some time – long before either of you were born, anyway." She started walking down the tunnel again as they talked. "It's part of why we like to be thought of as myths. But past that," she shrugged, "he also knows I like you two, I'm sure."

"Well," Jake conceded, "if that was security playing it friendly, then fine."

"So now?" Casey asked again.

"Oh, we're almost there," Key told her. "Just another junction or two at most."

"And then," Casey said, "we can fix The Heart?"

"Oh," Key said softly, and she stopped walking to turn and face them. "About that…"

"Nope," Jake said quickly, "nothing good ever starts that way."

"You're right," Key admitted. "I know, dears, you both came here to help fix The Heart. But it's too far gone for that. I came down here before I called you, remember, honey?" she asked Casey.

"Yeah, of course," she answered.

"I knew then we couldn't fix him – The Heart is dying."

"So we're here to offer last rites?" Jake asked. "I thought if The Heart died, so did Mur."

"That's true," Key said. "That's true."

$$\infty$$

Milashek Novak sat on the floor of his apartment and cried. He couldn't take it any longer. For weeks he'd found himself plagued by emotions out of control. They flooded him, and he couldn't resist them or control his reactions. One minute he found himself overjoyed and wanting to run in the sunlight, and the next he longed for companionship so strongly he curled up on the floor and wept.

He could find no rhyme or reason to it, and no doctor he asked had a sensible answer. They all had *answers*, of course, but each of those felt utterly silly to Milashek. He knew his mind; he knew as sure as he could feel himself inhale and exhale that these emotions came from *outside* his body and mind. No one believed him. No one he talked to about it would even humor him and take the idea seriously enough to consider. They tossed it aside as another symptom.

Milashek admitted to himself that they could be right, but then another wave of emotion hit and he knew they were wrong. This was external. And it was breaking him. He took a deep breath, trying to calm himself, and tried to feel happiness instead of the crushing sadness that currently washed over him. He tried something new this time, however, and instead of just fighting back, he tried to project that new feeling back to where the first came from.

It worked.

Some.

He was lying there, letting the relief float him along toward sleep, when someone knocked at his door. Though he felt in no mood for visitors, Milashek opened the door to see a tall old man standing there, wearing exceptionally casual clothing: a short-sleeved shirt with holes in it and shorts with frayed hems.

Milashek asked how he could possibly help the strange old man and got only as laugh in return. He started to close the door, not willing to play games, but the stranger stopped the door from shutting.

"Apologies," he said, shaking his head sadly, "I should not have laughed. But the thing of it is, it is not I who needs help. Rather it is the city that needs help – specifically yours."

The stranger did not expect it when Milashek tried to shut the door a second time, using more force. Staring at the closed apartment door, the old man knocked again and spoke through the cheap wood. "Forgive me, truly. My name, well, what people call me is Rory, but perhaps you know me as The Wanderer?"

"That will have to do," Key told him. "And may I present The Silent Heart?"

The room was dirt floored and utterly spotless. In the center, a nude man floated in a tank, his eyes closed. There was nothing else in the space except for lights along the walls, brightening the room up significantly from the tunnels before it.

"Do we bow?" Casey whispered to Jake.

"No," Key said.

"Why don't we get a doctor in here, or take him *to* a doctor?" Casey asked, walking around the tank. "He looks fine to me."

"The body of The Heart," Key started, "it's…just as my body is here and fine, but my spirit is tied to Mur tightly, The Heart is the reverse. His body is here, but only a shell. His spirit inhabits Mur the way my body does the city, do you see?"

"Nope," Jake said.

"We are the reverse of each other," Key tried again. "My spirit is trapped by the city, whereas his body is. But my body can walk the streets, and his spirit does the same. The larger Mur grew in terms of people, and complexity, the further the spirit of The Heart had to move, and so the body became an atrophied organ of his existence."

"Wait," Casey said, "so your…spirit…has the same problem as his body. Which means, what, your body is tied closer and further into Mur, but your spirit is…useless?"

"Useless only in the sense of…well, in no sense, really," Key waved her hands around a bit as she spoke, trying to find a way to explain all of this quickly, "but my body is tied so close to the city that the city is my spirit, as it is The Heart's body."

"You said The Heart was the city's spirit though," Jake said slowly, working it out, "and yet now you're saying—"

"The Walker is a creation of The Heart," Key said suddenly, "and the Knockers a creation of The Walkers. The energy is all one source, shared and distributed. The physical manifestations of that energy are strange, and we could spend all week here debating the physical reality of it versus the theoretical implications, but we *don't have time*. The body and spirit are needed by both of us, but the energy of Mur manifests in opposite directions for us. Regardless, saving the body is not enough – the damage was not done to him physically."

"So what *can* we do?" Casey asked, resting a hand on Jake's shoulder.

"And this is why I lied," Key said. "Honey, I'm sorry, but I was hoping you would become the new Walker. I knew my time grew short – I could feel it, but not why, so I looked for a replacement. I found you, and you will be wonderful."

Casey worked her jaw several times without making a sound before she finally spoke. "But the problem isn't you, it's with The Heart..."

"Also true," Key said, "though if The Heart passes, the energies keeping me alive will fade even faster. I had hoped, when we started this walk here, that you becoming The Walker would give you a boost enough to find a new Heart, but the situation is worse than I thought, honestly. I must be weaker than I thought, frankly, to not have seen it earlier."

"Then what—" Casey started.

"She's trying to say I should get in the tank," Jake told Casey. "Or at least, I mean, that *was* what you—"

"Yes, young man, exactly. Normally a new Heart is found, someone who is already connecting to Mur in the right ways. But anyone willing, who has the love for the city, the empathy and the strength, can be The Heart. It's not impossible. Though it may hurt a bit? I honestly do not know. What I do know," she said, looking at Jake, "is that it will work, and save Mur."

Jake nodded. Then he turned to look at Casey. "We both knew, didn't we?"

"Nope," she said, "and don't rewind and think you did, either. We were on a rescue mission."

"Still are," he said.

"Not the same one. No. I don't want to lose you like this. I don't want to lose you *at all*, jerkbutt. You...you fought across time to get back here. And now you'll just agree to crawl into a tank like that?"

"You know how much you love Mur?" Jake asked. "You're a native, and we both know it. And this?" he sighed. "This saves what you love."

"You're what I love," she said, and turned to Key. "I'll get in the tank."

"What, no, that's not—" Jake started.

"A stronger connection is better, right?" she asked Key.

Key nodded silently.

"Well then," Casey told them both, "Jake's right. I'm closer to the city than he is. And I have a sense of the job – you made sure of that, Key. I'm the better choice."

"The hell you are. No," Jake said.

Key looked between them. "The Walker and The Heart do talk. Endlessly. Every day. Constantly."

"Then what does he say about it?" Jake asked.

"It isn't words exactly, not often, but that may be him, this Heart. I'm...I'm not sure. The last Walker didn't know, either, only knowing this Heart as well. But either way, it isn't like that for us."

"Jake," Casey said, running a bandaged hand down his arm, "help Key find a new Walker. I'm going to do this. I don't need permission, but I want you to let me—to let me go."

"Nope," Jake said. "That's the thing I will *not* do. All right, do we shoot for it? Rock, paper, scissors? Or a short straw, or—"

"And you'd cheat," Casey said.

"Obviously!" Jake told her. They both laughed, and hugged suddenly and tightly, gripping each other closer and surer than atomic forces could ever hope to match.

"So then I disqualify you from games to decide, which means," Casey said against his ear, "I win." She pulled away from Jake and faced Key. "Do it. And if you need a new Walker," she glanced at Jake, "I know a guy."

"Damn it, Case," Jake said, wiping at his eyes. "Please."

"Do it, Key," she said, staring at Jake. "You know I have to."

"I know you don't want to deal with getting a new couch, but this is a new low in dodging that decision."

"You giant ass," Casey said through her own tears. "Key, before I change my mind, what's the play?"

Key looked between them and felt her own tears well up. She fought them back and nodded at Casey. "If you're sure—"

"Come on," Casey said.

"I can sever The Heart's connection, with his help, and transfer it to you. Then you get in the tank and...everything past that I will have to show you through our link."

"Do it," Casey said. "Wait," she added, shaking her head, "do I have to be nude? I just don't want to float for thousands of years all naked and on display."

"Not as far as I know," Key said. "I couldn't begin to tell you why The Silent Heart is nude in there."

"Leave the man's fetish alone and ruin my life already," Jake said.

"Hey now," Casey told him, "I'm gonna be an entire *city*. That's kinda cool. I'll play you a song, you'll know it when you hear it."

"I'll play *you* one," Jake said, "every morning."

"Learn to play an instrument first, please?"

"Always with the requirements that come with more work," he told her.

They held hands as they watched Key. She closed her eyes, then reopened them and nodded. "It's done. The Silent Heart is no more."

"I...I really," Jake admitted, "thought there'd be more to it."

"Real magic looks just like real life," Casey said, "or so I've learned."

"See, she gets it now," Key said happily, though her eyes were still wet. "Now honey, I will connect you to Mur. It may hurt some, and you'll...the emotions of the city will—"

"All at once, I'm guessing?"

"Yes, exactly so. Jacob—"

"Jake, if you're going to actually use my name for once, it's Jake," he said, feeling his heart crack as Casey let go of his hand.

"Jake, then, dear, I'll need you to help her into the tank. She won't be able to do it herself."

"What about—" Casey started to ask then fell silent as she saw the tank. It was empty. Jake just shook his head at it.

"Are you ready, honey?" Key asked.

"Hit me," Casey said, taking a deep breath. And the world did exactly that. The emotional content of Mur flooded into her, even stronger than they did at the gate, overwhelming her senses and dropping her like a stone to the floor. She managed to not scream, refusing to give in, even as she found herself praying to a dimly remembered childhood god that her head not split open onto the floor beside her.

Then Jake's hands were on her and she felt that she could cope, or at least that she could survive. She tried to open her eyes again but they wouldn't. Her hand, barely under control, slapped around at her side until it found his, lifting her, and squeezed it as hard as she could. He squeezed back, and then the coolness of the liquid in the tank, and she was floating in raw emotion and endless dreams.

Jake and Key sat together, looking at Casey float in the tank. "She's connected," Key told him, "and fine. I have a little time left now. Long enough to walk her through things, and you. But not much more than that."

"You can do both at the same time?" he asked.

"I told you, it isn't exactly talking, in the case of me and her."

"The Singing Heart," he said.

"Yes," Key agreed, "The Singing Heart. As for you, young man, we need to talk. I will not leave this place again. You will begin your Walk soon enough and should prepare."

"I don't want to leave here—to leave her," he said.

"You won't leave her. Not for endless years," she told him, smiling gently.

"Then what's first?" he asked.

"You need a name," she said. "A good name, something with some myth to it."

Balthazathor the Savior of Might landed gently on the windowsill. He considered his next move slowly, being unsure of what'd just happened. He'd been flying and then, out of nowhere, another pigeon cut across his flight path and startled him. He paced along the sill and fumed. How dare that bird bother him? Did it not know who he was? In anger, Balthazathor reared his head back and struck the glass next to him. He did it again, finding the noise, and the sensation, a good vent for his frustration.

A single, loud *FLUMP* from a pillow on the other side of the glass and Balthazathor screeched, stepping backwards off the windowsill and falling six feet before he recovered enough sense to spread his wings and fly off, even more offended than before. He glided off out of this story, and into his own.

"Fuckin' pigeons," The Jack of Diamonds grumbled, waving a hand toward the window and trying to will the pillow to return to his hand. The pillow, quite rightly, refused, and Jack got out of bed, walking the few feet to the window and retrieving it, tossing it back on the bed.

He stood near the window and looked out onto Mur. Morning light washed over the city, giving it a reddish gold glow that he loved, even if he didn't often get up quite early enough to enjoy it. He wandered across the loft and started the coffee maker going and made up his mental list for the day.

Jack, he thought to himself. The Jack of Diamonds. A hundred years ago he'd been told he would keep aging, for a time. It helped with the myth, letting him grow old with his friends, and then stopping when he was older, and alone. Harsh but effective, he had to admit. Though the fact that these last few years people had started to call him Uncle Jack burned a bit. He didn't feel old enough to be called Uncle Jack. Then again, he also felt positively ancient.

You learned to ignore the unresolvable dichotomies in life after a while, is all.

Hitting the bathroom and then running a quick shower, he walked out, drying himself off with a towel, and poured some coffee. Jack knew he had to go see the Caimbeuls early – they'd need help with their daughter. Then he should check in with the florist and see if he could finagle a deal for their lease. It'd be easier, he decided, if he helped their landlord with her ongoing war with the shoemaker down the road first. He also hoped to spend more time in the park, as he tried to when it was nice out. He'd sit around and play card games with anyone who stopped. He didn't play for money, these days – he simply enjoyed the practice and the feel of the cards.

Then there was the long build he'd mapped out, a way to help seventeen people at once – if he put together the pieces of his plan in the right order. There were easier ways to get things done, but they weren't half as much fun. Three times the work for twice the fun still had him coming out ahead, he figured.

The Jack of Diamonds sighed. It never ended. Then he smiled. It *never* ended. Oh, he knew one day it would end – everything does – but that end was far, far away. And until then he had Mur, his Singing Heart, and a bunch more mornings started too early by wildlife.

He opened his window and sat down, as he had done every day since he became The Walker, at his upright piano. Weather didn't matter. The window was opened regardless of, even in spite of, it.

The piano he'd purchased on the way home that first night, and plunked badly at it the next morning. It was, to him, in no way surprising that over a hundred years of practice for a few hours a day made you better at a thing.

Uncle Jack had gotten better at a lot of things. He tapped the deck of cards he'd left on the piano next to the keys and grinned. But no, that was for later. First things first. He gently touched the acoustic guitar he kept on top of the piano. He didn't play the guitar, had never learned, but changed the strings and cleaned the instrument once a month anyway, tuning it every night and keeping it there, atop the piano, so that it, too, could sing every morning.

Jack started to play, closing his eyes as he did, reaching out and greeting the city, greeting The Singing Heart warmly, with a song. The guitar vibrated against the piano, humming along in its own way. Outside, he heard the noises of the city seem to align, as they did every morning, for him. They became part of, and to added to, whatever song he came up with.

He played, putting all of himself into each note, and Mur sang back to him in perfect harmony.

ALSO BY ADAM P. KNAVE

PROSE

Crazy Little Things

Stays Crunchy In Milk

Strange Angel

NYCWTF

I Slept With Your Imaginary Friend

This Starry Deep

The Endless Sky

COMICS

Amelia Cole

Never Ending

Artful Daggers

Laser Joan and The Rayguns

Sensation Comics Featuring Wonder Woman

The Once and Future Queen

Adam P. Knave

has been telling stories since he was a small child. He never stopped, and hopes he never will. A New York native, he self-exiled to Portland, Oregon, not long before his fortieth birthday and now spends many evenings on his patio, whiskey in hand.

www.adampknave.com